Praise for
LORI AVOCATO's
PAULINE SOKOL myste

"Sexy and sassy ... a sure pres
for outrageous sleuthing
Agatha, Anthony, and Macavity Awa
author Carolyn Hart

"Hilarious."
USA Today bestselling author Merlin

"Great fun and a diverting es
Laura Van Wormer

"Delightful."
Publishers Weekly

"When the prescription is mystery, no one is any
better at serving up the cure."
Former FBI agent and *New York Times* bestselling author
Christopher Whitcomb

"Clever, comical, and gutsy, Pauline Sokol
is the perfect sleuth."
Nancy J. Cohen, author of the Bad Hair Day Mysteries

"*Nip, Tuck, Dead* is fun, fresh, and fabulous! Lori
Avocato's newest book mixes healthy doses of
laughter, sexual tension ... and murder. If you haven't
already fallen in love with Pauline, Goldie, and the
gang, this book will do it. Diagnosis: fantastic!"
Alesia Holliday, author of *Blondes Have More Felons*

Books by Lori Avocato

Nip, Tuck, Dead
Deep Sea Dead
One Dead Under the Cuckoo's Nest
The Stiff and the Dead
A Dose of Murder

LORI AVOCATO

Nip, Tuck, Dead

A PAULINE SOKOL MYSTERY

AVON BOOKS
An Imprint of HarperCollinsPublishers

AVON BOOKS
An Imprint of HarperCollins*Publishers*
10 East 53rd Street
New York, New York 10022–5299

Copyright © 2006 by Lori Avocato
ISBN–13: 978–0–06–083704–4
ISBN–10: 0–06–083704–7
www.avonmystery.com

First Avon Books paperback printing: December 2006

Avon Trademark Reg. U.S. Pat. Off. and in Other Countries, Marca Registrada, Hecho en U.S.A.
HarperCollins® is a registered trademark of HarperCollins Publishers Inc.

Printed in the U.S.A.

10 9 8 7 6 5 4 3 2 1

To my dear friend,
Chris Whitcomb,
who I forgot to thank for all his FBI/investigative input
for my last book, Deep Sea Dead. *Oops. Then again, if*
anyone knows "better late than never," it's Chris.

Acknowledgments

To all my wonderful readers. You guys are great! It's so fabulous to hear from you about how you love Pauline and the gang. Glad to be able to brighten your lives with a laugh! I certainly live by the motto that laughter *is* the best medicine.

To Jay Poynor, my agent, who is a doll and a damn good agent to boot!

To May Chen, my editor. Thanks for all your wonderful input to make this fab book more fabulous! The series can only keep getting better and better with your help. We're a darn good team!

Thanks to Danielle Bartlett, Avon publicist from Heaven. Thanks for all your hard work and wonderful ideas!

Thanks to all the Avon/HarperCollins employees behind the scenes who contribute to making my work a success.

To all the patients who have suffered to be beautiful—and those of us who only wish we could ...

Finally, thanks to whomever else thinks they've helped me out somewhere along this fickle road to publication. You know who you are!

One

"What the hell is wrong with my nose?"

I couldn't help shout at my skuzzy boss, Fabio Scarpello, who had just suggested I get a nose job. A nose job!

I looked into the file cabinet to see as much of my profile as I could. Only things I could find in the metal were fingerprints galore and some brown stuff, which I didn't want to even guess at.

Fabio was a pig in his office, and I'm sure in his private life (and not only with the setting, I might add), but he was the owner of Scarpello and Tonelli Insurance Company and gave me insurance fraud cases to investigate.

In other words, he was my only means of support.

I'd switched careers midstream, leaving nursing for snooping. Thing was, darling Fabio always gave me the medical fraud cases. Sure it made sense, but I wasn't looking for sensible.

I was looking to get out of that business! Being single and in my early thirties, I knew I couldn't keep switching fields and have any kind of retirement. Besides, I loved the investigating. What a rush to solve a case!

I never let the reminder that murders occurred along the way even enter my head.

My heart thudded. Murders!

Oops. Truthfully, the M word did that to me since I'd come way too close to being one of its victims—several times.

I looked closer at the file cabinet. Fabio's brown-stained reflection appeared. Yikes.

"No, you don't need a nose job, doll. But that's part of the business. Going undercover doesn't always come easily." He sucked on the wet, sticky end of his cigar and laughed. "Nope. Sometimes you have to make sacrifices to earn some bucks. Besides, I thought any doll would jump at the chance to have something fixed." His gaze ran down to my legs and back up to my chest—and stayed there. "Rather have a bo—"

"No!" I stepped back. Yuck. No way was I going to discuss my chest with him. "I don't understand why I need anything done."

He took a long pull on the cigar, coughed until his face was rotten-apple-colored, and grinned. "How the hell else are you going to get inside that plastic surgery clinic to do your job?"

I glared at him for a good fifteen minutes. Okay, maybe it was only for a few minutes, but it seemed longer. I knew what was going to come out of my mouth, but I *really* didn't want it to. No way. I was not going to say … "I can go to High-cliff Manor as a—"

My insides dropped to my toes. I couldn't believe what I'd nearly said. I'd almost offered my medical services, throwing myself back into a burned-out career.

Heaven help Pauline Sokol because I obviously couldn't help myself.

Fabio walked to his desk and shoved a manila folder toward me. "One of my clients, a small company out of Rhode Island, reports an increase in plastic surgery submissions from this one particular clinic. Ones insurance shouldn't be covering. Smells to high heaven." He waved the folder at me. "Case number five for you, doll."

"Stop calling me *doll* or you'll be wearing that cigar in your ear—lit." I stood firm, reached across the pile of old coffee cups and stale doughnuts on dirty dishes to grab the folder from his hands. *I wish I had a nickel for every time I'd told him to stop calling me that*, I thought as I grunted, looked at the file and started walking toward the door.

"Make sure you come up with a good reason to go to Highcliff. Those rich bastards are often smart. That's how some got filthy rich while others got their dough from Mommy and Daddy. Newport, Rhode Island, is filled with money."

I think he snorted, but my mind was on the file in my hands.

I had to come up with a plan to get inside the clinic? This was a new one. Usually Fabio handed me a case already in the works, where I went to investigate whatever he'd set up. This time, since

I'd refused to get any part of me nipped, tucked, or mutilated, I was on my own.

But the bonus was that in Newport, being such a posh town, the fraud was exorbitant—and so would be my fee.

And I needed money like a sailboat needed the wind.

"I know!" my best friend and roomie, Miles Scarpello (Fabio's nephew by adoption—thus Miles was a honey, as he lucked out of being from the same gene pool) yelled. "You can go to Highcliff as a rich bitch and then just get your ears pinned back ... a bit."

"Whaaaaaaaat!" I screamed, and ran to the mirror. I'd been holding Spanky, our joint custody shih tzu who weighed in now at seven pounds, so he jumped onto the couch in my haste. Spanky had adopted another "parent" in Goldie Perlman, Miles's significant other, my other best friend and our third roomie.

Yes, they were both the best, and I could never pick one over the other.

I leaned closer and pulled back my hair. "Nothing wrong with my ears. Is there?" I leaned forward, "Oh, my," I mumbled and moved my head from side to side. "And, besides, if I get any surgery, what kind of shape would I be in to work?"

He looked at me. "Your ears, nose, breasts and every inch of you is perfect, Pauline. There is nothing needing any kind of tucking or clipping." He bit on a perfectly manicured nail.

I looked down at my fingers and groaned. Being a nurse had me in the habit of wearing my nails way too short. I tried to hide that fact with a bronze nail polish, but since I hadn't been to the nail place in weeks, the bronze was now a dull gray and nearly chipped off.

"I guess I owe you a thanks for that comment, Miles." I took one last look in the mirror, pulled a handful of blonde hair over my ears (just in case) and flopped onto the couch with a sigh. "How the hell am I going to get into that place? I've already checked their staffing needs. They're full."

Miles sat down opposite me, took off my fluffy pink slippers and started to massage my feet. Ah, the benefits of platonic male roommates. Amid the nirvana he'd set in motion, the door opened with a bang.

"Oooooooh! What a day this has been!"

I peeked over my shoulder to see Goldie dancing around with poor Spanky shaking in his arms while Goldie sang, "What a rare mood I'm in, folks!"

Miles stopped massaging and we both cracked up.

Goldie set Spanky down and sat on the edge of the glass and chrome coffee table. Today he'd worn Armani—from the women's department. The only way I knew the designer was that I'd seen the camel jacket on Goldie's bed and read the label. If he wasn't almost a foot taller than my five-six, I'd have tried it on. He looked glamorous, sexy, and his light blond wig set off flecks of gold in his eyes.

Very cherry-colored lips smiled at us.

"What's made you so happy, Gold?" I eased my feet off Miles's lap and sat up, pulling my robe tighter. Not that these two lovers would have cared if my breasts hung out, but I came from a Polish Catholic family, and the day I had started kindergarten I learned what a "Catholic-school-induced" (CSI, as I now referred to it) conscience actually was.

Unfortunately, morality was my middle name.

Goldie gave Miles a kiss on the lips, leaned toward me and planted one on my cheek. "I nailed the sucker! I nailed the shit who was scamming Global Carriers Insurance Company for millions!"

Goldie, way more experienced than myself, also worked for Fabio and had been my mentor on many an occasion.

My eyes widened. "Oh, Gold, that's fabulous. I thought you'd be working that case for eons."

He looked at me under his heavy black lashes. "Suga, every once in a while a miracle happens. A shitload of evidence falls into your lap. It's up to us to make sure we catch it. Now I'm taking some time off."

Miles and I looked at each other, and I knew we were both thinking: *God, I hope he didn't do anything illegal.*

But then we both winked simultaneously and realized this was our Goldie we were talking about. Ex–army intelligence. Tall, smart. Sometimes beautiful. Sometimes handsome. Everyone loved Goldie, and he was as honest as the day was long.

Miles went to fix me tea and the two of them martinis while I told Goldie about my new assignment.

Once Miles came in with the tray of drinks, snacks of bruschetta, which he happened to whip up, and a doggie treat for Spanky, I leaned back and sighed.

"I'll never come up with a way to get into that place."

Goldie eased his drink from the tray, muttered a thanks to Miles and leaned closer to me. "You *know* who can help you."

It was barely a whisper, and I knew it killed him to bring it up.

My mind wandered for a few seconds to my sometimes "partner" in crime solving. The enigmatic, always mysterious, deliciously handsome, exuding maleness through pheromones *Jagger*— who Goldie constantly reminded me not to get interested in—you know, in *that* way.

"Stop fantasizing about him and give him a call," Goldie ordered.

I didn't take offense because I knew I needed that verbal slap to stop my foolish fantasy. Yes, I was somewhat smitten with Jagger, although— after only a few kisses—I really didn't think he noticed that I was young, hopefully hot, and female.

Jagger worked with his own agenda.

I breathed out a long sigh, which seemed to let my body cool off a bit, and took a sip of tea. Then I said, "I can't call him. I mean I won't. I really have to work by myself. I can't rely on him over and over. You know I've gotten myself out of scrapes on my own—"

They both glared at me.

"Okay, I shot an elevator—twice—and had a few near misses on board—"

"Not to mention getting shanghaied into the mental hospital, Pauline."

"Thanks for the reminder, Miles." I forced a smile. "I really do want to work alone. I'm a big girl now."

"Oh, that reminds me, Suga. I ran into your mother at the Stop and Save …"

I knew Goldie was talking, but the mention of Stella Sokol had the power to cause my decent intelligence to nosedive. I yanked my robe tighter, remembering her constant reminder not to come home from work and put on my robe or I'd never have a life outside of nursing since I'd be homebound for the night. I looked at the clock. Fourthirty.

I had no life.

"… so, tonight at six," Goldie finished.

I blinked as if that would pull back the words he'd just wasted on me. "Six?"

Miles got up and put a hand on my shoulder. "I knew you didn't hear a thing past 'mother.' Get dressed, Pauline. We're off to your homestead for, what is today?"

"Thursday," Goldie and I said in unison.

"Then pork roast it is," Miles finished.

You could set Greenwich Mean Time on Stella Sokol's meal plan. Mom made the same meal for the same day of the week—always. The thing was, the retro house (original stuff inside and out like shag carpeting and knickknacks were *never* updated) with white metal siding at 171 David Drive always smelled like kielbasa and sauerkraut no matter the day of the week.

Every time I stepped onto the royal blue shag carpeting in the living room, nostalgia had my heart flutter—until my mother suggested that I move back in. Then I'd have to rush off to find her pine-scented Renuzit, which always filled the air in Mom's house. She bought it in bulk. It'd come to be a comforting scent for me, and sometimes I sprayed the air a few extra times when my life wasn't going ... too well.

I couldn't even count on two hands how often that was lately.

"Goldie, you look attractive. And Miles as handsome as ever," Mom said while she gave all of us a big hug. "Pauline, you look horrible."

I wondered if my mother thought I needed a nose job, but then again she probably was talking about the red jogging shorts and black jogging jacket I'd thrown on. No one important would see me here.

"Thanks, Mom," I muttered, kissing my dad on the forehead as he read his newspaper (always took all day long to finish since he'd retired).

Daddy mumbled, "Hello, *Pączki*!"

I smiled. He called me the endearing term since I came kicking and screaming into this world at ten pounds five ounces. Now my purse weighted that much. No one else could get away with calling me a prune-filled Polish doughnut except Daddy.

Miles went into the kitchen to get us all something to drink, and I could hear him arguing with Mom. She never wanted any help, or she wouldn't be the star hostess, something she reveled in. However, she always backed down when it came to Miles.

They were both so cute.

The front door opened as I sat myself on the couch next to Goldie.

"Is that Pauline's car in the driveway?" my favorite uncle called out.

I jumped up and ran to the foyer. "You know it is, Uncle Walt. You know cars better than Henry Ford." I gave him a quick peck on the cheek, and he gave me a hug.

"How's the business?" he asked.

I laughed. "Got a new case today." Uncle Walt was always one of my supporters for leaving nursing. My father remained silent, my siblings couldn't care less, and my mother always tried to get me to go back. After four cases she still thought it was "just a phase."

Finally we were all seated in the dining room (Mom never let company sit in the kitchen to eat.) We chatted about nothing, ate gigantic amounts until I had to unbutton the snap on my shorts, and then ate some more when Mom brought out her famous chocolate cake with Hood's vanilla ice cream on the side. I slid my zipper down about an inch and dug into the dessert.

"So, Pauline," Mom said as she handed Daddy an extra large slice of cake. "Did you read the article in the paper about the nursing shortage, and that they are hiring at Saint Gregory's Hospital?"

I choked on the ice cream.

"Um. Hm."

"Don't talk with your mouth full." She sat down next to Daddy and started to pour coffee for everyone.

I swallowed, coughed and swallowed again. My throat froze instantly, but I managed, "Mom, I am a medical fraud insurance investigator now. No longer a nurse. I'm sorry about the shortage, but there's been a shortage since I graduated over thirteen years ago. I'm sure my leaving didn't have that big an impact."

She continued on about the article as if I'd never said a thing.

Miles and Goldie had seconds on the cake and ice cream. Daddy had thirds. Uncle Walt took his usual "seated at the table" nap, and Mom glared at me. "So, what is your next case?"

I could hear her teeth grinding, trying to get the words out. "Well, it is in lovely Newport, Rhode Island, Mom. Right near the ocean. I'll be able to walk along the cliff near all the mansions. This time of the year should be beautiful there. Not too hot yet."

She held her fork in the air. "I know spring is a lovely time of the year, Pauline, but you are evading the issue. What kind of trouble are you going to put yourself into now?" She set down her fork and made the sign of the cross on her forehead.

I could see Miles shift in his chair.

Goldie muttered something and gave me a pathetic look. Well, the look was more like sympathy and *I* was the pathetic one.

Daddy kept eating.

Uncle Walt snored, and I sat there feeling as if I was five years old.

"I'm going to do private duty nursing at a plastic surgery clinic, Mom."

I could see Goldie and Miles's shocked yet pleased expressions. Thanks to Mom, I just figured out how to get into the clinic to do my investigation! Now all I needed was ... a patient.

Damn.

"Oh, I see," she said, then remained silent.

Yes!

Feeling as if you've checkmated your mother was glorious. A smile crossed my face. I could see myself in the stainless steel coffeepot and smiled wider.

She leaned closer to me. "So, who is your patient?"

My smile faded when I met her eyes. Five years old ... again.

Goldie jumped from his seat. I thought he might shake Mom, but knew him better. "Me!"

"Me?" I shouted.

Miles looked confused. "You?"

I turned toward him. "No, him."

Daddy looked up as he stuffed the last forkful of frosting into his mouth. "Who's him? I'm confused."

Goldie started waving his hands about. "Pauline is going to be my nurse. You know, private duty type. I'm going to splurge and treat myself to a *nose job!*"

Two

"Oh ... my ... gosh! This place is fabulous!" I shouted when Goldie and I drove down Bellevue Avenue, the main artery for mansion viewing in Newport. In the Gilded Age, the wealthy built their forty room "cottages" along Bellevue—and competition became the name of the game. From the Astors to the Vanderbilts all the rich moguls tried to outdo each other with their homes and their parties.

I shut my eyes and could picture golden carriages pulled by white horses *clip-clopping* along the street. When I opened my eyelids, all I could see were long driveways to mansions bigger than the Hope Valley town hall.

Finally Goldie turned down a street where a sign for Highcliff Manor stood. When we drove down the long drive, I looked at the place and gasped.

Goldie chuckled. "Nice digs I'm gonna be in for the next few weeks, Suga."

I nodded in agreement when I looked at the

sprawling white wooden mansion, which over-
looked the ocean but from some distance. The
distance was a perfectly manicured expanse of
lawn, greenery, shrubs, topiaries and flowers of
all sorts. Wrapped in a surround-type porch, the
place looked homey in a very classy, expensive
big way.

As soon as Goldie pulled his banana-yellow
sixties Camaro into a parking space, I turned to
him and touched his arm. "Gold, you really don't
have to do this."

He leaned over and kissed my cheek. "I know,
Suga. I really want to."

I kissed him back, turned and opened my door.
When I stepped out, the warm spring ocean breeze
hit my face. "It smells great, Gold. So oceaney."

"Look to the left."

I turned to see him pointing and gasped again.
"Oh ... my ... God. It's amazing."

Behind the rows of salmon azalea bushes, now
in bloom, whitecaps, riding swells of waves,
frothed in the distance. Tankers, the size of a
child's toy from here, edged slowly across the horizon. The Atlantic Ocean was only steps away—
and about fifty feet below. Yikes.

"This is going to be the best assignment!" I
turned to see a nervous smile on Goldie's face
and quickly gave him a hug. "I'm going to take
excellent care of you, Gold. I am."

"You know, Suga, I've always wanted my nose
tweaked, but was too scared to go under the knife.
You know me. I don't do pain. But when the op-
portunity arose to have you at my side, I jumped

at it." He leaned over and kissed my cheek once
again. "I'm not going to worry anymore. And,
I'm gonna be here to help you solve your case so
we can head back home real soon."

"Thanks," I said, but thought about how long
my cases usually took. Never had evidence "fall
into my lap" like Goldie's had.

Besides, if it did, I wasn't sure I'd catch it.

"I am Pauline Sokol and this is my ... patient,
Goldie Perlman," I said to the darling young
blond guy behind the reception desk. Quite the
hottie, if a few years too young for *moi*.

Actually, the place looked more like a library
complete with wall-to-wall books, mahogany everything (the expensive kind), and floral arrangements, real ones that probably cost more than my
yearly salary.

The young man gave Goldie the once-over. Not
in an insulting way though. Thank goodness. I'd
grown to be rather protective of my dear friend,
although, in all honesty, Goldie could hold his
own—and mostly protected *me*.

"Welcome to Highcliff Manor. I'm Ian. Ian
James. Have a seat." He motioned for us to sit.
Well, he motioned for Goldie to sit. Me he just
nodded at. Hm. I was guessing that Ian either
thought my Goldie was as hot as Pamela Ander-
son (only more sophisticated) or as hot as Johnny
Depp (only more ... in all honesty, he didn't need
improvement).

I sat next to Goldie and took his hand. "When
do we get to see the doctor?"

Ian looked at me and smiled. "Ms. Sokol ..."

I knew he was talking but got hung up on the "Ms." part. How come he'd assumed I was a Ms. and not a Mrs.? Goldie's hand grew cool. I tightened my hold and yanked my thoughts back to Ian. No worrying about my lack of marital status right now. Gold was way more important, and besides, I'd convinced myself that I was now a career gal.

"... so, you see, we have it all down to a science here at Highcliff Manor."

I'll just bet you do, I thought, although I hadn't heard everything he'd said, and it probably was important. Oh well, I was sure Goldie got it all. Before I knew it, Ian was standing and motioning for us to follow.

He gave us a brief tour of the manor, which looked as if *House Beautiful* had set up stakes here to decorate the place. Gorgeous. Floral everything. Antique furnishings. Carpets softer than clouds. Goldie and I "oohed" and "aahed" all the way to his room.

When Ian unlocked Room 211, he stood to the side and handed Goldie the key. "If you need anything, I'm always around." They shook hands although I guessed Ian would have liked maybe a hug.

"Holy moly, Suga! Look at this place!"

"Wow," was all I could say when I stepped in after Goldie.

The room swam in ivory and salmon everything. And lace, silk and French provincial overpowered the huge size. It looked like a millionaire's living room, so I figured it had to be a suite.

"You could stay here with me, Suga. No need for you to go to the bed and breakfast you booked. Why spend the money?"

He was right, but I thought he'd need the time away from me and, more importantly, I knew Miles had planned a surprise visit for the weekend.

"I'll be fine at the Samuel Freeman Lodge, Gold. It looks fabulous on the brochure, and I'll have a place away from here to work on the case and not worry that someone might find any evidence that I turn up. Besides, it's only a few blocks away and I can walk."

Goldie seemed more mesmerized than myself with the suite, and when he went into the bathroom and rifled through the floral-scented bath salts, I told him to enjoy himself and I'd be back at three for our meeting with Dr. Cook, Goldie's plastic surgeon.

I only hoped he wasn't really Dr. "Crook" and my number one *suspect* in medical insurance fraud.

When I got to the front desk area, Ian sat at the computer reading something. No sense in wasting time since time really was money on my cases (Fabio was known for his bonuses for quickly solved cases—although, sadly, I hadn't had one yet), so I headed toward Ian, hoping I wasn't interrupting something too important.

"Well, Goldie is very pleased with the room."
Because of Miles, there was no point in encouraging Ian.

Ian turned toward me and at first looked confused—as if he didn't know who I was. Then he
quickly shoved the monitor to the right—where I
couldn't see what he had been reading.

*Go, Ian. You may be the ticket to a quick-solved case
bonus.* But now I had to maneuver myself like a
damn contortionist to see the monitor.

"Is there somewhere I could get a cup of tea,
Ian?" I leaned so far over, my sunglasses fell off of
the top of my head onto Ian's desk. "Oops. Sorry."

By the look on his face, I should have stuck with
the subject of Goldie. Oh well, at least I knew how
to get the most mileage out of Ian, I thought as
I reached for my sunglasses—just as Ian's hand
grasped mine.

I gasped and looked up.

His face had grown stern and his eyes darkened. I looked down to see that beneath the sunglasses was a printed page of several paragraphs.
Ian didn't want me to read it.

While still holding my hand (and not in the
least bit sensual way), he grabbed my glasses
with his other. "Here."

Once he let go, I rubbed my wrist so he could
see it smarted. It really didn't, but I thought I'd
make Mr. Ian think twice about touching me
again. And I didn't have to think twice about
coming back here during his coffee break.

"Thanks and sorry." No point putting off my
investigation. I looked down toward his comput-

er although he tried to turn it farther away. "Well, I can see you are busy. I'm off now but, as I said, will be back. Have a great day!" I added that last part to try to get on the good side of one Mr. Ian James.

"Welcome to the Samuel Freeman Lodge," Arlene Hallowell, the innkeeper, said.

"This place is gorgeous." I turned around to check out the foyer where I stood while Arlene filled out some paperwork on the other side of the counter. From there I could still see the main foyer whose forty-foot ceiling gave the place an air of gothic beauty. Dark oak paneling covered all the walls, staircase, and ran right up to the ceiling. Stained-glass panels hung freely at the top, and the windows were leaded glass. Wow.

I turned back, leaned on the bottom part of the door and sighed.

This job was going to be glorious.

Living in a mansion that Fabio was paying for (okay, against his knowledge, but my buddy and his receptionist, Adele, had set it up for me; I owed her big-time) would be fab. What Fabio didn't know wouldn't hurt him had become my motto after Adele had put the idea into my head.

"Thanks." Arlene told me how the place had been the home of a Samuel Freeman in 1892. Apparently he'd been one of the leading politicians in the area, although not very well liked. She actually intimated that old Sam might still be around. Yikes. Then she called to one of the other staff to give me a tour.

Tina took me on a short walk around, and after
telling me to make myself at home, showed me
the refrigerator, the complimentary coffee and tea
setup, and the porch were I could sit and rock to
my heart's content. While we headed up the stairs,
she added, "No red wine in the rooms. Stains the
carpets. You can have any other one though." She
seemed to get a bit nervous when she said, "Arlene is a stickler about the red wine."

I couldn't even concentrate on wine or the fact
that I'd rather have a Coors. There was an air
of opulence, a feeling that I'd stepped back into
the enchanted Gilded Age when I walked up the
staircase. At the top, Tina opened the door to my
room and stepped aside.

Suddenly I felt as if someone else was in the
room—but it was only the two of us. Hm.

The room was tiny by comparison to the rest
of the lodge, with a bed built into the wall with
drawers underneath. It looked as if it had come
off a sailboat in the 1800s. She showed me the
bathroom, which in fact was much larger than the
room and had a double shower.

I looked at it and groaned. What a waste.

Who was I going to share it with? Before I could
get maudlin, or start fantasizing about Jagger,
I thanked Tina as she left, stuck my suitcase on
the bed and flopped down when the door clicked
shut. "Ouch!" I'd hit my head on the back wall
in the tiny space, but excitement had me ignoring it.

This was going to be a fabulous gig.

And the best part was—I was going to do it *myself*.

A cold breeze swept across my face—and the windows were closed.

"Oooooooh!" Goldie shouted as Dr. Cook placed a tiny nose speculum into his right nostril.

I leaned forward and grabbed Goldie's hand. "Try to relax, Gold. He'll be done in a minute." I turned to the doctor and gave him a "you better not hurt him again" kinda look. In all honesty though, I knew Goldie's level of pain wasn't very high. If I thought the doctor was doing something he shouldn't have been doing, I would have been out of my seat and complaining in a heartbeat— or maybe even clocked the guy.

No one ever hurt Goldie.

For a few seconds I watched the doctor, until he'd finished the exam. All in all he seemed ethical, knowledgeable, and not bad to look at. He stood there wearing a white lab coat over what had to be a silk shirt and tie. His shoes alone probably cost more than my college education. Fabio was right about Newport being a wealthy town.

Then again, maybe old Doc Cook could afford to look so good because he was scamming the insurance companies.

I leaned over as nonchalantly as I could to see what he wrote about Goldie. Nothing. From that distance I couldn't see anything. Gold caught my glance as he wiped a tear from his eye. Nasal exams'll do that to you. Suddenly I heard a *cling* on the floor. "Oh, Nurse Sokol," Goldie said. "I dropped my watch. Could you please get it? My vision is still a bit teary."

Only my darling Gold.

"Sure," I said as I bent to get his watch, which had "fallen" nearly under Dr. Cook's feet. When I got up, I said, "Excuse me," let the watch fall onto the desk and practiced Evelyn Wood speed-reading dynamics.

Deviated septum. Deviated septum? Goldie? He'd never complained of having any breathing problems so why would the doctor think Goldie's nose wasn't divided evenly?

"Is there something I can help you with, Ms. Sokol?"

"Hm?" I looked down to see Dr. Cook seated in his chair and holding out Goldie's watch toward me—while I read his notes over his shoulder.

Oops.

"Oh, no." I grabbed the watch. "Nope. No. No. Just getting the note ... the watch. My Goldie's watch."

"Please sit down so that I can explain Mr. Perlman's options." He gave me a nasty look.

I flopped down next to Goldie and opposite the doctor. Goldie was still blotting his eyes. This should be good.

Dr. Cook stood then seated himself on the edge of the desk in front of us. "First of all, let me say we here at Highcliff Manor put the patient first for the utmost care. We pride ourselves on our skills and the unmatchable postoperative care that our nurses give."

I cleared my throat.

"Oh, true. You will have your own private duty nurse, Mr. Perlman. But unless Ms. Sokol is planning to move in here at Highcliff, you will be taken care of by our staff at certain times."

And he'll be snooping for me while they're caring for him, I thought.

Then I looked at Goldie wiping his eyes so much they were starting to turn red. Gold didn't exactly have the highest tolerance for pain or, for that matter, being uncomfortable in any way. I wondered just how much help he would actually be. After all, his recovery came first.

"So," Dr. Cook continued after explaining how the staff worked as a team around there, "on to your diagnosis, Mr. Perlman."

Goldie's hand flew from his face and waved the tissue in the air. "Diagnosis? I'm here for a nose job."

"Yes. Yes, you are, sir. However, you will be glad to know that due to your deviated septum—"

It was then confirmed that Goldie was not going to be of any help to me. He wailed and continued waving.

"Deviated what? Oh … my … God! What is that, Suga?"

I put my hand on his shoulder. "Relax, Gold. Calm down. It's just that your nasal septum—"

"Nasal whaaaaaaaat?"

"The part that divides your nose into two halves. It's shifted to one side, Gold. No big deal."

"May I interrupt?" the doctor asked.

I turned to see Dr. Cook giving me a dirty look. Who the hell cared? I'd do anything to ease my friend's worries.

"Mr. Perlman—"

"Call me Goldie."

"Fine." The doctor stood and walked back to his red leather chair, where he sat and glared at me once again.

I think he didn't trust me to be too close to him.

"I will cover the risks, including anesthesia. But you should do fine. It is merely a defect that could cause you sinus problems and/or breathing problems. After the surgery and your swelling subsides—"

Goldie moaned.

"—you will be amazed at how much better you can breathe."

"I only wanted a bit off the tip."

A bit off the tip. Hm. Insurance wouldn't pay for that, yet they would undoubtedly pay for a septoplasty to repair the deviated septum since it was affecting Goldie's breathing.

Did Gold really have this "defect" or was it a lucrative way to charge the insurance company more money than the doctor could get from a private patient?

Then again, this was Newport.

It didn't make sense that money would even be an issue for most of the patients. Why on earth would the doctor commit fraud instead of just having these wealthy patients write him a check?

Maybe there was more involved in this deception than met the eye.

I looked at Goldie, who was now crying. Quickly I got up and placed my arms around him. "What is it, Gold? Change your mind?"

"Ooooooh. Noooooo! It's just—" He sniffled and looked at me. "Defect. *Defect*."

The doctor had said Goldie's deviated septum was a defect—and Goldie feared not being perfect.

I leaned near his ear. "Miles loves you so much, Gold, your nose could be as long as Pinocchio's and he wouldn't care."

He took my hand and squeezed.

I smiled.

Three

Still in Dr. Cook's plush office, Goldie held onto my hand as I seated myself on the edge of his chair. I felt horrible to be putting my friend through this painful ordeal. Still, it was something he really wanted, and in my heart I knew that was true. Besides, I didn't have the authority or power to have anyone get plastic surgery if they didn't want to. That was just not me.

I looked at the doc, who was writing something in his notes. Probably about me. For some reason, Dr. Cook didn't take to me. Maybe guilt had him being wary.

"Are you going to go over the surgical risks, Dr. Cook?" I asked, scanning my vision on every paper on his desk and anywhere else in the office that I could see.

Goldie tensed his hold.

I bit back an ouch. "Routine stuff, I mean. Nothing to worry about, Gold."

The doctor looked up with a "do you want to

take over?" kinda look. Well, it didn't matter how or why he looked at me, Goldie's safety, health and happiness came first.

"I was jotting down a note, Nurse. I've done this many times before, and think I have it down pat." He looked at Goldie.

I curled my lips. Oops.

"Mr. Perlman, as I'd said before there are, in fact, risks involved with any surgery—"

Goldie sucked in a breath. A very loud breath.

I switched our hand positions and tightened my hold on him. "This really is routine. Don't worry about it." I gave the doc a look that said he better not frighten my patient again.

After the usual lecture on anesthesia, recovery, post-op care and what was expected, the doctor got up and started toward the door.

I still held onto Goldie's hand, knowing the part about possible death had stuck in his mind. Gently I touched his other hand and stood. "Come on, Gold. Let's go get a cup of tea."

"I need chardonnay," he said.

I patted his shoulder as the doctor held the door. "Of course you do, Gold. Of course you do."

After three glasses of chardonnay, what seemed several hours of me telling Goldie he could change his mind, and several more of him convincing me he was doing this because he really wanted to, we decided to go for a walk.

Maybe the ocean's breeze would clear our heads after this trying day.

I had to go back to my room at the lodge to

change my shoes and put on some walking
clothes. Goldie wanted to do the same, so we decided to meet at the end of the road where the
ocean swam below and to the right or left was
Cliff Walk.

In one of Goldie's brochures I'd read that the
walk ran 3.5 miles along the cliff with the ocean
below—almost seventy feet in some areas—and
on the other side, mansions and their gigantic green rear lawns. If that couldn't clear our
thoughts, nothing could.

I enjoyed my walk through the wealthy section of Newport from the lodge to where I'd meet
Goldie. Salve Regina University was spread out
among the manors, and many of its buildings
were mansions themselves. Students bustled
about, but I imagined them all wealthy kids in
the 1800s.

Up ahead I could see two people coming out
of Highcliff Manor and turning toward the ocean.
At first I thought it might be Goldie, having made
friends with one of the other patients, but on closer inspection the blonde looked a bit heavier than
Gold. Not that she wasn't svelte by any means.

"Suga!"

I turned toward the east to see Goldie waving.
Dressing in designer "beatnik" jeans with hand
painting up one leg and on the opposite hip, the
sun sparkled on the gems that were nestled amid
the designs. He wore a white linen blouse, which
made him look as sophisticated as any society
snob around there.

"Hey, Gold." I waved and hurried up to him. "Which way should we go?"

He turned toward the left. "This way the path is mostly paved. The other way has sections where you have to climb over rocks, and without railings, areas that drop seventy feet to the crashing waves."

I shuddered. "You don't have to tell me twice. It is a gorgeous day, Gold. Let's keep safe!" We laughed and passed an elderly couple walking along the cliff.

Now I felt much better about our choice of direction.

Goldie and I made small talk as we worked our way along the walk. As we passed the forty-room mansions, Gold and I marveled and oohed and aahed together. We were like two little kids in Disney World—and that wasn't that far of a stretch.

Newport was miles apart from Hope Valley, and being a hometown kinda gal, I'd never been anyplace so ritzy.

The waves clapped the rocks below, and each time I stood still long enough to look out to the open sea, I'd notice a new vessel of some sort chugging away. A mist touched my face and with each breath I inhaled the salty air.

Seagulls perched on rocks jetting out between swells of waves, and the rhythmic sound had me more relaxed than a glass of chardonnay ever could.

"Gold, are you really all right with this surgery thing?"

He turned toward me. "You know I am, Suga. I'm fine. Don't let a few screeches scare you. Sometimes I'm just so emotional. I could—"

"Oh!" I shouted and grabbed Goldie's arm.

"What? What is wrong?"

Not able to say a word, I pointed.

Goldie turned toward the walk up ahead. I know he couldn't miss the two people standing there arguing. He looked back at me. "Must be a lovers' spat, Suga. Nothing to worry about. We can pass them."

I shook my head. "Gold—" I swallowed. "She tried to ... I'm not sure ... but it looked as if she tried to push him—off the cliff!"

Goldie swung back to the couple.

The path was empty.

Not that either Goldie or I was superstitious (okay, he did carry a rabbit's foot—a pink one), but we decided to cut our walk short—after we headed to the part where the lovers' spat had occurred. If that's what it was.

There was nothing below except water, rocks and red tide, which I'd learned was tiny reddish seaweed.

"Okay," Goldie said, grabbing my arm. "I'm ready to go back."

"Me too, Gold." Something made me take one last look below. "Goldie!"

He swung around so fast his arm caught mine and I stumbled forward—and screamed.

Thank goodness for quick reflexes. Goldie grabbed my shoulder before I could stumble one more foot—to the end of the cliff and over the side.

My mouth dried instantly. "They need a wailing here," I muttered through the dryness, and then ran my tongue over my teeth for some moisture. "Railing."

"Jesus, Suga." He pulled me back and took me into his arms. "Jesus."

I stayed nestled in Goldie's hold for a few extra minutes despite the fact that several tourists passed us—and stared. Who cared? He'd just saved me from splattering on the rocks below.

Goldie eased me to his arm's length. "What the hell made you go so close to the edge?"

"Oh, geez. I nearly forgot." I started to step toward the ocean, but Goldie held me back.

"Oh, no, Suga. Just *tell* me." He held onto my arm rather tightly.

Despite a bit of discomfort I smiled to myself. It was great having a guy care so much for me—I only wished it was a heterosexual guy named...

Never mind.

"Gold, they must have thrown something over the cliff. There was a bag below. From Talbot's, that expensive chic clothing store, on the corner near the Tennis Hall of Fame."

"Well, let's head back as we talk."

I know Goldie wanted to get me off the cliff and away from any "accident" areas.

I smiled again.

We made it back to Highcliff Manor in about twenty minutes, but on the way Goldie had me feeling much better that the "lovers" were none of our concern, and it was probably something personal between them that they sent down to Davy Jones's locker.

"You're right, I'm sure. None of our business. You go ahead and get yourself a glass of wine, Gold. I'm going to head back to the lodge and take a little power siesta.

He laughed. "I hear you. I'm not the least bit tired, but I could rest after that emotional scene."

I know he was talking about me nearly catapulting off the cliff—but I couldn't get that couple out of my mind—or the stupid shopping bag.

Since it was Monday and still off-season, the lodge didn't appear very crowded. I fixed myself a cup of tea and decided to go sit on the wraparound porch before taking my nap.

Once I settled in the comfy rocker, I leaned back, took a sip of my English Breakfast tea and set the cup down on the nearby table. When I shut my eyes, I could picture the couple on the cliff.

Was she trying to push him? Or was he trying to push her?

Suddenly I wasn't sure, so I tried to use my investigative skills to re-create the picture in my mind.

He had the bag in his hands!

My eyes flew open. The guy did throw something over the cliff. Now, even from the distance that Goldie and I stood, I could see this couple had money, as my mother would say. They were dressed very yuppielike, with sunglasses I was sure didn't come from Wal-Mart, like mine. Hers must have had diamonds on the lens since the sun sparkled on them. And her hair didn't move in the ocean's breeze. It remained a perfect brunette coiffure while my blonde locks danced about, making me look like Medusa.

After a few more attempts at reviewing the scene, I told myself that I was getting way too tired. What the heck did I care about that couple anyway? At least no one, including *moi*, went overboard.

But there was something instinct told me to keep in mind.

And a Sokol's instincts were very precise—as evidenced by Stella Sokol on a daily basis.

Why I needed to keep thinking of that couple, I had no idea. But until I ate my dinner and headed up to my room for the night, I kept reliving the scene in my head.

Maybe my investigative skills were really sharpening!

I felt as if someone were watching me. I looked around.

Hm. No one in sight.

"Sweet or savory," Tina, the innkeeper's assistant, asked the next morning when I sat at the dining room table.

The question started each day off in the Samuel Freeman Lodge. She went through the two break-fast choices, and I picked sweet today. No great surprise with my penchant for sugar ... especially chocolate.

"You'll love the apple topping on the wheat pancakes. The cook always whips her own heavy cream too," she said, and hurried off to the kitchen.

I sat at the big table all by myself and decided I'd pretend that I lived there. After my meal came, I devoured it, and told Tina to give the chef my kudos. I'd hire her in a heartbeat if I really did have the money to buy this place.

Money. The root of all evil and something that I was not blessed with very much of. One of these days I really wanted to have enough savings to buy a condo of my own. As it stood, I didn't even have enough for a down payment thanks to a crooked friend, a Lexus car loan I'd co-signed, and a proclivity for shopping.

At least I'd cured myself of that last addiction lately—out of necessity and low cash flow.

I folded my linen napkin and set it near my empty plate then walked out of the lodge to go for my morning jog.

The ocean was one of my favorite spots in the world, I decided as I jogged along Cliff Walk—the safe section that was paved. Such a beautiful day had me smiling, greeting anyone that I passed and even not worrying about my case.

Deep inside I knew it would be a piece of cake, Goldie would be beautiful/handsome and all would be right with the Pauline Sokol world.

"Hey!" a woman yelled.

I stopped to listen and see where it had come from. Waves crashing below filled the air. After a few seconds and no more voices, I decided maybe I'd imagined it. Maybe the enchanting sea made sounds that had confused me. Or maybe it was a mermaid, I thought then laughed.

Or the ghost of Samuel Freeman following me around.

I wiped the sweat from my forehead and gave one last look around, then started forward.

"Hey! Over here!"

This time I stopped cold and yelled, "What? Who is there?"

An Asian couple taking pictures of the back of the Vanderbilt mansion, The Breakers, gave me an odd look. I'm sure it wasn't that they didn't understand English but noticed me yelling—to myself.

"Over here!"

Now I could tell the voice had come from a cluster of bushes that had little thorns and orangelike balls growing on it. I hurried over and noticed a flash of pink. "I'm right here."

"Help me up." This time the voice held an air of authority. Made me feel like one of the servants from the nearest mansion.

After a few "ouches" on my part, I pushed enough of the branches away to see a woman lying amid the thorns. "Oh my gosh! Are you all right? Are you hurt?"

"Only my freaking pride, honey. Get me out of here!"

I eased the thornier sections to the side and held out my hand to her. After several minutes of cursing (hers) and praying (mine) I had the most gorgeous woman standing next to me.

Even I had to admit to her beauty.

"Are you all right?" I asked.

She snarled at me as if *I'd* pushed her into the bushes. Suddenly I realized being a Good Samaritan did not come without consequences in swanky Newport.

"All right? Look at my jogging suit!" she said.

No thanks. Not even a hello. The suit was torn in several places and sticks of orange balls hung off her arm. If she wasn't so model perfect, she would have looked comical. If *I* had on that outfit, we'd both be in hysterics right now.

"I see your suit is torn—that can be replaced. Are you cut anywhere?"

Her eyes widened in horror as if it hadn't occurred to her that her perfect skin could be maimed. She swung around. "Am I? Am I bleeding anywhere?" She touched her face. "Is my face—"

"No. Not a scratch." Now that the original emergency had passed, I looked at her closely. Sure her skin was flawless, but almost too flawless. Not that I was jealous because of my pasty white skin and grayish eyes. Thank you very much Vikings for invading Poland and having me look as if I grew up in a cave.

But her lips were swollen way too big for my taste. Angelina Jolie would look thin-lipped next to this woman. Now that I took the time, I realized she was way too nipped and tucked when seen this close. "You look fine, ma'am."

She glared at me as if she didn't believe a word I said.

"I'm a nurse." Geez. As if that would have any bearings on my sanity. The woman was getting creepy, yet she did look fabulously wealthy. Stella Sokol would agree with me on this one.

"A nurse? Where?"

Great. Was she going to claim some injury that I'd have to tend to now? "I'm only in Newport temporarily." I almost said working a case, but finished with, "At the Highcliff Manor. Private duty."

She grabbed my sleeve!

I tried to ease her hand free but her two-inch nails dug into my arm.

"Highcliff? Do you know Dr. Cook?" Her voice came out so desperate, I started to feel sorry for her.

"Why ... I just met him." I tried to unlock the grip—no success yet. "Ma'am, I really have to get back to my patient." I looked down at my arm. She held tight.

"I need to talk to him."

"Oh. Well, I'm sure if you call Ian James, he can make you an appointment—"

She spat on the ground!

I yanked free and started to turn. But before I could, she said, "I spit on Ian, that bastard."

Bastard? Darling Ian?

This scene was getting weirder by the minute and not making a hell of a lot of sense to me. "How do you know Ian?" Suddenly I felt protective of the guy who hid his monitor from my view. Go figure.

"I've been a patient there many times. Besides, everyone in town knows him just like they do Olivia Wheaton-Chandler from Highcliff. The money lady herself."

Ah. Thus the overly tight skin, lips puffed out bigger than my sister Mary's after a bee sting, and eyes that slanted way too much for a Caucasian. I tucked the Wheaton-Chandler chick's name into my mental file to check out eventually.

Ah, again. Maybe Barbie here could shed some light on the fraud. I reluctantly stuck out my hand and hoped she wouldn't latch on again. "I'm Pauline Sokol. I have a patient at Highcliff who will be having surgery in a few days."

She took my hand so gingerly this time I wondered if she had come to her senses and decided she really didn't want to touch a peon like me. "Babette. Babette LaPierre."

Why did that not surprise me?

"Nice to meet you, Babette. How long ago was your last … stay at Highcliff?"

She touched one of her gigantic nails against her tooth. Babette never cleaned a toilet in her life, I told myself in that instant, and was pretty certain that included the rest of a house too.

"Let's see. I think it was about fifteen days ago."

Fifteen days? Geez, I was thinking years, maybe months. On closer inspection, I diagnosed Babette as one of those women who were addicted to plastic surgery. "Wow. So, how many procedures have you had done at Highcliff?" Not that I cared, but I'd suddenly made a bet with myself. Had to be in double digits. More than even Joan Rivers.

Babette had to stop and think for so long, I was guessing past fifteen.

"Twenty-eight. I think that's correct." She started to rub her hands against the sides of her jacket in a rather rhythmic fashion. "I tend to lose track."

OCD. I would just bet Babette had several other signs of obsessive compulsive disorder. So I figured her plastic surgery requests came from her also suffering the new fad illness, BDD. Body dimorphic disorder. Babette required more and more changes to an already perfect body, which, until therapy worked, she'd never be satisfied with.

Hm. She really might know something for my case.

We walked back to one of the side streets that led away from Cliff Walk. Obviously Babette was mortified to be seen in public with torn Armani, and I wasn't all too thrilled being seen with her. I didn't want anyone to think I had BDD. Then again, if they looked at me closely—they would see I'd never have to worry about that. Actually, I didn't want anyone seeing me with Babette in case I needed her help.

Suddenly she seemed to want to get rid of me. Or at least not be seen with me since she kept looking away and turning toward the street as if to cross.

"Well, I'm this way," I said, nodding toward the right.

"I live on Bellevue. I will see you around High-cliff though." She nodded and looked both ways before starting off.

I was wondering what she'd do if someone

were coming down the street in her direction, when all of a sudden a woman did come out of a garden path from a home bigger than the White House. The real White House in D.C.

Babette seemed as if she would scamper off, but instead she turned toward the lady. Ready to turn away, I noticed her hairdo. Stiff brunette.

Without thinking, I found myself walking across the street, all the while staring.

Babette turned around just as my mouth dropped to my chin (something that often happened when I was shocked. Mostly by Jagger though).

"Oh, you. I thought it might be someone important," Babette said.

The other woman looked at me as if she recognized me.

Babette said, "I forgot your name, Nurse, but this is my friend Daphne. Daphne Baines."

My first thought was that Daphne had BDD too. No one was born that perfect. No one.

Then my heart started to race when my second thought was: *Daphne Baines is the woman who tried to push that man off of Cliff Walk!*

Four

I started my run back to the lodge, and after making it only three streets away from Highcliff, I heard the crunching of gravel behind me. *Oh, well, must be another jogger,* I thought. Pretty soon the sound got louder—and I *felt* a presence getting near. Most joggers were courteous enough not to get too close but to move over. Not this one. I quickened my pace.

So did he.

I assumed it was a he, but to be sure, looked briefly over my shoulder. Yep. A he. All in black. Getting closer. And not looking familiar or like a real jogger since he had on jeans.

He was following me!

I sped up, and when I got one street away from the lodge I cut across a neighbor's yard. Despite some large dog barking, I ran as if trying to save my life—and I might have been.

Soon the lights of the lodge brightened my view—and my mind. There on the porch sat a couple, who I assumed would save my life if need be. Suddenly they looked past me, causing me to swing around.

The black figure sped past and out of sight.

Phew.

Who the hell was that?

If I hadn't needed a shower, I could have gone right to Highcliff. Geez, having Daphne Baines see me up close and personal, then being probably stalked, I made it back in record time.

Now I was more convinced that it was she on the cliff with that guy. Her husband? Lover? Hm.

And what the heck did they throw into the sea?

Before I'd hightailed it out of there, I did notice gigantic diamond rings on her fingers. If she were a divorcée, it didn't seem as if she'd wear all the markings of a married woman.

After a quick shower, I dressed in my pink nursing scrubs and decided to go see Goldie. Even though it killed me to stick on the damn outfit, I thought I'd look less conspicuous at Highcliff wearing it. And besides, I could get into areas that were for staff only.

"Miss Sokol," Ian said, causing me to yank my head up from *his* computer.

Yikes.

"Hm?" I bumped my temple on the shelf of the desk, but swallowed back a cry of pain.

"Miss Sokol, may I help you with something?"

Nonchalantly I hit the X in the upper corner to close the window on Daphne Baines's files before Ian could rat me out.

Seems old Daph was married—to a gazillionaire. He owned business after business, mostly in the real estate game. With the prices of housing around here, I figured the Baines clan didn't want for much. No kids, and I figured that was because Daphne didn't want to ruin her perfect body, which she'd paid dearly for.

Interestingly enough, I'd found that Daphne had suffered the ultimate to be beautiful—eleven plastic surgeries. Wow. It was a darn good thing that her hubby had the big bucks. Nothing she "required" would have been covered by insurance.

Ian moved closer, his black wing tips tapping on the wooden floor as he moved about, and he looked at his computer and then at me. "If you need something, just ask me. I'd rather you didn't feel free to do what you want around the clinic."

Ouch. Chastised by a twentysomething. *Oh well*, I told myself. There were a lot of things in this business that I had to learn to ignore, and getting myself into trouble or being embarrassed was one of them.

"I'm so sorry, Ian. It's just that I'm used to taking care of my patients and ... well, doing whatever is necessary to care for them." I sat myself on the edge of the desk—partly out of defiance and partly out of pride so that Ian wouldn't throw my butt out of the clinic.

He eased past me, clicked on the mouse, and his screen disappeared to the desktop. A lovely paradise island. "I understand you are used to working other places, but around here, no one is allowed behind the desk ... except me."

Now I really needed to get on the good side of Ian. There were other computers in the back room, but in my gut I knew Ian's *private* computer held whatever I might need.

Had to pull out the big guns. "Understood, and I'm truly sorry. Hey, let me make it up to you and take you out to lunch."

I could see a "never" forming on his lips, and no wonder. Not only had he caught me snooping, but also I was *not* dear Ian's type—even in my sexy pink scrubs. Quickly I added, "With Goldie."

Ian's eyes brightened. "I'll be ready in ten. I have some business to attend to first."

And I had a friend I needed to convince to pretend to put the moves on him—despite him being my other friend's lover.

What the hell was I doing?

Suddenly I thought of Jagger and how he'd gotten me out of trouble on more than one occasion. Well, I really wasn't in any trouble or danger right now, but I would have to do some fancy footwork to make picking up the lunch tab worth it.

"Yum! This place smells wonderful." I looked around The Market on the Boulevard and had to swallow in order not to oversalivate.

Along one wall ran the deli counter—with one section for meats, salads, and cheeses from around the world—and continued all the way down to the bakery section. I stood in front of the prepared foods, which ranged from cooked cocktail shrimp to fabulous looking beef tenderloin.

The place was a baby boomer's dream—gourmet food and no cooking.

I was starving after my jog and having found out something about Daphne Baines—even if I had no idea if it would help—I stood there getting hungrier by the minute. "Great choice, Ian." No harm in buttering him up over and over and over.

He turned to me, and I could tell he was glancing at Goldie over my shoulder. I looked around. Yep. Goldie was eyeing the specialty cheeses.

"Yes, Pauline. This is where the locals shop. Great gourmet food." His gaze followed Goldie toward the bakery section.

I'd be heading there myself real soon. Ian was proving to be a tough nut to crack, and I was about ready to pull out the chocolate. Not for him though. For me.

"Next," the college-aged girl behind the counter asked. She had an adorable Irish brogue, and I found out that several foreign students worked there and at various other places in Newport.

I waved my hand since Ian was still engrossed with watching Goldie. "That'd be me. I'll have a cup of clam chowder to start and three cocktail shrimp." Even as I said it, I winced. The little delicacies were over twenty bucks a pound, but I figured I could afford three of them—and fill up on the free oyster crackers that sat in various baskets above the salads and next to the white plastic silverware.

After I received my chowder and shrimp, I got

a free cup of water, and then sat at a table by the window. The tables were all very close together, but I found one that was next to an unoccupied one. If I got anything out of Ian, I didn't want any local ears eavesdropping. Not that they'd know what we were talking about, but I'd learned from the best in this business (Jagger) never to assume anything or talk about a case in public.

Okay, I was bending that last rule since "the best way to a man's anything is through his stomach" rule overrode the public one. Ian should be pleasantly satisfied by the time I had to pay the bill.

And hopefully I'd have something to work with other than, well, frankly—nothing.

Goldie sat down with his goat cheese, salad, and side order of pesto tortellini. Ian had some kind of roast beef wrap. Everything looked great.

I glanced down to see the liquid butter slosh around my clam chowder as I stuck my plastic spoon into the delicacy. On first taste I think I moaned. Damn. Fat and calories aside, it was delicious.

Goldie started the conversation with small talk and soon we found out that Ian had been at the clinic only three years. The way he ran the place, I would have guessed longer. *But, still, three years is long enough to help me out here*, I thought.

I stuffed the last of my horribly expensive yet fabulously delicious shrimp into my mouth. After the cocktail sauce had my eyes watering just so, I swallowed and said, "Ian, you must have seen some interesting cases being at Highcliff Manor for so long."

Yes, he did eye me over his wrap as if I really thought three years was "so long." But he was a gentleman, since at the same time Goldie gave him his world-famous smile, and Ian nodded. "Oh, yeah. I've seen plenty."

Goldie and I looked at each other and laughed. It didn't sound as fake as I thought it might. Like one of my little nieces, I leaned toward Ian and said, "Tell us. Tell us your most memorable story!"

Now I know what the term "pregnant pause" meant. It always sounded stupid to me, but I imagine when you lived through one, it would be very similar to nine months of pregnancy then hours of labor. You could hear Goldie's Rolex ticking.

Goldie touched Ian's hand. "Hey, man. Don't worry. Pauline and I are trustworthy. We'd never tell a soul." He leaned over more. "Just us friends talking." With that he held onto Ian until the guy looked as if he'd explode.

I said a silent prayer that dear Ian wouldn't get hurt. I knew Goldie would never do anything to cause Ian heartache, but the look in the younger guy's eyes said he might already be hopeless.

He turned toward Goldie, smiled and said, "Well, sometimes we get these women who have had that bypass surgery and lost oodles of weight."

I got stuck on the "oodles" and wondered if the obese women would have thought of their accomplishment in that term.

"And they take off pounds and pounds of skin," Ian added.

Goldie winced.

Ian chuckled.

And I bit my lip in order not to scream.

About ten more Ian stories later we had nothing. Nothing except the gruesome details of surgery. Seemed as if Ian had been a bit preoccupied with the actual procedures, and confessed to sneaking into the back of the O.R. to "peek."

Oh, great.

The horrible thought that Ian might not be my best snitch going sprang from my brain.

I was about ready to get up and order an entire ten layer chocolate cake when dear Ian finally made my offer of lunch pay off.

"There are some frequent fliers at Highcliff."

I put chocolate thoughts on hold. "Frequent fliers?" I knew he had to be talking about repeat customers but wanted to hear it from him. Another thing I'd learned in this business was to get clarification when a snitch told you something. Could save face and your salary in the future.

"Yeah," he said and looked at Goldie.

Darling Gold smiled, took a sip of his Perrier and said, "Tell us about them, Ian."

Poor Ian seemed to melt into a puddle of male receptionist with a foible for surgery viewing.

"Well," he said with a mouthful of wrap. "There's a couple. I guess about seven patients that keep coming back. I can't get over how much they have had done, and the next thing I know they are back."

Seven? Wow. I couldn't imagine seven patients being hooked on plastic surgery or suffering from BDD in such a small town and small clinic. Then again, Newport was not exactly the boonies. These patients probably came from all over the world to the posh, world-renowned *expensive* clinic. I'd done my homework before allowing Goldie to volunteer as a patient—and all the docs were superb and all board certified in plastic surgery.

I leaned closer to Ian. "Seven? That sounds like a lot. How can they afford to keep coming back?" Yes, I did feel stupid saying that when I knew these ladies probably could buy and sell Hope Valley. Still, I often had to swallow my pride—and sometimes my sanity—in this job.

Ian looked at Goldie who nodded. Geez. They both were acting as if I were invisible.

"Silly Pauline," Ian said.

I rolled my eyes but kept my mouth shut. I did have a great comeback but didn't want to slow down his pace. We only had about five more minutes before he'd have to get back to work. Instead of telling him to get bent, I merely giggled.

Geez again. Pauline Sokol giggling.

Thank goodness Jagger wasn't around to hear. I'd never live it down.

"Clients that come to Highcliff Manor are filthy rich," Ian said.

His eyes darkened and that last word seemed to be forced through his clenched lips. Very interesting. Old Ian was making my day and lightening the fact of my coughing up the dough for this meal.

"Oh, I see. Lucky you."

"What do you mean?" he asked while still looking at Goldie.

"I mean that you don't have to deal with insurance companies."

It was only a slight sign, and I wasn't even certain I noted it correctly. But when Goldie's eyes met mine in a look of "Ah-ha," I knew that I'd read little Ian correctly.

He'd momentarily tensed when I mentioned insurance companies.

The rest of the day I spent hanging out at the reception desk, more than likely causing Ian to suffer roast beef wrap indigestion. But I had to find out more about these frequent fliers. If they could afford all their surgery—no problem, and I was stuck in a corner as far as my case was concerned.

But if for some strange reason one or more couldn't—then maybe we were talking about a fraud investigation break in the case.

I said a silent prayer to my favorite saint, Theresa, that I was talking case break. I could sure use a bonus.

"Pauline?"

"Hm?" My head swung up to see Ian standing above me at the reception desk and looking as if he wanted to smack me. I know for sure that look said he really wanted to get *rid* of me. "Oh, hey. Yeah?"

"Is there something *else* I can do for you?"

Something else? He hadn't done a thing for me yet. "Er ... let's see. Tell me more about Daphne Baines." Oh ... my ... God. How'd *that* sneak out?

Ian glared at me as if he wondered how I knew Daphne Baines. If he asked, I had nothing. But just then my darling Goldie walked into the reception area—and I gave him a wink, a smile, and mouthed, *Help!*

Being the professional and doll that he was, Goldie came closer to the reception desk, leaned over and said, "Hi."

Ian never took his eyes off of Goldie but said, "Daphne Baines is the queen of frequent fliers. She's been here more times than me, and I get paid to come here daily. When she'd get to a point where she looked fabulous—"

He stared harder at Goldie, who had on a bright pink velour jogging suit that looked perfect with his blond wig—ponytail and all. Silver earrings dangled from his earlobes and a silver necklace sparkled on his neck. Good old Goldie looked sophisticated and hot all at the same time. He winked at Ian. "And?"

"... and, when she looks fabulous, she comes back for more."

"Must get expensive," I interjected in a soft tone so as not to break the "Goldie spell."

Worked too since Ian continued, "Her hubby owns half of New England. But he doesn't pay for her cutting anymore."

Yes!

I had to get Ian to continue, but he looked as if he might snap out of his twilight infatuation at any moment. That's when I noticed Goldie smile and bat his false eyelashes. What a guy.

"Is she independently wealthy?" I asked.

Ian shook his head. "Insurance covers her ... now."

Bingo!

Why would insurance cover her now after her husband spent thousands on nipping and tucking? It didn't make sense.

"Interesting, Ian. Why does she file for insurance now?" No point in beating around the bush. Sure it was a long shot, but the Goldie spell hadn't worn off yet.

"Her husband got fed up with her obsession for surgery. He refused to pay anymore." He laughed. "Said she was obsessed and starting to look like a freaking mannequin. I heard he even threw all her credit cards into the ocean." He laughed.

So the doctors had to come up with some medical reason why she should be nipped and tucked again. That had to be it!

Very interesting indeed.

And the Talbot's bag had not been my imagination.

Once it seemed as if we wouldn't get any more info out of Ian, Goldie made an excuse to talk to me about his surgery. We politely said goodbye since Ian would be off duty soon. I followed Goldie down to his suite where we both collapsed into salmon stuffed chairs and hugged silken pillows simultaneously.

"Well, that seems like a start. Huh?" I leaned back and shut my eyes. Sometimes I thought nursing was a piece of cake compared to investigating, but then again, this was much more fun—and I got to be my own boss so to speak.

Goldie flipped off his pink sneakers and set

his legs over the arm of the chair. "A start. But we need to find out how these women get the insurance to cover their surgery. And why would someone with so much money deny his wife her beauty?"

I looked at him. "Gold, these are obsessive cases. They look gorgeous as it is, but are not happy. Actually, never happy and suffer the pain of—"

His eyes widened.

I waved my hand. "Oh, shoot. You won't be having too much pain, Gold. I'll make sure of it. I swear."

He smiled. "I trust you, Suga. I do."

He grabbed the remote control and pushed the power button. The local news had just started, and they were about to do the weather. Goldie pressed the mute button, leaned back and sighed.

I did the same but when I shut my eyes all I could do was think. Thinking was good, I told myself. I had to think since I was really working a case and not just doing private duty nursing for Goldie. Every so often I'd have to remind myself of that. Seemed as if going back to nursing was like riding a bike—you never forgot.

There had to be some analogy about remembering how to have sex after a long ... break, but since it'd been a while, I wasn't qualified to come up with that one. *Back to work, Pauline,* I thought, and thank goodness Jagger hadn't popped into my mind.

Wait a minute, guess he just did.

I mentally shook my head and thought about Goldie's question of how the women got the insurance companies to pay. We knew the doctors were involved with diagnosing them with medical conditions in order to justify the surgery—but how come the insurance companies bought that?

Because the doctors were *credible*.

I sprang upright.

Goldie startled and pulled back. "What's wrong, Suga?"

"Oh, sorry. Nothing is wrong, Gold. I've been thinking. The doctors that file these claims have to be pretty credible in their made-up diagnoses. I mean, if they had to send in a photo of the patient, any fool would see someone like Daphne or Babette didn't need anything tucked. And if all they filed was for a deviated septum—"

Goldie's hand flew to his face.

I touched my nose and smiled. "You're going to notice a huge difference in your breathing once the swelling goes down."

"Swelling!"

Oh, boy. I had to remind myself whom I was dealing with. I got up, hurried over and hugged him. "I'm going to have you packed in ice to prevent any swelling. Really ... oh ... my ... God!"

"What?"

I pointed to the TV. "Turn it up. Turn it up!"

A blond-haired, blue-eyed yuppie newscaster stood outside some mansion. The bottom of the TV said, Newport, Rhode Island. "The police were called only minutes earlier to the Bellevue Avenue home of Mr. Chester Baines, real estate mogul ..."

Goldie and I hurried toward the television and sat on the floor beneath it.

The blond continued with, "The body was found by the upstairs maid, who says she immediately called 911."

"They really have upstairs maids?" I muttered. Then I looked at Goldie. "Daphne was murdered?"

"Sounds like." He ran his hand across his chin. I had to smile since it was such a "male" thing to do. You had to love Goldie.

"Wow. That adds a new wrinkle to this case. Wonder why someone would kill her? Wish we knew more about her—"

That jaw thing happened as I pointed to the television.

"What the hell?"

The police and some fancy dressed man (lawyer type) were walking Daphne down the huge marble staircase in front of her place.

"If she's alive, who ..."

"Behind me you can see," the news reporter said, "Mrs. Daphne Baines is being taken in for questioning about the death of Chester Baines, her husband."

Goldie and I looked at each other. "Shit," we both said.

Five

After being glued to the television set for the next few hours, waiting for more information about the death of Daphne's husband (the man I, in fact, recognized as the one on the cliff), Goldie grew tired, and I didn't want to have him get worn down before his surgery. Tomorrow Dr. Cook would let us know what day it was scheduled for. In the meantime, he went through the routine program they insisted on of healthy diet, exercise, and pampering the hell out of the patients (this in my words).

Great. This program would buy me time.

"I'll head back to the lodge, Gold. You get some rest. Thanks for all your help with my case." I kissed him on the cheek, tucked a violet silken duvet around him after he'd settled himself on the top of the bed, and then I slipped out the door.

They didn't have too many male clients at Highcliff, but dear Gold was in his element—especially in violet.

The reception desk was empty. Ian had left

hours ago. I wondered what he'd have to say about the recent news story. An elderly woman, though very attractive, bustled about in the back room. She must have been the evening receptionist, but I had no desire to stick around and find out. I had enough to think about for tonight.

Patients came and went, with bandages being the name of the fashion here. One woman, who hovered about silently, had her face so wrapped up I wondered what the heck she'd had for a procedure. Maybe I'd ask. Then again, she probably couldn't speak if she wanted to.

Time to get out of there, since all I wanted was a hot, exotic-scented bath and then to lie in bed and read. When I got outside and realized it was already getting dark, I leaned against the wall of the front doorway and did some stretches. An extra jog could never hurt and thank goodness I wore my jogging shoes with my scrubs.

I was the height of fashion in Newport.

In order to stay on the well-lit streets, I decided to jog out to Bellevue Avenue. I hadn't forgotten that I would have to pass Daphne's place. Place. Ha! How could a mansion the size of Hope Valley's town hall be called a place?

I started out at my usual pace and when I came near the Baines residence, where several patrol cars sat with lights blinking like synchronized strobes, my pace quickened. The urge to slow down was difficult to face, but I figured I'd never learn anything for my case around here.

When I went to pick up my pace, I noticed someone fly out of the topiary butterflies on the

left lawn. Male. Thin. Light hair. I crossed the
street for better viewing even though in the dusk
it didn't help. Amid all the cars—with passengers
who had stopped to gawk at the crime scene, I
was sure—I made it to the sidewalk in time to
see the brown-jacketed guy with red shirt make it
over the wall on the northern end.

That didn't seem right.

When I went around the corner, he was gone.
No sign of anyone.

I hurried over to the front of the house to find
someone in charge and ran smack dab into a uni-
formed cop. "Oh!"

He grabbed my arm, more out of saving me
from landing in the topiary ducks than from anger. "Whoa! You all right?"

I yanked free and breathlessly said, "I saw
someone, a man run through the butterflies and
over the fence. Wall. Over the wall. Light hair,
brown jacket, red shirt and male. A male man."

He looked at me a few seconds as if in disbe-
lief.

"I'm not kidding!"

Finally he turned toward two other policemen,
standing by within earshot, and said, "Go check
it out, boys."

I brushed a twig of green leaves off my arm.
"Good. Well, good luck." I started to turn when I
felt a hand on my arm.

"Not so fast, ma'am. I'll need some information from you in case we need any questions answered."

"Oh, right." I wanted to tell the cop that I was

a P.I. but realizing what I looked like, thought better. Instead I went along with being a private duty nurse jogging to the lodge and gave him all the answers I could, including how I'd seen Mr. and Mrs. Baines on Cliff Walk.

Soon I was off to the Samuel Freeman Lodge in a run, and wanting nothing more than that damn bath. The way I felt, even a nightly ghost visit would have been welcome.

I slowed one block away and noticed my shoe was untied. My luck would be to step on the shoelaces and fall flat on my face so I bent down to fix it. A car slowed enough for the lights to shine in my eyes. "Damn it," I muttered.

Then a shadow came from the bushes.

Looked like the one at the Baines mansion. Thin. Red shirt. I readied to shout to him, but didn't need to. He turned in my direction, plowed forward—and before I could scream, I was pushed down to the ground with a smack against my head.

The car lights dimmed—then went out.

My head hurts, I thought while I rubbed at it. Then I opened my eyes to see I was on the ground and recognized I was a block from the lodge. No one was around. That guy from the Baines mansion! He must have knocked me over!

Shoot. Was it coincidence that he hit me or had he seen me there and knew that I'd seen him? Oh, great. One more thing to worry about. Why couldn't I just do my job without threats to life or limb?

I eased myself up. Rubbed my head again as if that would do something then started toward the lodge. Once in the front door, I nodded to the innkeeper and headed up the stairs toward my room with no intention of telling her what just happened. I'd pass the info on to the cops.

When I got to the door and had to fiddle around in my pockets for my key, I felt something—no, someone—behind me.

I swung around.

No one.

Now my hand started to shake. The damn key kept falling back into my pocket. And the presence cast a cool breeze on my now sweat-covered top. Was I just skeptical now?

With shaky hands, I managed to shove the key in the lock, told myself I was getting paranoid for no reason, and kicked the door with my foot to swing it open.

And then I screamed.

My eyelids fluttered. For several seconds I fought the urge to open them or to just lay there and sleep or maybe die. But I didn't feel as if I'd been sleeping peacefully. Confusion had me wondering what the hell had happened, and then I felt something cool and damp run across my forehead and realized I was lying down.

My eyelids flew open.

"You're gonna make it, Sherlock."

Samuel Freeman himself couldn't have startled me more than ... seeing ... "Jagger?"

Suddenly I was wide-awake and sitting up.

"What the hell ... you nearly scared me to death. Again! You do that on all my cases."

He grinned.

I melted inside, but held my own—although barely—since it took a hell of a lot to gain control.

"What? You thought I was old Sam Freeman?" He laughed and threw the damp washcloth he'd been using on my forehead into the bathroom sink.

He was trying to revive me. How sweet. Then again, he'd shocked me into passing out—how Jagger-like.

I looked at him staring down at me. Maybe there was something in my eyes that he misread, but soon he'd seated himself on the bed next to me.

Now that was just plain too much excitement for my night.

I swallowed hard despite my desert-dry throat. "Hey, I've felt Samuel Freeman around here. I'm not altogether sure there aren't things like ghosts or spirits of some sort. We'd be pretty conceited to think we're the only creatures on this planet."

He looked at me as if I were nuts. With Jagger, I'd long ago learned to ignore those looks.

"What the hell are you doing here anyway?"

Jagger leaned against the wall, lifted one foot on the side of the bed and said, "Coincidently, I'm rooming here for R and R."

Now I couldn't even swallow. Having a mysterious, hunky fine specimen of eye candy sitting so close on my *bed* made any sensible thoughts jumble. For several seconds I let the letters R&R

settle in. Sure I knew what they meant, but Jagger? In Newport?

"How'd you get into my room?" I asked—not sure if I really wanted to know or cared.

He grinned at me.

"Yeah right. Housekeeping must have let you in."

Seemed as if my mind was clearing.

I gave talking a shot with, "R and R? In Newport? You?"

He shrugged. "I like sailing."

Maybe it was the nonchalant shrug. Maybe it was the dim lighting, closeness of male, and tone of his voice. Or maybe it was because I was so shocked at having him sitting on my bed, but whatever the reason, I bought his explanation.

"Wait a minute. Okay. I buy that you are here to rest up, and I'm sure you deserve it. And, I also buy that you like sailing, and sure, Newport is the closest fabulous harbor to Hope Valley, but what I don't get or buy is why the Samuel Freeman Lodge? Where *I'm* staying?"

Jagger chuckled, leaned near ... and kissed my cheek.

"Don't flatter yourself, Sherlock. This is an annual for me. Merely coincidence that you got a case here in town." With that he pushed himself up, walked to the door, and over his shoulder said, "Get some rest. I'll see you at breakfast. Wednesday's savory dish is eggs rancheros. My favorite. I'm next door."

Next door!

Guess he'd said that in case I needed him—for protection.

I think I sat frozen in my bed for hours before falling asleep in my scrubs.

"Sweet or savory?" Arlene asked. I hadn't noticed before but she was petite, brunette, and weighed a bit more than she should. But no one could argue that she wasn't pleasant and sweet, and besides, she'd told me that she'd worked there for over ten years.

My head pounded from a night of tossing and turning and knowing that Jagger was only a wall away. Why me? I had thought half the night. Then why him? The other half. At least I'd managed to tell the cops about the guy who knocked me over last night. I really couldn't say that he'd attacked me, so they didn't sound too interested.

"Oh, sorry, Arlene. Sav ... sweet." I had no idea what she'd just rattled off as the choices, but ordering Jagger's favorite didn't seem like a good idea to me.

I still couldn't get over that he had come here for R&R. What were the odds? And how much deviousness had gone into Jagger's R&R plans?

A few guests bustled in and out, helping themselves to coffee on the mahogany sideboard that offered homemade bakery delicacies as well as yogurt, fruit and dry cereal. Fresh floral arraingements decorated the room in pastels, and the silverware in front of me probably needed to be polished on a daily basis. It shone like it was very expensive.

Before long Arlene brought my pancakes with pecans, apples and raisins swimming in Vermont maple syrup on top. I knew it was real Vermont maple by the aroma. Delicious. She set the dish in front of me and soon I was salivating. I took my fork and sliced off a section. When it hit my tongue, my entire body shivered. "Wow. Delicious." I took a sip of tea as Arlene stood and asked a couple who'd just arrived last night whether they wanted sweet or savory.

It took all of my control to not take another bite, but I wanted to ask Arlene a question, but not with my mouth full. "Oh, Arlene, have you met the new guest who is staying in the room next to mine?"

She seemed to hesitate. Wait. Make that pause. Arlene looked deep in thought (maybe trying to figure out who was in the room) but when her eyes widened, her tongue ran over her lips and she grinned like the freaking Cheshire cat—obviously Arlene had a great memory.

"He's come here for years…"

With that she was gone as if in a dream. Geez. Maybe old Samuel had snatched her away. Or it could be having tasty Jagger coming to your establishment for years was something to drool over. Even for married Arlene.

So it was true.

I tucked that thought into the back of my head and decided to finish up and leave before *he* came down. I'd never get to work if I got hung up on the fab breakfast and even fabber company of one Jagger—last name unknown.

Suddenly I wondered how much Arlene knew about him. Coming here for years might have been a good sign—a break for me to find out more about the mysterious guy. Yeah, right. Hopefully he'd slipped somewhere throughout his visits, revealing something, and maybe she could tell me more about him than I could ever find out in Hope Valley.

"Morning."

I jumped, knocking my green tea over and soaking my delicious pancakes. "Damn it, Jagger. Stop sneaking up on me!"

He pulled out the chair opposite me. At first I was disappointed that he didn't choose the one next to me, but then again, now I could see him. Seeing him would be easier on my libido than having him sit next to me.

Shoulders touching.

Scent-inhaling pheromones.

And maybe, God forbid, brushing knees.

"Pauline, wake up. I asked you a question."

I looked up to see Jagger, holding his coffee cup in his hands and glaring at me. Oops.

"What?" I figured if I sounded annoyed he wouldn't question my trip to La La Land—on his behalf.

He took a long slow sip while the other couple chatted about going on a tour of the mansions with a nice elderly woman who sat across from them. "I asked you about Goldie."

Goldie? Why the hell? Oh, yeah. My best friend and patient. "Right. I knew that. Gold is fine. We're going to find out when his surgery is—"

Even though I knew, just *knew*, that it was going to be a waste of my breath, I couldn't help ask, "How the hell did you know about Goldie being here?"

For once Jagger didn't give me a "how the hell do you think?" look. Maybe since he was on vacation, things would be different. He set down his cup as Arlene put his eggs in front of him, and he gave her a Jagger-smile. She melted. Then he looked at me. "Fabio told me."

Fabio? A logical explanation but one that I was hesitant to believe. Then again, Fabio was clearly afraid of Jagger. I'd often wondered what kind of power or control Jagger had over Fabio. Now that Jagger was here and not working—maybe I'd do a little snooping about *him*.

It wasn't like he didn't do the same about me.

Okay. Okay. A girl could hope.

I'd left Jagger at the breakfast table chatting with Arlene about her kids and hubby and made it to Highcliff. Yes, I could see that Arlene knew Jagger fairly well. One of these days she and I were going to chat over tea. Soon.

"Morning," I said to Ian as I passed by.

"Wait!" he shouted and stood.

I swung around. "What's wrong?" Ian had a long scratch on the side of his neck that I hadn't noticed yesterday. Hm. I walked closer and tried to use every investigative technique I had about something that suddenly interested me. "How'd you scratch your neck, Ian?" flew out of my mouth before decorum and tact could even get a shot at me.

He touched his hand gently to his neck, which

looked as if he wore liquid foundation. "Oh, this. I guess shaving." He hurriedly restacked a pile of records over and over on his desk.

Ian was nervous.

"What is it that you wanted?" I leaned over the desk to get a closer look.

Fresh wound. Not fully scabbed over. Lighter pink than an old cut would be.

Ian was the guy running through the topiary butterflies last night and the one who'd knocked me down!

"Oh, Dr. Neal is going to see Gold … Mr. Perlman today. Change in schedule. The appointment is in a half hour. His office is next to Dr. Cook's." He shoved the files to the side and scurried away from the desk—and away from my gawking.

I stood there for several seconds, but he never came back, so I hightailed it down to Goldie's room. He had to be my number one concern until post-op. After all, Gold was making a huge sacrifice for my case.

After I knocked on the door, Goldie yelled to come in. When I opened it, I nearly laughed. He sat on the chaise lounge with some young woman at his feet, giving him a pedicure. Only my Gold.

"Morning." I nodded to both of them.

"Hey, Suga. This is Marilee. She's almost done. Does a bitchin' job on feet."

Marilee laughed. It didn't take much to become friends with dear Goldie. He motioned for me to sit.

"Want some tea?" he asked.

I thought of my soggy pancakes. "No," I said

then sighed. "Hey, Gold. Guess who is staying at the Samuel Freeman Lodge?"

He touched his nail to his tooth and tapped a few times as if that would give him the answer. Then he turned toward me, shook his head, rolled his eyes and glared.

"How'd you know? That is uncanny!"

"He comes here every year to get away. Long time ago I'd heard about how Jagger was on some sailing team out here. Guess he likes the water." With that he shivered.

I too had fears of drowning, so I was with Goldie on this one. "How come you never told me this?"

Goldie's forehead wrinkled. "Guess it never seemed pertinent to the conversation, Suga. When would I have worked in, 'Oh yeah, Jagger heads to Newport every year for some sailing and sea-food'?"

"R and R he calls it." I slumped back in my seat. "Actually let's drop Jagger—"

Goldie waved his hands. "No problem for me, Suga."

"Stop that. He's not like cocaine for me. He's not going to make me feel wonderful and then make me crash and burn. On to my case—"

Marilee caught my eye. Damn, I had to watch what I said, although she looked engrossed in finishing her job.

"Case of poison ivy. Any good cures, Gold?" I lied.

He winked at me. "Calamine lotion. Give it a try." He settled back to enjoy the rest of his pedicure, and I sat with my mouth shut until Marilee left with a polite goodbye.

I hurriedly told Goldie about his appointment (which Ian had already sprung on him, I'm sure just to come visit Goldie earlier) and quickly segued into last night and the scratch on Ian's neck.

"Jesus, Suga. You think Ian killed Mr. Baines?"

"No! I really don't, but I'm guessing our little Ian does know something that could help my case. I just feel it in my female premonition gut."

Goldie and I never did figure anything out about last night, and before I knew it we were seated in the office of one Dr. Neal Forsyth—a real looker if I ever saw one.

I told myself that Jagger was here, in town, in Newport, but then the doc gave me a big smile and I melted much like Arlene.

I gave him a smile back and noted that his teeth were perfect, whiter than the proverbial snow— hey, he was a plastic surgeon for crying out loud and probably traded favors with the dentist. His hair was a deep black with more than specks of silver. Although there wasn't a sign of age on the guy, he was graying before his time—and looked delicious.

"So, Goldie. May I call you Goldie?"

"Go for it." Goldie leaned back in his chair.

I had to smile to myself because it sure looked as if Gold was very comfortable with this doctor—as opposed to old Doc Cook, who was, in fact, not any older than Neal ... Dr. Neal or myself. Thirtysomethings filled the room, although

I will say, he acted older. More mature. Good for him. It was good that Goldie trusted him. That would make my conscience ease a bit.

And, I had to admit, I didn't mind working with this doctor—only because he was so much nicer than Cook!

"Fine. We work as a team around here and divide up everything evenly. I hope it's all right with you that I'll be performing your surgery."

I think I moaned some kind of sexual tone.

The way Goldie and the doc looked at me, I was sure that I had. I cleared my throat and chose to ignore that the guy made me hot. After all, Jagger was in town!

Then again, that was such a long shot; I decided I'd be a wee bit friendlier with this Neal Forsyth. Why reach for the stars when you have a gimmee right in front of you. *Pauline!* What the heck was I thinking? I didn't even know if he was married. I decided to look at the prospect of the good doctor as attainable.

I scanned the room for family photos and, phew, there were none. No ring. Which was not unusual for a doctor. Many that I knew didn't wear them because of surgery.

The décor of the place said bachelor. Leather. Glass. Chrome. No wife in her right mind would let a guy decorate his office in a way that would make the female patients think single.

"Is that all right with you, Nurse Sokol?"

"Hm?" I looked up. Neal and Goldie were looking at me. "Call me Pauline," flew out of my mouth.

Neal merely smiled. Nice.

Goldie winked.

And I swallowed so loudly to buy myself time that the entire room shook. Okay, it didn't but it sure felt as if it did. With all the decorum I could muster, I said, "I'm sorry? I didn't get what you said before." Because I was gawking at you.

"I'd like Goldie to take a few more days of our healthy diet, which is very high in protein, exercise and take more advantage of the use of all the pampering of our facility to make sure he's in excellent shape—although I have no doubt that he is."

I'm sure Goldie only heard "pampering."

"Is that all right with you, Gold? It will prolong your stay here." I leaned forward.

Doc Forsyth smelled good. Rich. Not that money influenced me, but the scent of rich was very sensual. I'd dated doctors before and found this to be true, unless they were penniless interns or residents. Then I had to focus on other things, like great sex.

Suddenly my face felt flushed. Neal was looking at me while Goldie was thumbing through a brochure on the "facility."

"Warm this month. Isn't it?" I wiped at my forehead. Sweat! I actually had sweat on it. Geez.

Neal chuckled. "I'll have Ian turn up the AC, Pauline."

I nodded and got up to hightail it out of there to save face. Before I could make it to the door, Neal said, "Oh, Pauline?"

I swung around. "Hm?" He was right behind

me! In my space. Now some women might find that unsettling, but I just thought—welcome. "Yes?"

"Goldie tells me you are single."

My eyes widened in horror. *Thank you very much my dear, dear friend*, I thought. "Very busy career," I lied.

He laughed. "I hear you. But could I show you around Newport sometime?"

Without a thought, I looked at my watch, then his hand covered it.

"Tonight I have hospital rounds and am on call for several days, but maybe next week?"

Oh hell. Did I seem too eager?

One could only hope that crimson went well with gray eyes and blonde hair—and that single plastic surgeons were not astute enough to notice.

Six

I decided to head over to The Market and pick up something for lunch. Being a place the locals frequented, I decided to join them since the other day the food was wonderful. Besides, it wouldn't hurt to sit around and "eavesdrop" on the locals.

I had a feeling that Newport was a close-knit community—if you had the bucks to be included. Thus, the eavesdropping.

Goldie had decided to go back to his room and "study" the brochure. I had to laugh, thinking he didn't want to miss out a second on the pampering. The meals they had fixed him here were not only gourmet, but nutritious and exactly what the doctor had ordered.

A butterfly darted inside my stomach—and not from hunger.

I pushed the idea of Dr. Forsyth into the back of my mind as I headed out the front door. Ian wasn't at his desk so I had to literally force my feet toward the door instead of toward his desk and valuable computer. This was going to be one of my more difficult cases, as far as trying to snoop around eagle-eyed Ian, I concluded, walking toward Bellevue Avenue. The good news was, it didn't seem dangerous—to me anyway. Poor Mr. Baines might think differently.

However, working by myself and having to do real nursing for my friend was proving more difficult. I pulled my shoulders straighter, turned onto Bellevue and hastened my pace.

I would succeed at this case.

And hopefully not die trying since every case I'd had so far ended up with me in some kind of hot water.

Had to laugh inside my head at that thought. If I didn't, I knew I might change my mind about the danger element. I concluded that staying at the lodge was more of a threat—from a ghost.

And … Jagger.

I nodded to a few women walking toward me. Of course, they'd given me odd looks since I had laughed out loud. Oh well, no one knew me around here.

Once I passed the Tennis Hall of Fame, I got to the end of the block and took a right onto Memorial Boulevard. The day had turned rather warm for the late spring, so I slowed my pace and in a few minutes noted the sign for The Market. Before I could turn into the driveway, a black Lexus limousine pulled up to the curb. The thing was so long it had to be the stretch version. I'd learned plenty about "real" cars from my uncle Walt, but limos were another story.

For some reason, I paused to see who stepped out. Mentally I chastised myself for being so "touristy." I usually didn't get enamored of money or celebrity, yet I bent down and started tying and untying and retying my shoe just to waste time so I could watch.

When I heard the car door close, I looked up in time to see Babette LaPierre and Daphne Baines walk into The Market.

Damn!

Now what? I wondered. They could be involved in the very fraud I'd come to investigate, and here I'd walked a good twenty minutes, was hungry enough to not even watch my carbs, and had to get back to do my jobs in a decent amount of time. I'd passed other small restaurants on Bellevue, but I was dying for the clam chowder from here, and besides, being waited on would take a lot longer.

Oh, well. I stood, made sure the last thing I'd done was to retie my shoes, and then walked into the store. Neither woman was in sight at first and there was a line near the deli counter. Good. I walked over and got in place, noting the fantastic looking guy in what had to be a black Armani suit in front of me. Of course, I only noticed him to make sure the clerk knew I was next to get waited on.

Yikes. The guy looked like someone who had stepped out of *GQ*.

Tall, past the six-foot mark. Light hair with greenish eyes that spoke to you (I ignored my mother's old teaching of don't talk to strangers) and a build that said daily gym membership.

I nodded and smiled at him while I ran my gaze around the store. I couldn't see past the cash registers too well, but neither woman was near the produce. No great surprise. I couldn't imagine Babette or Daphne doing any grocery shopping.

When I leaned over to see the section of tables as best I could since there were shelves blocking the way, I bumped into the man. "Oh, excuse me."

He smiled. "Hey, baby, don't sweat it."

My jaw dropped, but lately I'd gotten used to this phenomenon, so I quickly shut my mouth. Sometimes eye candy should not open their mouths.

It really was amazing and, yes, probably biased on my part to be surprised that someone who looked like this guy would talk like that. Sounded more blue collar than Jeff Foxworthy. Not that there was anything wrong with being blue collar. My dad, uncle, and one of my brothers all fit into that classification. But what didn't jibe, to me anyway, was the contrast of this guy's looks, including clothes, and the way he talked.

"Next?" the Irish clerk asked.

"That'd be me, Red," the guy said. He turned toward me and gave me a big smile. "Hope you're not too hungry, babe, this could get complicated and take a while." With that he laughed as if he'd told some hysterical, more than likely sexual joke.

I swore I'd never judge a book by its cover again.

Mr. Contradiction wasn't kidding. The other clerk was busy doing a phone order, so I had to stand there and listen to the order, of tomatoes on the wrap, but no skin. Roast beef rare, but not too. Nothing with peanuts, but a dab of Beluga caviar and five black oil-cured olives on the side. Five, he repeated.

I rolled my eyes and Mr. C went on and on and my stomach growled at him louder than a pit bull eyeing the rare beef.

When he was done, he took his order and turned toward the table section. I ignored his comment of "Later" as I eased up to the counter and ordered my clam chowder. That was all the time I could waste here, but I knew it would fill me up until dinner.

When the Irish girl, who I'd learned was named Sheila, handed me the take-out container, I thanked her, got my plastic spoon, bag of oyster crackers and a napkin. I turned toward the window to see Mr. C sitting with Daphne and Babette.

Oh ... my ... God. Was he "man-made" like the two of them?

After gawking at Mr. C and the two plastic surgery addicts, I decided I better get a table before my chowder got cold. Since I'd been so preoccupied with the threesome, I noticed several customers had just about filled up the small section of tables. The area wasn't large by any means, so now I was stuck.

There was, however, an empty chair to the back of Babette and one table over. Only one young girl

sat at the table for four and she was reading the
morning newspaper.

In this job I had to learn to be assertive and not
worry about what anyone thought about me, so
I made my way over to the seat saying "Excuse
me" several times as I bumped into diners in the
close quarters.

"Hi. Is this seat taken?" I asked.

The girl looked up at me, looked around the
room and said, "Uh hah." With that she went
back to reading.

Perfect. At least I wouldn't have to make empty conversation with her—and instead be able to
eavesdrop my heart out. Now thankful that the
place was crowded, that my chowder smelled
heavenly, and that neither Babette or Daphne
paid me any mind, I sat down, lifted the container
lid off, ripped the plastic off my spoon and took
a spoonful. It really was heavenly. Again the butter swam atop the liquid. I should have probably
skimmed it off, but what the heck. I told myself
this job was like a vacation. Who wouldn't think
that about swanky Newport?

"Just the tip of my nose," I heard Babette say.

My forehead wrinkled. Surely that wasn't dining conversation—except maybe for poor BDD
sufferers. I wanted to swing around and shout
that her nose was perfect and no one could im-
prove on perfect, but I had to fill my mouth with
a huge spoonful of clam chowder instead.

I tried to lean back more but didn't want to be
obvious. Thank goodness there was a table full of
jock boys between us. I guessed they were from

Salve Regina, and they were eating half the deli in one swallow. Luckily they weren't rowdy though. I could still hear Babette and sometimes Daphne talking.

A few times she sounded a bit tearful, and I had to remind myself that although she was out to lunch with supposed friends, her husband died yesterday.

Allegedly murdered. Yikes.

One might assume she'd be home mourning—or at least dressed in darker clothes.

But nope. Daphne wore a shocking pink set of slacks with a pink (exact shade) and white striped long-sleeve top. Her hair was pulled back into a chignon, which made her facial features (yes, perfect ones) stand out. Not to mention what it did for the gazillion carat diamond stud earrings that she wore. Wow.

Accidentally I made a slurping sound that drew the girl at the table's attention. "Oops. Sorry."

At first she looked annoyed, then she looked more—amused.

I took that as a sign to speak to her. "Sorry again. I'm just so hungry and need to finish fairly soon."

"Where you nursing?"

I was ready to ask how she knew I was a nurse then realized I had on my pink scrubs. "Oh, I don't work around here. I'm only temporarily at Highcliff Manor doing private duty nursing. Only one patient."

"And a rich *bitch* I'm sure." I noticed her knuckles whiten as she held the newspaper tighter.

Hm. Interesting. "Actually a male and a sweet-heart. I'm Pauline." I held out my hand.

She hesitated then released her life grip on the paper and shook, very weakly. "Lydia."

Hm, again. Why the hesitation?

"Nice to meet you. This place is amazing for its food. Isn't it? So, what is your favorite dish here?" I'd read a long time ago, to entice someone into a conversation, not to ask only questions that could be answered with a yes or no. Before she could answer, I noticed her look past me and frown.

"The beef tenderloin," she said in a matter-of-fact way.

I tried to sweep my hair back with my hand to use the gesture to turn a bit. All I could see was Mr. C, glaring at Lydia. What the heck? I had to act fast and wondered what Jagger would do in my position. Since I could never second-guess a Jagger-action, I said, "You know him?"

She looked back at me. "Do you?"

"Oh. No. I merely stood behind him in line. Took so long I thought I'd pass out from low blood sugar."

"Blood sugar?" She released the paper and let it fall to the table.

I had to remind myself that Lydia was a kid. Geez, that made me sound so old. But she couldn't be more than seventeen or so. Technically I could be her mom. Yikes. "Low blood sugar from being so hungry."

"Oh. That doesn't surprise me."

I felt my forehead wrinkle again. Had she assumed I'd have low blood sugar? Did she even know what that was? What the heck was she talking about? I had learned from Jagger to get my facts straight, so I asked, "Excuse me? I'm not following, Lydia." I set down my spoon and remembered that I had forgotten to get a free cup of water. No way was I going to get up now, in case Lydia might open up again or leave.

She motioned with her head toward the threesome. "Him. Devin. Doesn't surprise me that he'd push his way in front and take forever to order. Jerk. Selfish jerk."

Very interesting indeed!

Seems that not only did Lydia know Mr. C, but she also wasn't too fond of him. "Selfish jerk. Wow. That's a pretty heavy accusation."

She looked at me. "It's not an accusation. It's a *fact*."

My heart started to race as it so often did when I was about to learn some tidbit of info for my case. I knew the feeling and this sure was it. One darling Lydia was about to spill her guts about the guy I suspected had made the rounds on the O.R. tables.

Suddenly I wondered if my buddy Ian had snooped in on any of Devin's cases. Had he frequented Highcliff Manor too? That was the more important question. This was getting very interesting because if Devin suffered BDD too, how was he paying for his surgery? Rich wife? Family inheritance?

I looked up at Lydia. "Fact?"

"The asshole is married to my aunt." She started to rip edges of the newspaper off and leave them in little piles on the table.

Rich wife.

I caught a few shreds of paper as they fluttered in the air before Lydia got thrown out for littering and said, "Wow. Your aunt must be pretty young." With that I sipped my clam chowder so as not to appear too eager to learn more.

In the reflection of the window, I noticed good old Devin get up and walk toward the cash registers. Daphne and Babette followed. Damn, no more eavesdropping. Well, at least I had Lydia to grill for info. I just had that gut feeling that she was going to be helpful to my case.

"What's your last name, Lydia?" Suddenly I felt like a weirdo asking the kid personal questions.

She looked at me. "Chandler."

As in Olivia Wheaton-Chandler?

Lydia suddenly got up.

My spoon flew from the chowder, splashing white liquid onto the pile of newspaper pieces and Lydia's probably very expensive jeans. I'd heard that name before and not in a very good tone either. What was the connection?

I grabbed a napkin and wiped at the denim. "Oh, I'm sorry. So sorry."

She pushed my hand away. "It's all right, Pauline. Not sure what you're so wired about, but maybe you should ease up on the caffeine." She laughed and walked toward the bakery section.

Good. Maybe she wasn't leaving after all.

I scraped the rest of the fabulous liquid from my container and decided I really needed some water. Seemed safe enough to get up now that the threesome had left. No one else in this place knew me—or at least I hoped they didn't.

I poured myself a cup of ice water that the store owners smartly left on the sideboard with lemons and more plasticware. I stabbed at two lemon wedges, plopped them into my water and added a pocketful of Splenda. Instant, and ashamedly I admitted, free lemonade. It wasn't that I was destitute, but Fabio didn't pay my expenses yet so I had to make sure I didn't spend more than I was earning on each case.

Money, the root of all evil.

If only I had a sixth of the amount as some of these folks, I could afford my own place instead of living with my two dear friends. Speaking of Goldie, I had to get back to see him soon.

Lydia ordered a cup of English Breakfast tea to go with the chocolate chip cookie she'd bought. Good, that meant a longer time to "chat."

I walked near her and ordered the same tea but no cookie. Too much time to spend on guilt to run off the calories when I should be working. So I paid for my tea, put skim milk in it with two packets of Splenda, and went back to "our" table.

Darling Lydia had already sat down and was eating her cookie. She didn't look as if she wanted me to sit at another table, thank goodness. There were plenty empty now, but I pulled the chair out with my foot and sat, without giving her the option. I noticed she didn't have milk in her tea.

"Is your aunt—"

"The one and freaking only Olivia Wheaton-Chandler."

Yikes! The "money lady."

"That would make Devin your stepuncle." Going right to the heart of matters seemed the less painful route—and it did look as if it pained Lydia to answer.

A darkness filled her brown eyes—much darker and dangerous looking than anyone her age should have. Wow.

"Look, the jerk is not my step *anything*. I don't give a shit what the rules are. He married my aunt Olivia for her dough. Plain and simple. He is not family and is way too freaking young for her. Ick." She shoved a large piece of cookie into her mouth.

I felt badly that our conversation was probably prohibiting her from enjoying the delicious calories, but cookies aside, I had to find out as much as I could since plastic surgery was involved—and this town was so tiny.

"Yikes. That's quite an accusation." I tried to chuckle but Lydia's lips firmed, stopping me mid-chuckle.

"Not that you probably give a rat's ass, Pauline, but Devin McCloud was a carpenter. No, not even a real carpenter. One of those handymen who worked his way into my aunt's house and into her ... freaking bed." She shivered.

So did I. Ick was right.

"Anyway," she continued without my prodding, "the guy isn't around more than two months, and they get hitched. Freakin' hitched. I think he found out some dirt on Auntie, but I never could prove it."

Either that or he was damn good in the sack.

I stared at her over the rim of my teacup. For a teenager, she sounded so astute. How in the world would she suspect such things—and how in the world did old Devin manage all that? "That must have upset the entire family."

She licked chocolate from her finger and looked at me. "I'm the only freaking blood relative, Pauline, and I'd rather commit suicide than be considered family to those two."

Speechless was not usually in my autobiographical vocabulary—however, Lydia had me momentarily unable to comment. I kept watching her and thinking, *Man, what do I say to that one?*

Finally I yanked my sanity back and said, "Suicide? That's pretty heavy-duty stuff, Lydia. I'm sure you don't mean it." I tried to sound as serious as I felt, so she couldn't back away from my comment. However, with teens nowadays, you never knew.

Instead she leaned closer, actually grabbed me by the arm and said, "Suicide would be a welcome relief compared to *living* with those two."

Seven

All the way back to Highcliff, I couldn't help but think of the pain in Lydia's eyes and the suicide statement from someone so young. Someone who should be looking forward to her entire life—and enjoying the heck out of her youth.

Then I thought of her situation. Where were her parents? Why live with an aunt? Why would that aunt marry some assumed gigolo who was young enough to be her son, according to Lydia?

By the time I walked into the driveway, I had no answers and only more questions. So I decided I'd get right to a source that might help me with my dilemmas.

When I walked into the lobby, I noticed Goldie sitting on the high-back chair near the fireplace talking to a few women. They were chatting and laughing, so I merely waved and headed to the reception desk—to my new buddy.

Ian sat with his back toward me while he typed away on the keyboard. If only I could stand there innocently and read over his shoulder. But the guy had radar like a bat and turned as soon as I let out what I thought was a very silent breath.

How come he couldn't have been some hard-of-hearing old geezer of a receptionist?

"Hey, Ian." I eased closer and wanted to sit on the edge of the counter, but knew he wouldn't go for that.

"Pauline. Leaving for the day?"

I'm sure you wish. "Oh, no. Just back from lunch. I love that Market on the Boulevard. Their clam chowder is to die for."

Did he just flinch?

It looked as if he did, but Ian was a pretty up-tight kind of guy so just my being here could make him flinch or any other number of negative behaviors. It wasn't that I didn't think he liked me, more that he liked Goldie better and I was a reminder that maybe he didn't float Goldie's boat. I'm sure he blamed it on me somehow.

"Ah ... yeah. Great stuff. Need something?" he asked.

"Nope. Why would you think I needed something?"

He swung around to his computer, wiggled the mouse and clicked to that paradise scene on his wallpaper. Guess he didn't worry about being too obvious that he was hiding something from me.

And here I was just a plain old private-duty nurse. Why would the guy act like that with me? Unless ... he had such a guilty conscience that anyone that came near his precious files was automatically disliked.

Dear Ian, just what are you hiding?

The guy sat there on the mahogany desk chair, at the mahogany counter, looking oh so cute and innocent yet acting like one of the queen's foot guards at Buckingham Palace.

I was no dummy. I needed reinforcements.

While Ian kept his back to me, I looked over at Goldie and gave him a mental *Help!* over and over until he looked up. Man. That actually worked. Or else he just happened to look up. I chose to think I had some kind of special connection and/or powers. I winked at him and motioned with my head.

In seconds my friend was next to me and making small talk with Ian the guard, who at this point would have let me raid his computer without a thought while he drooled over Goldie.

Sure I felt guilty—but only for a few seconds.

Before I knew it, miraculously, Goldie had Ian up and walking toward the back patio to get a cup of tea! For a few minutes I stood there in awe until I realized it was my chance to do the real work that brought me there.

The women in the living room area were so preoccupied at looking in the many mirrors that decorated nearly every wall in the place and with chatting like a Stepford wives' coffee klatch, I felt I could make this move unhindered.

My theory—which I'd just developed, by the way—was that if you acted nonchalant and like nothing was wrong and like you *belonged*, no one would question you. So I walked purposefully behind the desk, gave a quick look toward the patio door, to see it was empty, and sat in Ian's chair. Thank goodness I was shorter than he because once I was down, no one could see me behind the counter.

Luckily he hadn't stuck the computer into some security mode where I'd need a password. Thank you, Saint Theresa. Then again, maybe Goldie's presence had made poor Ian so nervous that he forgot. Either way, I was happy. Not being the most computer savvy girl in the world, I clicked and fiddled until I found the Window's Explorer icon. When I opened it, my heart sank.

Ian had some weird code name system for all the files. How the heck did the other receptionists follow along? Then again, noting the way Ian had been with me, I'd bet he "volunteered" to do all the files and computer work himself, leaving them to only answer the phones and "guests'" questions.

Very clever guy that Ian.

But was he somehow involved in the fraud and knocking me over—not to mention Mr. Baines's murder?

My heart skipped a few needed beats on that one. Just the mention of the word did that to me since I changed professions mid-career. Sure I'd dealt with death in nursing, but murder took on a whole new meaning—and not a very pleasant one.

Little Mary Sunshine. Darth Vader. Brad Pitt. Johnny Depp. I took a moment to sigh. Little Red Riding Hood and Alice out of Wonderland. What the heck kinds of file names were those? I didn't have time to open and close each one so I had to make a judgment call here.

What would Ian title his most secret file?

I ran the cursor along the right column to scan down the list of file names on the left side. Suddenly one caught my attention. All the others had been capitalized but not this one: ff.

At first I thought it a typo, then I leaned back in my chair. Frequent fliers. Ian had called the repeat customers "frequent fliers." I clicked on the file folder icon and opened a document that listed familiar names like Daphne Baines, Devin McCloud, and Babette LaPierre. Ian had been wrong though. There weren't only seven names listed.

There were twelve.

And all files were dated within the last six months.

Because of Lydia, I clicked on Devin's file first. "Oh ... my ... God!" snuck out before I could swallow it back. The before and after and after and after photos of the guy were unbelievable. He'd started out looking as if he'd spent way too much time in the sun and at a young age, and thus had more wrinkles than a Chinese shar-pei. Not only was his nose bigger than needed, but it also seemed too far up on his face.

Remembering back to lunch—nothing was misplaced on old Devin's mug now.

I ran through the file and saw he'd had numerous surgeries in a very short amount of time. Dr. Forsyth had performed the first few then Dr. Cook took over.

Suddenly I wondered if I really wanted to go

out with Neal. Then again, I'd do it for my case. In my mind I could hear my mother saying, *Pauline, if you lie, your nose will grow like Pinocchio's but since yours is not wood, it will hang down to your knees.*

Man! That had to have had some physiological effect on me. Maybe that's why I wasn't such a good liar. Nevertheless, I had to go out with Neal and find out more about these patients.

Quickly I opened and read six of the others' files, including Babette's and Daphne's since I "knew" them. All really did suffer from BDD. There were a few notes from Neal about "highly suggest waiting on this procedure," then the next entry would be a pre-op note from Dr. Cook stating that he and Dr. Forsyth had discussed the issue and surgery was scheduled in a week.

Neal had agreed.

Damn.

I heard a rustling sound and paused.

"Ian, can you get me the file on Mrs. Benoit, please?" a woman called out.

Shit!

I mumbled an "Uh-huh," all the while hoping the woman wouldn't lean over the desk.

"I'll be back in ten," she said and I heard the clicking of shoes getting fainter.

Quickly I jumped up to see her standing by the elevator. She couldn't see me since Ian had the most beautiful silk flower arrangements adorning the area. One of the larger ones had a school of tiny fish swimming about in the clear glass vase. The plants were real since long roots fluttered in the water, giving it a wonderful fantasy atmosphere. It was almost as if Ian had built himself a stylish, chic barrier around his workstation.

Very interesting.

I could see that the woman was one of the nurses, since she had on navy scrubs with matching clogs. Thank goodness I had excellent vision for distance and could read her name tag: Kerie Cetin. I hadn't met any of the nursing staff yet, but she would be a start.

My only problem was, how to get her message to Ian?

When I clicked the close button on the ff file, I heard Goldie talking so loudly that one would think he was deaf. For a second I thought about yelling at him to quiet down, but then realized—Goldie!

Working better under stress, I scribbled a note for Ian about Mrs. Benoit's file, signed it a messy Kerie and jumped up. Before they made it back to the desk, I was out the front door, huffing and puffing—not from lack of exercise, but merely from nearly getting caught.

"Sounds as if someone is not in very good shape."

I swung around toward the voice. "Oh, hi, Dr. Forsyth."

"Neal. Please."

Neal? Please? What the heck? "Oh, yeah. Neal. Actually I am very much in shape ... I mean ... my body has never been ... er ... actually I'm fitter today—"

I felt a finger touch gently to my lips.

Since I was making such a fool of myself, he should have just strangled me.

"I have two eyes, Pauline. I can *clearly* see what shape you are in."

My knees buckled.

Thank goodness I wasn't an airhead and could recover my wishful thoughts quickly. I took in a deep breath, let it out slowly then smiled at Neal. "You're a doll to say that." Hopefully that came out chatty and not enticing.

"Are you finished for the day?"

I leaned against the stone wall that ran the length of the driveway and, wondering why everyone around here thought I was leaving—or maybe should be—said, "Oh, no. I have to review some pre-op stuff with Goldie. Mr. Perlman, that is."

He chuckled. "He's quite the character."

My shoulders stiffened. No one insulted my dear friend. But then Neal chuckled again, and I got the feeling he wasn't really making fun of Goldie. "He is a fantastic guy," I said.

Neal smiled. "I'm sure. Look, how is next Monday for you?"

Next Monday? I barely knew what I was going to be doing in the next hour. Back in my nursing days, every hour, every minute, was planned out to meet patients' needs and do patient care. Since leaving that highly organized profession, I found my days had no plan to them. I could come and go and do my investigating as I pleased. Seems as if my organizational skills had burned out with my resignation from that career.

It still amazed me to surf the TV channels to see Jerry Springer or Martha Stewart mid-morning. However, it hadn't taken me long to get used to the fact that I could come and go at will. "I think Monday would be fine, depending on Goldie's recovery." I stood there smiling and waiting.

"I'll pick you up around seven." He smiled back and again my knees did the thing they do when a hot guy gives me that look. Jell-O.

"Okay. So. Seven." I turned toward the door. "Oh, Neal. I forgot to tell you where to pick me up. I'm at the—"

"—Freeman Lodge. Got it."

Got it? How the hell did he get it?

Once in Goldie's room, I flopped onto the bed and while sinking into the fluffy duvet said, "I need a moment here, Gold."

Got it? Now I really was curious to know how Neal knew where I was staying. I shut my eyes to try to remember if I'd ever mentioned it. Why would I have though?

I felt the bed sink on my left side and peeked out to see Goldie lying there, sans makeup, wig, and wearing a white tee shirt and jeans. Male jeans. He looked adorable.

"Hey, Gold." I opened my eyes and pushed up onto three pillows. "Do you remember me ever telling Neal that I was staying at the Freeman Lodge?"

Goldie flopped onto his stomach next to me and looked me in the eye. "Neal? Neal?"

I slapped his arm. "Stop that. It's nothing. Merely a tour of Newport and a meal."

"Ha! Hey, I'm glad you have the hots for my doc."

"Yeah. Okay. You found me out. I'm only going out with him to make sure his hands don't shake when he holds his steak knife!"

Goldie let out a loud fake shriek.

I slugged him again. "Really though, Gold. He knew where I was staying, and I don't remember ever telling him. Did you?"

He rolled onto his back and tapped a long red nail on his tooth. Even in his male clothes, somehow the nails fit. Only on my Gold though. "Geez. No, Suga. I don't think I ever mentioned it. Doesn't seem as if I'd have a reason."

"Neal never asked about me?" I cleared my throat. "You know, professionally?"

"Don't worry about sounding conceited, Suga. You're a knockout of a woman so plenty of guys will be asking about you, but not Neal. Besides, I've never been alone with him. You've always been there too, Nurse Sokol."

"Hm. You're right." I knew he was correct, the more I thought about it, which made it all the more interesting as to how Neal knew—and why.

The next few hours I spent on Goldie's bed with him, discussing his surgery. After giving him a few more chances to renege on the deal, I was convinced that he wasn't just doing this to help my case.

When I mentioned how I'd spoil him rotten

post-op with fluffing the millions of pillows in this room, getting him magazines that he insisted I'd read to him, always have the remote handy, and black out the windows so he could sleep, Goldie would purr.

Warmed my heart. I'd smile.

Purr was not exactly the word I'd use when I tried to prepare him for things like: I'd have ice bags ready to prevent swelling, moisturizers and scar-reducing creams and petroleum jelly for incisions (with the doctor's okay) not to scar, and laxatives at the ready since pain meds could be binding.

We agreed Goldie would follow all my rules and the doctor's without hesitation. I gave him a hug, got up and thought to myself that taking care of dear Gold could be more work than having an entire caseload of fourteen post-op patients.

But I'd do my best.

And tender loving care would come easy for me.

I gave him a kiss on the cheek, left him on the bed so he could take a "power siesta" and headed out the door.

Back at the lodge, I walked in the doorway to find Arlene dusting the bust of, I guessed, Samuel Freeman. For a second I pictured Jagger's face under her dust feather. Ha! Imagine him a bronze bust!

Arlene turned and smiled at me. "Hello, Pauline. Have a good day?"

I thought of the handsome Neal and said,

"Sure. Yeah. It was a good one." I walked closer and touched the cheek of the bust.

Cold. Hm. My finger felt cold.

I pulled back and told myself that bronze always felt cold. "Was he some patriot or something?"

Arlene gave me a confused look then turned toward the bust. "Oh, him?"

I nodded but refused to touch him again. Way too woo woo for me, this ghost stuff.

She laughed a deep hearty laugh. "I think there actually was some patriot up in New England named Samuel Freeman, but that's not our Sam. Oh, no." She tapped the bust on the head, laughed and said, "Patriot ... ah ... no."

I half expected it to turn toward her and shout, "Cut that out!"

But the bronze remained firm and Arlene continued, "*Patriot* is not the word I'd use for Samuel Freeman—"

"Pirate. Scallywag," a voice said from behind.

A familiar voice. Oops. There went the pitter-patter of my heart.

I swung around to see Jagger in the doorway and asked, "He was a pirate?"

"Swashbuckler extraordinaire." He remained standing there in black jeans, black tee, and sunglasses still on. I wondered if they had a tiny camera in them and if he was filming right now.

I only wished.

I fluffed my hair just in case and laughed. "Wow. Imagine. A real pirate lived here." I looked around and felt a cold breeze on my face. *That came from the open door behind Jagger*, I told myself.

The two-story foyer gave the place an air of opulence. The deep mahogany wood said expensive, as did the handmade stained-glass ceiling of clouds and waves above. Actually this was the first time I'd noticed waves on the ceiling. Sure as heck didn't look like some pirate's lair.

Jagger stepped forward, letting the screen door slam behind him. I looked at Arlene, waiting for her to yell at him, but she kept dusting.

He turned toward the stairs and said, "Don't let the place fool you. Freeman was a buccaneer—and deserved what he got."

The screen door flew open—by itself, it seemed.

Arlene scurried out of the room.

I gasped.

And Jagger *swaggered* up the stairs—as if nothing had happened.

Eight

I stood in the very hot shower and shivered. Damn it. Felt as if someone—no, make that old Pirate Sam—was watching me. Jagger did that door thing on purpose. I was convinced. He just wanted to rile me up—and I'd never tell him it worked. Arlene was busy and hurried off to do her job and the wind blew the door open because Jagger let it slam and the lock didn't catch.

A logical explanation for everything.

I turned the water a bit hotter and wondered how Jagger knew so much about this place. He sure didn't seem the history buff type to me or the quaint New England bed-and-breakfast type either. Then again, the guy had been a mystery to me from the get-go. I really needed to find out more about this place I was going to be living in the next few weeks—and, it pained me to say, more about Jagger.

What irritated me about him was that I knew

how difficult it would be to get anything out of Jagger about himself.

When I shut my eyes to rinse off my face, he popped into view. My eyelids flew open, a droplet of soap snuck in and burned, so I screamed then said, "Okay! So it doesn't pain me. I want to know. Leave me alone, Samuel!"

When I stepped out of the shower, I wrapped the huge, fluffy towels they provided around myself and walked the few feet into my tiny bedroom. When I looked at the side of the bed where Jagger had sat, I tightened the terry cloth as if to cover up more.

Knock. Knock.

I jumped at the sound. The towel loosened and fell to my feet. "Damn it. Hold on." I grabbed it and rewrapped myself. Had to be the maid since my room needed to be serviced. "Wait a second." Holding tight, just in case, I touched the handle of the door, ready to turn it.

"Come on, Sherlock. I'm getting hungry."

I yanked my hand back. Jagger! Thank goodness I hadn't opened the door! Saint Theresa was keeping a decent eye on me—okay, make that keeping me morally decent. Damn. "What are you talking about?"

"Supper? Let's go get something to eat. Open the damn door."

I stepped back. What nerve! He assumed I was free tonight and, well, I was, but that didn't make it right. "I'll meet you in the lobby in a few minutes."

Even with the door shut I could *feel* Jagger looking at my terry-cloth-clad body—and my insides fluttered, seconds before I dropped said towel.

After I dressed and undressed and redressed since, unfortunately, I wanted to look good for Jagger, I ended up in my black jeans, white shirt with matching camisole top beneath, silver jewelry and tan suede heels. It said sophisticated and hot all at the same time—at least that's what Goldie had said when he picked it all out for me. Perfect Newport outfit.

Should also pique the hell out of Jagger's interest.

Wishful thinking, Pauline, I thought as I left my room and started down the carpeted stairs. At the bottom near the banister stood Jagger with his back to me and obviously looking at the photos on the walls. I'd looked at them before too, but learning about Pirate Sam now, they held more interest.

One was of a beautiful lady who may or may not have been involved with the old buccaneer. Lover? Mistress? A pirate too? Or maybe his wife? I paused at the base of the stairs and wondered who would marry a scoundrel of a pirate. What kind of insane woman would let love override sense?

As if someone was behind me and had pushed, I lunged forward.

Jagger swung around in time to catch me.

Quickly I righted myself and mumbled, "Shoe caught on carpet," while Jagger clearly said, "Save head over heels for after dinner, Sherlock."

Certainly my face couldn't have been as red as the heat felt zooming through my skin. I grumbled something incoherent, pulled my shoulders straight and walked out the door ahead of him—all the while wishing a gust of sea air would come along and blow me out to sea.

I could just see the headlines in the local paper:
Newport, R.I. Infatuated woman claims "ghost" pushed her into the arms of the delicious guy she's had the hots for since day one. Guy merely shakes his head—three times.

When I turned toward the parking lot, I paused. There sat Jagger's black Suburban. Old memories flooded back. *Old memories?* What the hell was I thinking? The only old memories I had in that thing with Jagger were embarrassing, humiliating, or life saving, and all were related to work.

I felt a hand on my lower back as he pushed me forward. "Forget something?"

I looked straight ahead. "Nope. My memories are clearly accurate." With that I sped up to move away from his hold, or lose my edge here or at least my sanity. That was for sure.

This time he did come around to my side to open the door, but only because he had to unlock it first. Guess he could have done that from his side, but maybe being away from Hope Valley had unleashed some gentlemanly qualities in old Jag.

I got in and looked at the door. Wide open. I grabbed it, yanked to shut the damn thing, and when it clicked, Jagger was already sitting in the driver's seat.

He backed out of the driveway without a word

and started out down Bellevue, taking a left past the Tennis Hall of Fame, and before I knew it we had parked in some lot near the wharf. He never even asked where I wanted to go, but no great surprise, the place looked fabulous.

Lights dotted the buildings erected side by side in typical New England fashion. Each had its own character architecture, but they were all connected. The pavement was like cobblestones only larger grayish bricks. A gigantic black anchor stood as a decoration in the middle of one walkway, and three little children sat on it while their mom took their pictures.

Tourists and locals, I guessed, hustled and bustled into the shops and restaurants. The neat thing was, it all bordered the water where boats rode the light chop while tethered to the dock and the scent of salty air mixed with various aromas of cooking food. Music floated on the night's breeze from several of the restaurants and bars while a strong aroma of fish came from the seafood market at the end of the wharf.

"This is a great place, Jagger."

He walked next to me, doing that hand thing on my lower spine again. A girl could get used to something like that, but a guy like Jagger wasn't about to become predictable.

"Turn here," he said when we faced an old white wooden building.

The Black Pearl. Suddenly I felt underdressed. Then again, Jagger had on jeans and a button-down white-and-black-striped shirt. We probably made a decent looking couple—however, I was smart enough to know that term was a long shot.

I paused to look at the menu posted near the door. Hm. Pricey. Good, let him pay big bucks for assuming I'd come to dinner with him. When I started to turn toward the door, he took my arm.

"Over here."

He led me to the area of tables outside and behind a corral-type fence. wa t er s ide pat io and r aw ba r the sign said.

Oh how very Jagger-like.

And here I was worried about my outfit. We sat near the water, which actually was a neat area. Right next to me a sailboat rose up and down in a slight rhythm while moored to the dock, and as dusk approached, little tiny white lights magically flipped on around us.

The waitress came over for drink orders. Jagger got his usual beer and, after giving me the once-over, ordered me a glass of Kendall Jackson chardonnay—without asking. I was about to yell "Hey!" but realized that's exactly what I wanted and feared if I said anything, I'd end up choking down a martini out of Jagger-spite. Usually I would have joined him for the beer, but this case, this location, this dinner "companion," had me craving wine.

Newport chic.

Soon our drinks arrived. Without a toast—naturally—I took a sip and leaned back in my chair damn angry that he *knew* I really didn't want a beer.

"I'm starved. What do you want, Sherlock?"

"Oh." I was nearly in a relaxed state of Nirvana

but sat forward and looked at the menu. "Clam chowder," came out first. I figured I'd try it in every restaurant in Newport until I was sick of it. I'd never had better, creamier New England clam chowder than in this town.

"What else?" he asked.

"That seems enough." I took another sip of wine and watched him scowl at me.

"You do oysters?"

Do oysters? Even that sounded sensual coming from him. "I've actually never eaten one. They aren't cooked are they?"

Jagger chuckled as the waitress came over then ordered a dozen native oysters (which I noted cost more than I'd spent on lunch for Goldie, Ian and myself), my clam chowder and two steamed lobsters.

When the waitress left, he looked at me with those Jagger-eyes. "Don't tell me you don't like lobster."

"Okay. I won't tell you." I took a long, big sip. Somehow it gave me more stamina to deal with this guy whose knee occasionally touched mine beneath the table.

Yikes.

"You've never had one, have you?" He drank his beer from the bottle, just the way I liked it.

"Actually I have. I love lobster." I leaned back and smiled. "*Nick* used to take me to Madeline's for lobster."

Jagger remained silent.

Ha! Nick Caruso was Jagger's nemesis and did occasional freelance work for Fabio. Nick was as handsome as Jagger was hot and as sophisticated as Jagger was ... yum.

However, they had a past, not a very jovial one, and really didn't seem to like each other. Hence the attempt at lobster memories with Nick—whom I'd dated so briefly that I'm sure he would refer to me as "Pauline who?" if anyone mentioned my name.

Jagger drank the rest of his beer, flagged the waitress and ordered another round. I wanted to shout that I was fine, but actually thought I might need two glasses of chardonnay to get through this dinner without embarrassing myself, or antagonizing Jagger—the latter of which was way less of a possibility.

"How's the case going?"

I looked up to see him staring, with genuine interest in his eyes. Least that's how I chose to view it.

"Oh, well, good."

"What's good about it?"

"You're not going to let up until I give you all the details. Right?" My glass was successfully empty and my tongue getting looser.

He glared at me.

My insides, warmed by the wine, shivered. So I told him everything about my case including Lydia, Dr. Cook, Ian's filing system, and the BDD trio, leaving out Dr. Forsyth because, well, I wanted at least one thing kept from Jagger and why not a gorgeous guy?

Especially one who'd asked me out!

Besides, it wouldn't surprise me if Jagger already *knew* about Neal.

"So who is Lydia's aunt?" he asked as the waitress set this tray of jiggling oysters between us.

For several seconds I could only stare until they settled down. "I'm not avoiding your question, but if you think I'm putting one of those jelly thingies into my mouth, you are nuts."

"You'll try one."

The words almost had me grabbing a stupid oyster and sucking it down as the guy at the next table was doing. He actually looked as if he was enjoying it. But on principle I waved my hands at Jagger. "Nope. My clam chowder will fill me up, and I won't be able to see if Newport lobsters are better than the ones at Madeline's."

Had Jagger just flinched?

Or, more than likely, was I imagining things? Okay, more like wishing about things like he'd flinch out of insane jealousy that I'd dated Nick. It was more likely that the wine was playing horrible tricks on my mind and making me insane.

Before I could take another crazy sip, Jagger leaned forward. He held his hand out toward me and in it was one of the smaller oyster shells with the little meat glistening in the light and a dollop of cocktail sauce decorating the top.

I looked at Jagger.

He sat silent.

My mouth opened—on its own, I swear!

And before I knew it the slick oyster was inside my mouth.

My hands flew to my face, but suddenly Jagger's were holding them in both of his. "Chew."

Now "chew" is not exactly in the top ten sensual words of any vocabulary in any language that I know of, but damn if it didn't sound so hot coming from this guy that I quickly started to chew (merely to get it out of my mouth). Then my jaw slowed. The salty flavor permeated my tongue, which soon recognized the spicy sauce. I savored the taste. My tongue ran across my lips to get every morsel. I actually and without any effort or logical memory—sighed.

And I thought the wine nearly had me in Nirvana again.

"Well?" he asked as he took his napkin and with the very tip wiped oh so gently across my lips.

Even a freaking Jagger-napkin wiping had me nearly undone.

I swallowed nothing and smiled. "Good. It was good."

When he gave me his "cat that ate the canary" look I wanted to smack him, but—and this had to be the aphrodisiac effects of the damn mollusk—when his look turned into a grin, I wanted to kiss him.

I was in trouble now.

Wine. Oysters. Moonlit night. And, Jagger.

If I made it through this meal (without ripping his clothes off) I should be awarded some kind of prize for stamina and self-control.

My first choice in prizes said, "Another?"

I could only nod. This time he pushed the dish toward me and said, "Help yourself."

Somehow the second oyster didn't have the same effect on me, but it was delicious, and I polished off three of the smaller ones before my clam chowder arrived.

"So," Jagger said, after finishing his second beer. "What about Lydia's aunt?"

I set down my spoon in case he said something to upset me, and I had the urge to fling a dollop of chowder in his direction. "Why do you keep harping on her? The aunt?"

He turned to the waitress, who was a few tables over, and lifted his beer bottle. She nodded as if she recognized the universal sign for "hit me again." Then again, reading Jagger was something I sure wasn't very good at. Hopefully this waitress was better at it than me.

She must've been because within seconds—or so it seemed—she had set another bottle in front of Jagger. *Poor thing*, I thought, *he's gotten to her too. I'm sure she's never moved so fast in her waitstaff career.*

Jagger took a sip and looked at me. He had this way of pulling words from my mouth with those damn dark eyes. Sometimes, I noted, they took on a deep brown—very much like my favorite chocolate. Other days and only in a certain light, they appeared more black with specks of gold. Then there were times when I saw a hint of hazel.

Today was a chocolate day and no wonder the waitress was falling all over herself.

"Well, I've only met Lydia once at The Market. Man, they have the best clam chowder—"

Jagger glared at me. "I've had the chowder in

every place imaginable around here, Sherlock. I don't need a Zagat's rating review."

"I . . . um . . . so . . . where's the best?" I took a long sip of wine, which emptied my glass. The guy had my dander up, so I looked toward the waitress and held up my glass.

She turned away without a glance.

And I knew she saw me.

I curled my lips and looked back at Jagger. "Get me another one."

He smirked and waved at the girl, who didn't even have to come see what he wanted. Soon I had my third glass of wine in front of me, and as much as I told myself to go slow, that I wasn't used to so much wine, the thing was half gone in a heartbeat.

Yikes.

"Show . . . so . . ." Oh, boy. Was the dock moving? I inhaled the fresh ocean air to clear my head. "So, why are you so interested in the aunt?"

He shook his head—twice.

No one ever wanted Jagger shaking his head at him or her—especially me. Then again, I think I was the only one he ever shook at. I'd scored the number of shakes from one to three with one being merely annoyed and three . . . suffice it to say, no one wanted three shakes.

I got to buy some time when our dear waitress who just about threw my lobster in front of me (okay, the wine was blowing things out of proportion) went to help Jagger with his bib. She fussed and fussed tying and retying all the while

I'm sure she was suffering—make that enjoy-ing—some pheromone-induced episode.

Jagger suddenly took her hand. "Fine. That's fine, honey."

I'm sure she wouldn't wash her hand that night.

I stuck my bib on—crooked—while Jagger yanked his off and grabbed a claw from his dish. When he went to crack it with the tools set be-fore us, he said, "Olivia Wheaton-Chandler owns ... Highcliff Manor."

Nine

Olivia owned Highcliff!

I hadn't had a chance to find out who the "money lady" and Lydia's aunt actually was.

I bit into a chunk of lobster, chewed but swallowed without thinking since the bombshell Jagger had just set off took all my attention.

In seconds I couldn't breathe and grabbed at my throat—the universal sign of choking. Jagger flew out of his seat, grasped me from behind and did the Heimlich maneuver. The piece of buttery lobster popped out of my mouth and onto my dish.

Thank goodness it didn't land on Jagger's or I'd have been so embarrassed.

I'd gotten pretty used to being humiliated in front of him (actually *by* him), so having it on my dish and having my life spared was no big deal.

I pushed at his hands before he cracked a rib and breathlessly said, "I'm fine. Thanks. I owe you one."

He sat down and looked at me then grinned again.

Yikes!

I had to see if the adult ed classes back in Hope Valley offered a quick course on reading body language. Because in my book that look said "sex," but probably in Jagger's it was more like "you're going to have to wash my laundry" or some stupid guy thing to do with housework in order to pay him back.

I took a sip of water this time and gently pushed the wineglass away. One episode of near-death per night was my limit. "Okay. How do you ... is she really? Mrs. Wheaton-Chandler is? Is the owner of Highcliff? Lydia didn't say ... I mean she would know that—"

Jagger touched my lips.

I chose to "read" it as sensual; however, my logical mind *knew* it was out of exasperation to shut me up. Forget the course. I was going to read him how I wanted, or I'd never be able to work with him, knowing the truth.

"She owns it," he said, very matter-of-fact. He lifted his fork and stabbed at the tail end of his lobster, recovering a gigantic piece. Jagger didn't even dip it in butter, which didn't surprise me—however, it did annoy me.

I would probably gain anywhere from ten to thirteen pounds at this one meal tonight. Oh well, at least I was sticking Jagger with the bill. That gave me some justification for all the calories.

After my chocolate mousse dessert—with

whipped cream—I decided we—at least I—needed to walk a bit. No, a lot.

"It's such a nice night, let's take a walk," Jagger said.

Amazing, yet not surprising. The guy had some kind of power to read minds. My mind, that was. I only hoped he hadn't suggested the exercise because he'd noted I'd already started to gain a few pounds.

At the end of the wharf area we had to wait for the light to change before we could cross the street. America's Cup Avenue was always busy with fast-moving traffic. I turned toward a lamp pole and noticed a sign.

"Oh, Jagger!"

He swung around—looking very much like he thought he was going to have to do some kind of emergency procedure on me yet again. "What the hell?"

I waved at him. "I'm fine. That sign. Can we take it?"

"You want to take the sign?"

I groaned. "No, silly. What it says. Can we sign up for it? We have about six minutes before it starts."

He looked at the pole and remained silent a few seconds too long.

Made me start to get nervous. "Jagger?"

"I'm not going on some goddamn ghost tour around Newport. I can tell you all you want to know for free." With that he started to cross the street, leaving me, with my mouth agape, in his wake.

"Oh no you don't, buddy," I said, hurrying after him. Normally I was a jogger, but after three glasses of chardonnay, I wouldn't make it a mile. Thank goodness I didn't stumble as a Maserati sped past me and Jagger turned to yank me up onto the curb.

"Damn it, Sherlock. You wanna get yourself killed?"

Not while you're holding my arm like that, I thought. Yikes. Then I pulled away. "You walked away from me, and why can't we take the tour? I'll bet it's a hoot."

His chocolate eyes melted into me. Wow. Before I knew it I was on the other side of the street, standing on the sidewalk of Thames Street in front of the old Trinity Church. Tall white steeple. Set on the hill and very New Englandlike.

I poked at Jagger's chest. "Come on, Jagger. Live a little."

He growled at me. "Walking around Newport looking for ghosts is not living, Sherlock." With that he swung an arm around me, pulled me closer, leaned me backward and pressed his lips on mine.

Oh … my … God.

"This," he murmured, "is living."

Then I never want to die.

If I thought three glasses of wine made my knees weak, they'd actually been like steel compared to how this guy made me feel. In a few seconds he had me upright and our lips were no longer in contact, but the feelings surging throughout me kept right up—thank goodness.

"Now, walk." He'd said it as if nothing happened.

I stood speechless and, yes, still savoring the world-stopping kiss as I ran my finger around and around my lips. *Ghosts schmosts*, I thought.

Jagger was nearly up the small hill to the church when he turned and looked at me.

I yanked my hand from my face and sucked in a huge breath, which I let out very slowly all the way up the sidewalk—as if that would help me walk better.

We headed up Mary Street past the Vanderbilt Hall Hotel, an imposing brick mansion that sat on the hillside. Lamplights flickered in the darkness, and Jagger walked close enough so that our shoulders touched—why the hell he didn't put his arm around me I had no idea.

But, believe me, I was sending mental telepathy suggestions to him nonstop and to no avail.

We rounded the corner and made a circle, ending back up where we started, at the base of the hill of the Trinity Church. It wasn't a very long walk, but Jagger had been leading the way, and since I wasn't familiar with the area, I couldn't complain.

Well, I could, but found out a long time ago that complaining to Jagger was like talking into the wind. Your words merely flew back at you unanswered.

Since we'd remained silent the entire walk, I decided I'd had enough. "Okay, Jagger, spill about the ghosts. Are you talking Samuel here?"

He stopped mid-stride, turned and gave me a look that had me shiver. Yikes.

"Don't go messing with this one, Pauline."

Oh, boy. When Jagger used my real name, he meant business. And most of the time—well, all of the time—I'd listen.

But there were those damn glasses of wine that just made me not myself. So I said, "Messing with a ghost?" I laughed. "Come on, Jagger. Even you don't believe—no, especially *you* don't believe—in ghosts or spirits or anything woo woo."

"What the hell is woo woo?"

"You know," I leaned closer. "Woo woo. Spiritual stuff. Horoscope stuff. Anything that sounds woo woo."

He shook his head, but thankfully only once. "I believe that we shouldn't be so self-absorbed on this earth to think we are the only ones here. I believe there are spirits out there." He looked into my eyes. "And they don't like to be messed with."

The ride back to the lodge was pretty dull. Jagger kept his eye on the road and played a Tim Mc-Graw CD while I looked out the window, fascinated by the historic houses in Newport, by how I could peek inside ones whose lights were on and the fact that Jagger really believed in ghosts.

Who would have thought?

I might have found that hysterical if it weren't for the fact that I actually felt someone or something push me into his arms earlier. A shiver chased up my spine and I gasped.

"What?" he asked, not even looking.

"Oh. Nothing. Just cold," I lied and kept looking out the window. I had to switch my thoughts
from imaginary beings, so I let myself remember
The Kiss. I gasped again—only this time it was
followed by an "Ah."

"Jesus, Sherlock. If you keep up those orgasmic
noises I won't be able to drive."

My face had to be redder than the damn lobsters we'd devoured for dinner. But my memories
were fun to relive—and, okay, not far off from delicious Jagger's accusations.

We pulled into the parking lot. I looked up to
where my room was and noticed the light on.
Maybe the innkeeper's helpers were turning
down my bed and leaving me chocolate. One
could only hope!

I said good-night to Jagger. Gave him a quick
peck on the cheek since I was chicken to take his
face into my hands and give him a real kiss on the
lips—even though I really, really, really wanted to.

He mumbled something akin to "Good night"
and turned toward the kitchen. Certainly he
wasn't hungry.

Deciding to ignore Jagger and get some sleep
to work on my case tomorrow—since now I needed to find out a hell of a lot more about Olivia
Wheaton-Chandler—I walked up the carpeted
staircase.

My door was locked, so I fished around in my
pants pocket for my key. Old places like this still
used real metal keys and not the key cards of the
more modern hotels. After jiggling the key in the

lock, I pushed my shoulder into the door to get it to open.

And I gasped again.

A maid would not have left my room in such disarray. Someone had been in here looking. Looking for what? A cool gust of air flew into my face. I tried to scream but nothing came out. As if it were swirling around me, I reached my hands up to my face.

"Sam ... u ... el?" I asked as meekly as Dorothy speaking to the Wizard. "Is ... that ... you?"

Nothing.

Although my heart was in tachycardia (speeding like a demon) I eased my hands from my face, pulled my shoulders straight and said, "I am *not* afraid of you." But inside my head I was the lion saying, *I do believe in ghosts. I do believe in ghosts. I do. I do. I do.*

The curtains flew toward me. I stepped back ready to die. Then I noticed that behind them the window was open. "Great, Sokol. There's your ghost." I walked to the window, tucked the curtains back and pushed the frame until it closed out the night and the sea breeze pretending to be a spirit.

"Thank goodness no one saw me," I mumbled and laughed—more out of relief than humor. I decided to relive the earlier part of the evening and ignore my recent visitor.

Tonight was wonderful having dinner with Jagger. Fabulous food. Delicious wine (which now had my head pounding) and, well, the company, the kiss.

Nice.

Still, as much as I didn't want to admit it, someone had been in there. Someone had opened the
window. And someone had opened my drawers.
Couldn't have been the maid.

Right about then I'd love to have known that
it actually was a ghost's shenanigans. I wouldn't
mention someone being in my room though because it might tip the culprit off that I was investigating the fraud.

It took some doing, but I was beginning to
convince myself that I couldn't let threats and a
sense of danger interfere—and paralyze me from
my job.

I had work to do so I slipped off my shoes and
jeans and thought I'd forgo a shower until the
morning. When I unbuttoned my shirt, took it off
and left on the camisole, I decided I at least needed to wash up. I turned toward the bathroom and
walked into the doorway—and screamed.

Ten

Go home.

Just as my eyes were rereading the lipstick-written message on the mirror I heard a crash and felt arms around me.

So I did what any normal girl would do. I slammed my foot onto his toes and jabbed my elbow back—into a very soft spot that made him yell.

"What ... the ... hell! Pauline?"

"Jagger!" I swung around to see him double over in pain.

Oh, boy. Guess he wasn't in any mood or condition to congratulate me on my quick self-defense reflexes—which I'd learned from *him*.

He looked up at me with his forehead wrinkled and his lips pursed. "Put on some clothes."

Put on some clothes? That was all he could say after I'd been scared to death by a ghostly open window, a lipstick threat, and the door to my room being busted open? As a matter of fact, it did feel cool. In my current brush with fear I'd forgotten that I had been getting ready for bed. I looked down. Oops. I went to yank a towel from the rack, which pulled out of the wall and clattered to the floor, taking said towel with it. When I bent to grab it, I looked up.

Jagger was still staring.

Since I couldn't get the towel fast enough, I decided to follow my earlier advice and act nonchalant. Act as if nothing had happened. Hell, I'd have on less in a bathing suit. However, I would not be standing in a hotel room (very close quarters with a *bed* in it) with Jagger ogling me in a bathing suit. I'd be in the wide-open spaces of a public beach where male ogling wouldn't be so personal.

I did manage to walk into the other room and say, "Stay there until I change."

"How the hell ... can I move ... after your ... attack?"

Good point. I hurried to throw my jeans and top back on. I didn't worry about the outside shirt since I probably should be running down to the kitchen to get a bag of ice for Jagger.

Without my shoes on, I went back into the bathroom. "I'll go get you some ice."

He glared at me, freezing me on the spot.

"Okay ... no ... ice. Geez." Well, obviously I had no idea how a guy felt or at least how Jagger felt and he surely wouldn't listen to my medical/ nursing voice of reason. "Here. Let me help you to the bed."

When I went to take his arm, he didn't pull away but merely sat there. I couldn't have budged him if I'd wanted to. "Okay. Stay there." I went to the sink and poured a glass of cold water then turned to hand it to him. "Here."

He shook his head and winced. This time I know he winced because I at least could read anyone's body language when it came to pain. Lord how I prayed Jagger was not really injured. Really prayed hard.

For no *permanent* damage.

"What the hell is a glass of water going to do, Sherlock? Get me some scotch or tequila. That is what I need, not freaking water."

I set the glass down on the sink. "Sorry. I'm fresh out."

"Go ask Arlene."

"You're serious?"

He pushed himself up to stand, and when I reached out to help, he raised his hands in the air. "Stay away. Go."

"Well. I was only trying to help," I mumbled on my way out, but when I looked over my shoulder, I saw Jagger ease himself very slowly onto my bed.

I leaned against the door frame and sighed.

The kitchen was dark and empty, but no surprise. It was late and I knew Arlene lived in the carriage house behind the lodge. When I walked to the back door, I thought I heard someone behind me. "Arlene?" Had to practice on speaking more assuredly with possible "Sam sightings." "Arlene, is that you?"

A shadow appeared at the door.

My hands flew to my face. I was getting very used to living in this B movie and gasping every other scene. Geez.

"Not Arlene, little lady. It's me. Mr. Cooper. Just arrived this afternoon and got lost. Looking for the stairway to my room."

I slung myself against the door frame and pointed. "Behind you, through the dining room and off to the left."

"Thanks, little lady."

I smiled although Mr. Cooper probably couldn't see well enough in the dim lighting to discern that I was not a little lady. Pretty soon I was going to have a séance and summon damn Samuel to confront him—and tell him to leave me the hell alone.

The screen door slammed behind me, hitting me in the butt.

"Give it your best shot, buddy. I'm ready for you now."

All the way to Arlene's door I kept looking to the sides, behind me, and behind me again. No footsteps sounded on the gravel drive, so I figured I was alone. Still, I walked carefully, since my feet hurt, and headed onto the grass, where I was able to bite back a scream after a darn cat had darted out in front of me. "Shoo," I whispered, looking around for its owner.

All alone.

I was all alone.

I shuddered and hurried to Arlene's front door, grabbing the knocker and slamming it so hard the entire town of Newport probably heard it.

The door swung open. A gigantic Airedale lunged at me, pinning me against the ivy-clad arbor and started licking my face. Eeeeeeyew!

Arlene grabbed at his collar. "Get down, Delilah!"

Make that her collar. "You heard your mom, girl. Down." I wiped my hand across my cheek. "Hey, Arlene. Jagger ... well, he wants ... er ... *needs* a glass of liquor. Your choice. He's in no shape to be picky."

She looked at me a second, mumbled an "Excuse me" and left. Within seconds she was back with a very expensive looking bottle half full of scotch. When she held it out to me, she smiled.

Hm. She didn't look the least bit curious as to why he'd need the liquor nor did she ask.

Interesting and so very mysteriously Jaggerlike.

"Thanks. I'll bring the rest back."

She shook her head. "No you won't."

All the way back to my room I wondered if Arlene meant that I would drink some of it too—or she knew Jagger would finish every last drop.

Just how well *did* she know Jagger?

Once Jagger had finished his last sip of Arlene's scotch, and wasn't moaning any longer when he moved, I stood up from the chair near the bed and said, "Can I help you to your room now?"

He raised an eyebrow and for a few seconds only stared.

"Okay. So you don't need my help. Fine. Go ahead and get up yourself. You know, Jagger, I feel horrible about hurting your ... well I'd feel horrible no matter where I hurt you, but it wasn't on purpose." I had to concentrate very hard not to let my voice get shaky, and if any traitorous tears started to form in my eyes I was all set to refuse them to materialize.

"I would think you'd be proud of me for taking care of myself, remembering what *you* taught me, and, well, having great reflexes."

"Beautiful."

I wrinkled my forehead. "Excuse me?"

"I said beautiful." He remained motionless on my bed.

Gulp. "Are you saying I'm pretty or something?" I sat back down in the chair, preparing myself for the answer. Odd that he was talking about that at a time like this though.

Jagger lifted himself up on his elbows, looked directly into my eyes and said, "Beautiful that you think I should be proud of all your accomplishments when you've accosted me like this. Just beautiful." He groaned and eased himself down. "Sure you are beautiful, Sherlock. A real looker. Okay? Happy?"

The stinging in my eyes was getting way too difficult to contain. So I pulled my shoulders straight—as if that would help—refused to let myself cry and said, "Sure I'm happy with the compliment. Would be happier if it were real. Now I'd like to get some sleep. So if you wouldn't mind returning to your room—"

He reached into his pocket, pulled out a key and flung it at me. "I'm not budging."

I caught the key, thank goodness, and looked down at it. There usually was no sense in arguing with Jagger. He always won. So I decided to save face and go sleep in his room.

His room?

Oh ... my ... God.

All his stuff would be in his room! And if some identity clue happened to fall out of his suit-case...

"Good night. Sorry, and I do hope you feel better." I grabbed my robe, threw it over my arm and opened the door.

Before I could shut it, I heard, "And I know exactly just where all my stuff is, Pauline."

When I opened the door to Jagger's room, I stood in the threshold for a few seconds. The place was bigger, more gorgeous and opulent than mine. Not Jagger-like in the least. But what had me pause so long was that everything in the place was so neat and in order.

Not Jagger-like at all.

Least not what I would have expected after seeing the inside of his SUV. Another thing that held me there a few seconds too long was the scent—the Jagger-scent that wafted across the room.

I'd either never sleep tonight or I'd have the best damn dream of my life.

Telling myself that I was foolish, and still miffed that he would think I might go through his stuff (okay, miffed that he *knew* I would), I forced my feet to move toward the bed.

Oh ... my ... God.

I hoped Arlene or someone had changed the sheets because if Jagger pheromones were still on them—I was a goner.

When I pulled the brown and gold brocaded duvet over, the sheets were tucked housekeeper fashion under the mattress. Good. He hadn't used it since it was changed.

I scurried under the sheets, leaving one side tucked in and feeling as if I were in some kind of linen envelope, but there was no way I was getting up from there no matter how uncomfortable.

Too tempting to snoop.

And I'd never give Jagger the satisfaction of knowing he was right!

When the sunlight warmed my face, I slowly opened my eyes and sat upright. Where the hell?

Jagger's room.

Oh, yeah. Well, I had to get out of there before, in my sleepy state, I forgot his order not to snoop. No matter how tempting—and believe me it was—I had to keep Jagger's trust.

That was a gimme.

I could never work with him, or do anything else with him—I cleared my throat—if we didn't trust each other.

And, admittedly, I wasn't that good of an investigator to pull one over on Jagger and cover my tracks of rummaging around his room.

Not sure anyone was *that* good.

So I got up, pulled my robe over my camisole top despite the fact that I still had on my jeans, and went to the door. With one quick look over my shoulder I burned the scene of his room into my mind in case I needed to have some fantasy later on.

I slowly opened the door to my room, realizing I'd never locked it last night, but not worried since I was sure Jagger could take care of himself. This time the urge to gasp was replaced with widened eyes.

The bed was not only empty, it was all made up.

After I'd showered, dressed in my scrubs, and ate breakfast (where I grilled the young housekeeper, Tina, about if she'd seen Jagger—to no avail), I headed out to Highcliff Manor, but not before wondering (maybe wishfully) if Jagger had sneaked into his room and watched me sleeping.

The thought that Olivia Wheaton-Chandler owned it struck me as I turned down the driveway. What the heck was that about and why would it matter?

And, more importantly, did Jagger know something I didn't?

And how the heck did he know about her anyway?

I figured he'd never tell me about the last part as I opened the door to the front room, to hear shouting.

Ian was standing behind the desk, yelling at some woman who stood with her back to me. *How unlike him*, I thought as I tried to walk by unnoticed—yet eavesdropping. His face was the color of his crimson shirt.

"The files are in order, ma'am," he said so loudly I didn't even have to strain my ears to hear.

"Print me copies and delete that file, Ian Michael James. Or else." She swung around and glared at me. "Get to work!"

I started to oblige when words came out of my mouth that even surprised me. "Excuse me? *Excuse* me?"

"Look, Nurse, I'm not in the best of moods and if you want to keep your job here at Highcliff, get to work." She started to turn toward the door.

I looked at Ian, who was giving me a "Shut up, Pauline, if you know what's good for you" look. Who was that woman? Some patient? Some doctor? Some bitch?

I decided to go with the last choice as I said, "I am *not* an employee of Highcliff Manor. I'm doing private duty, Ms.—"

Ian stepped forward. To this day I don't know if he was trying to be helpful or just shut me up so the bitch would leave. "Pauline Sokol, this is Mrs. Olivia Wheaton—"

"Chandler," I mumbled, trying to shrink down to the size of an oyster.

Mrs. Wheaton-Chandler, a woman whom I'm sure never apologized, gave me another look with gray eyes of steel. "Then go tend to your patient, Nurse Sokol."

She pronounced it like "So-called" so I said, "Sokol," turned and walked onto the elevator— which I'm certain Saint Theresa had sent for me to save myself since I hadn't even pressed the up button yet.

Once in Goldie's room, I collapsed onto his bed next to him, because he hadn't gotten up yet, and told him about last night, Jagger, Ian, the bitch, and what was wrong with the current president of the United States.

Darling Goldie held me, cooed in my ear, and told me not to worry. He said all the right lies to make me feel better.

If my mother wasn't around for comforting, Goldie was always my first choice.

Finally he got up when his breakfast was brought to the door. I snuck a croissant and half a glass of tea while he went to brush his teeth. "Hey, Gold. Any questions about your surgery?"

"Stop trying to justify your job, Suga. Get going on your case. Now you have more to investigate. The bitch, that is. And why would Ian have the balls to yell at the owner of this place? Interesting."

It sure was. I knew Ian was the height of manners, and I hadn't ever heard him be so rude—well, except maybe to me, but there were extenuating Goldie circumstances there.

Goldie and I chatted awhile until lunchtime. He told me all about his plans with Miles that weekend. Miles was arriving on Friday, tomorrow, and had to leave early Sunday since Goldie needed his rest for Monday's surgery.

"You two will have a blast here," I said. "Make sure you take him on one of the mansion tours." I licked the strawberry jam off my finger.

Goldie reached into the top drawer of the bedside table and pulled out two tickets. "For the works."

We laughed and watched the local news on television before Goldie said he had a spa appointment in a half hour and wanted to shower first. He got up and pushed the tray table with his dishes toward the door. "You gonna wait around here?"

I finished my tea and shook my head. "No. I need a long walk to clear my head. Think I'll head in the other direction on Cliff Walk. The ocean's magic should work wonders for me."

"I hear you." He leaned over, kissed me on the cheek and went to gather up his clothes.

I got up and pushed the door open, then walked out, looking all ways in case the bitch was lurking in some dark corner. Laughing to myself, I passed by the reception desk ready to ask Ian what that was all about.

Empty.

I looked at my watch. It was lunchtime even though Gold had slept in and had such a late breakfast. I chuckled out loud and ignored the odd looks given me by two patients, bandaged to the hilt on their faces from laser surgery, as they walked by. I could still tell the look they gave me was odd even though I only saw their eyes.

"Ladies," I said and nodded as I walked out the door.

On the way to the side street entrance to Cliff Walk, I decided a walk really was what the nurse ordered. The day was so sunny that I almost wished for a few fluffy clouds to float by and give me a bit of a breather from the sun.

Thank goodness gigantic old trees surrounded many of the mansions there, oaks maybe that kept the streets bathed in shade. At the end of the sidewalk I turned left onto Cliff Walk. It was the part that wasn't paved, as the first section was, but I felt a bit adventurous today.

Anything to take my mind off things and to clear it.

After a few minutes, and my maneuvering over a rocky section, I noticed a couple walking ahead of me. Good. Made me not allow any stupid fear to materialize about being followed by someone who would attack me. Obviously they were honeymooners by the way he held her and how they stopped to take a picture.

"Want me to take one of both of you?" I asked when I got closer.

"Sure," the groom said. Both stood with the ocean to their backs, making a beautiful scene that they'd cherish for years while the sun sparkled on their new gold wedding bands.

"Just back up a bit more so you're not in the shadow of that bush, but be careful," I said, looking through the camera at what the shot would look like.

They stopped.

I clicked and walked forward to hand them the camera.

"Thanks," the girl said as she reached out.

I thought she had the camera, so I let it go. With horror, we all watched it drop to the ground and bounce like a child's ball over the edge.

"Oh ... my!" I shouted and hurried closer.

The three of us leaned over—and collectively screamed.

Camera aside, lying on the jagged rocks below—with waves washing over it as the rocks held it captive—was a man's *body*.

Eleven

After the newlyweds and I stopped screaming, I yanked out my cell phone, called 911 and told them about the body.

Sure looked like a body now (a dead body), and not a person with any hope of saving. The groom took his bride and moved her away from the edge with a "Sit over here, honey."

They both sat on the small hill of the land side of the walkway—away from the cliff. Not that I wanted to look down myself, but this all seemed so surreal that I just had to.

A whitecap of wave slammed into the body as I leaned over and looked with clearer vision.

The man's shirt, although soaked, was a deep color. Black? No. When the sun hit it, I saw more red. Crimson. Wet hair looked much darker as the waves washed over the body, bobbing back and forth on the tide. Part of the clothing had been harpooned onto a jagged rock, which must have prevented the body from floating out to sea.

When a whitecap washed over it, I noticed the shoes were still on. Black wing tips.

"Oh ... my ... God." Although it must have been about fifty to seventy-five feet below, there was now no doubt in my mind.

Ian James.

The dead body was dear Ian.

Suddenly I felt sick and pulled back as the sound of sirens pierced the air. I'd die of embarrassment if I vomited in front of the newlyweds, who, by the way, were both as pale as the fluffy white clouds I'd hoped for earlier.

I sat down next to the guy, bent my head toward my knees and took some very long slow breaths. The sickness in the pit of my stomach was for Ian. Dead. So young. And now so dead.

I called Goldie to tell him and let him know I'd be running a bit late.

Before I could sit and compose myself, wondering if Ian had fallen—or was pushed, a gang of cops in uniforms and a few in plainclothes hurried along the path.

And directly behind them was my buddy, Jagger.

He was walking a bit slower than usual. Oops. Maybe I should just throw myself off the cliff in order to avoid any further embarrassment.

"You look like shit, Sherlock." He reached down for my hand and pulled me up to stand.

"Thanks. New makeup." I stood on wobbly legs and actually had to hold one hand against his chest to steady myself. Really! "And you look very fit," I said.

Jagger growled.

The cops started asking questions, and between the newlyweds and myself—we were of no help at all. No, we hadn't seen anyone. No, we hadn't heard anything. No, the camera was not there with the body.

"She dropped it over the cliff," the bride said in what I thought was an unnecessarily accusatory tone, and the pointing at me that she was doing seemed highly rude.

I started to protest when Jagger glared at me. I leaned toward him. "*She* let it go."

Jagger stood silent.

"All right, all right," I said. "The camera is a moot point since a man is dead. You know how that bothers me, but she did let it—"

In order not to sound too childish—make that more childish—I dropped the subject and answered a few more cop questions involving the fact that I knew who Ian was and had only seen him a short time ago.

"Well, for one thing, he was working earlier. And … er … he did have a sort of argument with someone at work." Maybe I was prejudging the situation. Maybe Ian and Mrs. Wheaton-Chandler were really not at odds. And maybe Ian actually survived the fall. "Seemed to be, or make that appeared to be arguing. I mean allegedly arguing."

Yeah, right.

So I told the cops everything I could think of, ending with, "And I said, '*Excuse* me?' That was right after she'd ordered me to get back to work."

The main one, who I assumed was the detective in charge, said, "That'll do for now. We'll need names and phone numbers for our records." He looked at me through squinted eyes.

Did he suspect me?

Why is it that my Catholic-school-induced conscience always had me feeling guilty when I knew I wasn't? Damn. All I had to do was look at Jagger to see that he believed me. Of course, his look was not one of accusation, more of how difficult it was for him to control shaking his head at me right then.

After we gave all our names and info to the cops, I said goodbye to Mr. and Mrs. Bret Johnson from Lowell, Massachusetts, who were, in fact, married last Saturday.

Talk about a memorable honeymoon.

Not exactly what I'd have in mind for mine. *Mine*. Hmm. How odd that I'd even think about getting married when I had decided nothing was more important to me than my career.

Jagger took me by the arm.

Suddenly I wondered if my sister Mary's youngest daughter would make a good flower girl.

I really should have flung myself over the cliff.

While an ambulance crew worked on getting the body up from the ocean, we walked along the cliff to the exit. When we got to the side street, I saw the Johnson couple getting into their car. "Just a sec," I said to Jagger and hurried over to them.

"I'm so sorry about everything. Look, can I

send you a new camera?" *Please say no since it will cost me money.*

Bret looked at me with green eyes that were not quite as accusatory as his bride, Shauna's. "It was an accident. No problem."

"Oh. Fine. Have a great life you two."

Shauna shut the car door and opened the window. "Cameras are replaceable—"

"Glad you feel that way." And I really was. Guilt was something inbred in me by my mother and fostered for twelve years by nuns. You haven't lived guilt until it is nun-induced. They had my Jewish friends' mothers beat by a mile. "You can easily pick up one of those disposable cameras at the drugstore."

Shauna cleared her throat and in a whinny voice said, "It's the pictures of us that can never, ever be replaced."

Zinger to my heart. I was speechless. From the corner of my eyes I noticed Jagger—grinning.

He was enjoying this! The only thing I could do to make myself feel a bit better was to lean toward him and say, "Want a repeat of last night?"

Never in my wildest dreams would I imagine seeing fear, fear that I induced, as a matter of fact, in Jagger's eyes.

But damn if my threat didn't produce it and somehow make me feel a bit better.

Since Goldie was off on the town with Miles, Jagger took me to The Market for a cup of tea. The guy always did know what was best for me—but I'd die before admitting that to him.

When he set a cup of English Breakfast—de-caffeinated—down in front of me, I looked up at him. "By the way, I didn't get a chance to ask, but what the hell were you doing with the police?"

He'd set a cup of black coffee down in front of his seat and stood over the chair a few seconds, merely looking at me.

I rolled my eyes. "Never mind. I'm going to assume you're friends with at least one of the detectives, that you were visiting while the call came in, and you probably saw my cell phone number and tagged along because you thought I needed saving."

He grinned.

I should have been furious. I should have been embarrassed. I should have shouted for him to leave me alone—but I puffed up my shoulders and was so proud of myself for hitting that Jagger nail on the head that I wasn't furious, shouting or embarrassed.

Nothing could make my day like a look of pride from Jagger.

After our rather silent coffee/tea break, we walked outside and got into Jagger's SUV. Without a word he took a right out of The Market's parking lot and didn't turn down any side street to take us back to the lodge.

Just down the hill the ocean sprang out to the right, and although the beach was deserted at this time of the year, the surf of course continued its rhythmic crashing against the sand. Brown and white seagulls, gigantic birds, squawked from their perches on the abandoned lifeguard chairs.

Jagger turned into the lot, pulled into a space and shut off the engine. "Walk or sit here?"

Without a thought I said, "Walk," while never taking my eyes off the water.

Ian had died in this water.

I got out and stood, holding the door handle while a gust of ocean breeze nearly knocked me over. Jagger was already standing by the cement stairs that led to the beach.

"I'm fine. Don't worry about me," I said more sarcastically than planned.

"Unfortunately I have to, Sherlock. I have to." With that he bent down and took off his cowboy boots and socks.

For as much as what he'd just said had me as curious as all get out, I took my socks and shoes off too, set them on the side of the steps and walked into the amazingly warm sand. The sun had baked it all morning, causing an almost sensual feel.

Okay, watching Jagger's back and ... er ... lower back—okay, lower than his back—as he walked toward the water might have warmed me down to my toes.

Seagulls swooped down on us as if we were some tasty meal. The damn scavengers were annoying. Occasionally Jagger swatted at the air until they flew off shrieking.

Several times I looked out toward Cliff Walk and as if with zoom-lens eyesight could so clearly see the collection of rocks that Ian had been killed on. I shuddered.

And Jagger's arm was around me in seconds.

We walked silently, enjoying the ocean, the rhythmic sounds of slamming waves and the salty scent of the Atlantic. Once we reached the end of the beach area below a row of fabulous cottages, Jagger led me to an outcropping of rocks where we both sat.

The warm sun beat down on us. Despite the breeze, the air had warmed enough that my feet never got cold in the sand.

I leaned back to rest my head against the rocks, shut my eyes and let my mind wander.

Of course, with Jagger next to me, my mind headed down "Lust Lane," but it was damn fun.

Beep. Beep.

Nearly paralyzed from pleasure, I remained still.

"That's you, Sherlock."

"Hm? Oh." I opened my eyes, sat forward and took my phone from my pocket, amazed at how dreamy I felt in this atmosphere. I looked at the caller's number. "Oh, no."

"What? Something wrong?" He looked at me with genuine concern.

Such a guy. "I'm not sure. It's my mother." I flipped open the phone. "Hi, Mom."

"Actually it's Daddy, *Pączki*."

"Oh, hey, Daddy. Daddy?" I nearly dropped the phone but Jagger steadied my hand. "Daddy, what is wrong? Uncle Walt? Is something ... oh, God, no ... something wrong with him. Mother! Why isn't Mom calling me, Daddy?"

Daddy wasn't one to talk on the phone. Never

had much experience with my mother around. So I could tell he was probably holding the phone wrong and could only hear part of what I was saying.

"Daddy. Why did *you* call?" I held my breath.

I heard him clear his throat and talk to someone in the background. When I was just about ready to scream at him to tell me what was going on, my mother came on the line, "Pauline, everything is fine. I'm all right. Really—"

"Mother! When someone says all that, there is something wrong. What happened? To whom?"

I said a silent prayer that my uncle was okay since he was the only one I hadn't heard talking.

"Oh, it is nothing really. I broke my arm. That is all. You have a good weekend."

"Don't hang up!" I rolled my eyes, and Jagger stared.

He whispered, "What?"

I held my hand over my cell phone and said, "My mother broke her arm."

"How's she going to cook?"

I could only stare back at him. Why on earth would that be the first thing that popped into Jagger's mind? How rude. Not even an "Is she all right?"

Then again, he heard me talking to her, so he must have figured she wasn't too bad off. But cooking? Cooking! Oh … my … God. Cooking to Stella Sokol was like breathing.

"Mother, which arm?"

"What does it matter, Pauline? I can hardly do anything with this gigantic thing on my arm.

Must weigh a thousand pounds. And who ever heard of a cast in shocking pink? I'm shocked all right. Pink. Ha!"

"Right or left?"

"My cooking arm, Pauline. My right one."

My mouth dried. Poor Mom. Not only had she gotten hurt somehow, but she also couldn't do her daily duty that she so loved. "What happened, Mother?"

She proceeded to tell me how she tripped on my darling Spanky! Apparently Miles couldn't get anyone to watch him, so my mother had volunteered to take care of him—all the while, I'm sure, protesting that she didn't like dogs.

"They smell like dog," she'd say.

Before I could apologize, she had me volunteering to come home for the weekend since Goldie really didn't need me—and she couldn't cook for Daddy and Uncle Walt.

"I'll show you how to maneuver around with a cast on, cooking and all," was the last thing I said.

As I followed Jagger into my parents' house, I could not believe I was back there and that he'd insisted on driving me. As if I was too upset to drive. Well, having to leave Newport was a bit upsetting, but my folks needed me and thank goodness Mother wasn't badly injured. All in all, I told myself it wasn't going to be a bad weekend.

Mother managed to open the door and say, "Thank goodness you two are here. Of course, you'll both have to stay here to help out. Elderly can do just so much for themselves. Correct?"

Obviously Jagger was holding back a grin while managing, "Correct, Mrs. Sokol," as he walked into the house and finished with, "and pink goes wonderfully with your outfit."

I think I groaned since Mother gave me a chastising look, but I know I rolled my eyes. She had on a brown, yellow and white plaid housedress that pink did *not* go with.

Mr. Jagger had something up his mysterious sleeve. I just knew it.

After I made fried bologna and bacon sandwiches on rye bread—Daddy's favorite—I made Jagger help clean up. He protested once in the kitchen, but I gave him a look that I thought was close enough to what Stella Sokol would give me if I had been complaining.

Then I dried my hands on the aquamarine towel that hung on the duck's head near the sink and said, "I think they can all get along for a while. I'm going to check on Spanky and then head over to—"

"I'll drive you."

Damn. I had no car, and he'd figured it out just as I had. "Yeah. To the office. I'm going to talk to Adele."

He merely nodded, and before I knew it we were in the car driving away from hell at 171 David Drive—but knowing I had to come back and make roast pork since it was Thursday and Mother always made it on *every* Thursday of the week.

* * *

I kinda hoped that Jagger would just drop me off and I'd have some free time with Spanky. But he shut the engine off and was at the front door before I was.

"You know, Jagger, I hate that you had to leave your R and R to bring me back here. Wait. I know. I can use my uncle's car and you can go do ... whatever it is you do around here until Sunday night. Then we can drive back to Newport together. So, I'll see you—"

I'd come up behind him as I was talking, took out my key and had it in the lock before I finished.

Jagger walked right inside.

I hesitated and watched my darling Spanky bark and run up to—Jagger!

The little traitor!

He'd done that before and it didn't hurt any less right now. How I wished I was back doing my job.

My job. I had to call Adele. Ignoring the two males, I walked inside, shut the door and went to the stairs. Over my shoulder I said, "I'm going to make a few phone calls. You two enjoy." I tried to have the tone come out very nonchalant, but instead it came out schoolgirl jealous—and by the look on one of the male's faces, he knew exactly how I felt.

Damn him.

I hurried up the steps and opened the door to my room—and froze. I hadn't been gone that long, but my room looked different. Not that I could put my finger on what it was, but there was something ... the drapes were pulled farther back than I liked them. The bedspread was pulled so taut I knew a coin would bounce to the ceiling fan. And there were no little Spanky indentations on the bed.

He hadn't been in my room while I was gone.

Odd. Miles would never had even entered my room. That much I was certain about. Then what the heck had happened? Surely I wasn't imagining all that? I walked to the closet, opened the door and puffed out a breath.

Pine-scented Renuzit.

Stella Sokol had invaded my space!

I just knew Mother had been there and was trying to "help" me out in some Polish matronly far-fetched way. Before I could call her to yell she had no business being in there (not that I would since she was wounded), I started to yank open all my dresser drawers.

Organized to within a thread of color.

All my socks. All my nighties. All my ... shit!

As if in slow motion I reached into my "essentials" drawer and touched what I knew were *not* mine—which was everything.

Thongs.

Black on black lacy ones. Red with pink dog ones. And some kind of blue fishnet with black lace trim.

Invader of Victoria's Secret. Stella Sokol. Yikes.

My hands started to shake as I jabbed at the new bras Mother had purchased for her thirty-something, single, childless daughter.

Purple satin glared at me. I poked at the fabric to feel something soft inside. Gel. My mother had gotten me a gel cleavage-enhancing bra with naughty black trim, and next to it were matching panties—or what tried to be panties but ended up as some kind of V-string thingies.

I lifted them in the air and blew out a breath.

"That'd be my reaction too."

I swung around to see Jagger standing in the doorway, grinning and staring. I threw the lingerie down into the drawer where it belonged.

Jagger had no idea that this was all my mother's doing! What the hell did he think I was doing with the purple satin devil's design underwear?

Stella Sokol never ceased to amaze or embarrass me—even if she wasn't physically present.

Jagger whistled—and not even under his breath.

Twelve

"These aren't mine. They, well, yes they are in my drawer ... but still that doesn't mean. I don't wear ... nor would I be caught. Look, I know how they got here. My—" What the hell was I explaining any of this to Jagger for? Or make that trying to explain to him. I didn't owe him any explanations for anything—even sexy lingerie.

Besides, he'd never believe that Stella Sokol sabotaged her single—make that *never* married—childless daughter like that.

I could hardly believe it.

With my hip, I shoved the drawer closed and walked to the door, being very careful not to even brush against any part of Jagger while I headed past him. Over my shoulder I said, "I have to go make dinner for my family."

My legs barely got me down the stairs as my knees kept trying to buckle under the embarrassing scene I'd just lived through. But I knew if I even acknowledged it to Jagger, I'd be a goner.

He followed me downstairs, gave a quick hug to Spanky, and we were out the door in silence—thank the good Lord—and soon on the way to 171 David Drive.

And I thought the *lingerie thing* was a nightmare.

"I salted the pork just like you said, Mother," I repeated as I rolled my eyes. If she told me one more thing about how to cook a meal, I might not be responsible for my actions.

She leaned over the aquamarine Formica counter. "More pepper."

My teeth clamped down inside my lips so nothing could come out. I grabbed the pepper shaker and shook until the damn pork was speckled in so much black and gray that it was unrecognizable.

Jagger had the audacity to sit next to my mother, take a sip of his Budweiser and grin.

I shook the pepper shaker in the air above the pan and blew a bit in his direction.

Once he started sneezing, I felt much better.

Finally my mother gave me the okay to set the table while potatoes boiled, pork roasted, and corn sat at the ready to be heated. How I wanted to corner her and get the naughty lingerie truth out of her, but she made herself look so pathetic sitting on the counter stools next to Jagger, sipping her cream sherry while he helped her get comfortable with the pink cast.

Geez.

I shook my head and politely excused myself

before I exploded. When I went into the living room to find my purse, I smiled at a sleeping Uncle Walt on the couch and my father reading the newspaper (for the past three hours I might add) as if the most exciting things had happened around Hope Valley that day.

"Hey, Daddy." I reached into my bag and got out my cell phone. From the corner of my eye I could see Jagger laughing with Stella Sokol and decided I had to do something.

Daddy muttered a few unintelligible words.

Uncle Walt snored, and I hurried down the hallway, opening the bathroom door and ducking inside. There on the back of the commode was what I needed.

Mother's pine-scented Renuzit.

I sprayed a few puffs into the air and sat on the edge of the bathtub with phone in hand. Suddenly I felt a bit more relaxed, as if my Prozac had kicked in although I didn't take Prozac or any other medication. As usual, the nostalgic pine scent did the trick.

When I searched through my cell phone book, I found Scarpello and Tonelli Insurance Company and poked the button.

"Ello?"

Adele Girard, French Canadian and like a second mother to me although in a very different sort of way, still had a slight accent even though she'd lived in the States for some time. Actually this is where she'd spent years in prison—which was another story and one that always made me root for her even though she had broken the law

to pay for her mother's chemotherapy. Tough call,
but a broken law was a broken law.

"Hey, Adele. It's me. Pauline."

"Oh, *chéri*, we miss you. How is it going in
Newport?"

"Actually that's why I called you. I need your
help." After I filled in Adele about Olivia Wheaton-
Chandler and asked her to run any kind of check
on the woman that she could find, I at least felt as
if I was doing my job. Being the doll that she was,
Adele assured me she would get right on it and
not tell Fabio that I was back in town. She was excellent in her job, with contacts reaching far and
wide. I could always rely on Adele.

I'm sure that wouldn't sit well with Fabio since
private investigators didn't get weekends off.

After letting the pine scent waft around me, I
gathered up what mental faculties I had left and
went out into the kitchen.

Mother was instructing Jagger on how to set
the table!

I stood in the doorway and watched, barely believing my eyes as he took each order in stride
and did as told to perfection.

Why was it that Stella Sokol could get so much
out of him while I couldn't even find out if he had
a last name or a first name? Well, I had to admit,
now I was more determined to find out *a lot* more
about one Jagger. A.k.a. Jagger.

"Don't just stand there, Pauline. Start the gravy," Mother said.

I looked at the pink cast and cursed in my
head.

Jagger grinned at me. Yes, the man could read my mind. That fact, sad but true, was proven over and over with him.

"Sure, Mom." I turned to hurry into the kitchen. Maybe I could get the gravy done before they came in.

The door swung open just as I was bending down to look in the cabinet below the counter. "Where is the gravy, Mom?"

I heard a throat clear and swung up just in time to smack my head on the counter. "Ouch!"

Jagger Whoever stood there, grinning yet again.

"Didn't your mother ever tell you if you make a face like that it will freeze?" I asked, rubbing my head to feel for a bump or fresh blood.

"Excuse me?" He walked closer until we were eye-to-eye.

Yikes.

"Never mind," I said and started to bend down again, all the while rubbing the top of my head.

Jagger took my arm and pulled me back up. Then he touched the top of my head and said, "Sorry about that."

For a second my usually brilliant mind turned to gravy. "The gravy!" I yelled, very thankful for the stupid diversion. "I have to find it before Mother comes in. Where is she anyway?" I leaned past him to see if the Gestapo mother was on her way in.

Nothing.

"Your mother is in the living room. She said she'd be here in a few minutes to help." He smiled.

I pushed his hand away from my head before the top started to burn from his touch. How pathetic was I? Maybe I should start using the thongs. Geez, I couldn't even think about those garments with Jagger so close. "I have to make the ..."

What the hell was I going to do?

He looked at me, and I swear wanted to grin. "Gravy, Sherlock. You are in here to make some gravy. You know, that pork smells good. Think it's done?"

I pushed at his chest. "Don't you start. Don't tell me how to cook. I know when a pork roast is done."

"The longer you cook a pork roast, Pauline, the more tender it becomes," Mother said, walking in.

I hoped she didn't see me touching Jagger even if it was only a poke. "Right. Cook longer. Yeah, got it, Ma."

"Mother," she corrected and perched herself on the "observation" stool.

Jagger sat next to her.

I growled inside and bent down again, this time being very careful about my head. "So where is the gravy, Mother?"

"What?"

I stuck my head out of the cabinet and repeated, "The gravy? I don't see any."

"Pauline Sokol. How could you see something you haven't even made yet. I think that *job* is way too much for you. You need to go back to nursing, so you'll remember you don't find gravy under a counter."

I shook my head and ignored Jagger's look. "I'm happy in my job and thought you'd keep the cans of gravy down here with the cans of vegetables."

Mother gasped.

Obviously in order not to grin like a fool, Jagger bit his lip. "Where I come from, gravy is made from scratch with the drippings from the meat," he said.

I reached inside the cabinet for a can of anything to fling in his direction.

"Pauliiiiiiiine," Mother said.

Soon my hand was back, empty, and I was standing up. "Okay, I give. How the hell do you make gravy?"

"Stop using that longshoreman language, Pauline, and I'll walk you through it."

For some reason I was more amazed that Stella Sokol used the term "walk you through it" than the fact that she thought "hell" was used by longshoremen.

I stared at the tiny white lumps in the pan. Oh ... my ... God. Mother was not going to ever let me forget about this. When I took the spoon and started to poke at them, hoping against hope that they'd dissolve, I watched them pop back up like little inner tubs afloat in a sea of mud.

Pauline's homemade gravy. Yum.

At least I'd been successful (and had the foresight) to shoo Jagger and my mother out of the room earlier with the pretense of having appetizers in the living room after throwing a few slices of cheese and crackers on Mom's wooden cutting board.

Actually I think at least one of them was glad to leave.

Mother, however, kept kibitzing from the living room.

The gravy stared back at me and bubbled. Twice.

There had to be some secret, some trick that she deliberately didn't tell me so I'd fail at this chore. Mother was not a vindictive person, far from it, but cooking was her life and her main function in this world—and I'd bet my last paycheck that she didn't want anyone taking over the lead.

A splatter of gravy sputtered into the air, landing on the front of my top.

Mother had nothing to worry about.

"Pauline, I'm getting very hungry," she said.

"Have another cracker and cheese, Ma." Okay, I called her that deliberately so she'd start to fume in the living room and forget that I was in the kitchen from hell speckled in brown.

Suddenly I had an idea and grabbed my cell phone from my pocket. I hated to disturb anyone but this was an emergency.

"Miles, I need help *now*!" I whispered into the phone, still managing to sound as if I were drowning in the damn gravy.

"Oh, God. What is wrong, Pauline!"

"Sorry. I don't mean to alarm you, Miles. Tell Gold hi for me. Hope you two are having a ball, but I have a food emergency—"

"Oh, Lord, Pauline. I never should have let you go to your mother's house to help out cooking alone. It's all my fault." I could hear him interpreting every part of our call for Goldie in the background, who occasionally shrieked or gasped. And why wouldn't he?

They knew my mother very well, and knew me even better.

After several minutes of Miles's instructions on how to revive a dying pan of pork gravy, I searched through the kitchen for his suggestion of a strainer. Everything I found had holes that looked way too big for what I needed. The tiny clots of flour would just pass right through.

Wait. I had visions of working the renal unit back in my nursing days and thought about straining for kidney stones. Now a kidney stone was the size of an uncooked piece of rice that tried to pass through a piece of spaghetti—uncooked too. So that theory might apply here.

Maybe my nursing skills really were still useful.

I looked around the kitchen and found the only thing that seemed plausible to use. Mother's white dish towel. Had to be cotton. Had to be clean as a whistle since it was in the drawer, and had to be dye-free since it was white.

I draped it over a bowl in the sink, poured the mess of clots into it, and stepped back.

"I'm guessing your family wants to eat this century."

I swung around to see Jagger only inches away, looking at my invention.

"Dinner will be served in a few seconds." I turned away and looked at the gravy.

Not one clot had budged. It seemed rather thick.

"Damn it, Jag—" I looked over my shoulder.

Once again my buddy had disappeared like the north wind.

After many minutes, which, of course, there at 171 David Drive felt like years, I threw in the towel. Literally. I threw the entire mess into the garbage and decided I was going to tell my folks that gravy had way too much fat in it and their cholesterol levels might skyrocket if they ate it, so I was cooking "heart healthy" tonight. Gravyless pork.

It looked naked on the serving platter.

I sucked in a breath, blew it out as if that would give me more courage, and started to shout, "Dinner is—"

"Going to be in five minutes," Jagger finished from behind.

I swung around to chastise him when I looked at his hands.

Two cans of pork gravy.

Before I could think, I swung my arms around his neck, winced when the gravy cans poked into my chest but managed a smack of thanks on his lips ... that I will *always* remember.

*   *   *

Mother tried to cut her meat using her cast-covered arm and following my instructions. She managed to get most of it cut since it was so over-done the pulled pork fell off the bones. I kept encouraging her to do things herself, knowing that I couldn't stay any longer than tomorrow.

Thank the good Lord.

Daddy did his best to help, and before the meal was done and Uncle Walt had taken his usual nap at the dining room table, Stella Sokol had gone from wounded martyr mother to accomplished pink-cast-covered heroine who could care for her family despite rain, sleet, snow or fractured humerus.

You go girl!

And I could go too.

Buzz. Buzz.

Mother, who was reaching for another helping of my "gravy," looked at me. "None of those phone things at the table, Pauline. Where are your manners?"

The hours I'd slaved over the meal got to me. "I have perfect manners, *Ma*, but this is business." I got up, took my phone and went toward the hallway. "Hey, Adele. What's going on?"

Jagger must have heard me talking because before Adele could tell me about her daughter coming to town, he was at my back.

"So, *chéri*, you must meet Lilla. She is a darling—most of the time."

I smiled to myself. "I'd love to. And about Mrs. Wheaton-Chandler?"

Silence.

Damn, Fabio probably had the cheapest phone service available. "Adele? Adele?"

"I am here, *chéri*."

"Oh, thought I'd lost the connection." I turned my shoulder away from Jagger to give him the hint that this was a private conversation. Too eager to hear what Adele had to say, I didn't want to argue with him right then. "So? What do you know about Olivia Wheaton-Chandler?"

"She didn't exist twenty years ago."

Thirteen

"Excuse me, Adele? Excuse me? Olivia Wheaton-Chandler did not exist twenty years ago? What does that mean?"

My gut told me I knew exactly what it meant, but I wanted to—no, needed to—hear it from Adele to make it more real.

As if I wanted *that* monkey wrench in my case to be real.

If Mrs. Wheaton-Chandler had no record of living in Newport, then what about Lydia? Where did she come from and what the hell was going on?

"Adele, I can't wait to meet Lilla. I'll be there in a few minutes. You mean Mrs. Wheaton-Chandler didn't live in Newport twenty years ago?" *Okay*, I told myself, *that is really reaching for straws, but I'll go for it.*

"No. No, *chéri*. There is no record for her *any-where*. Not in Newport or any other state."

I felt Jagger's breath on my neck, ignored it as best I could, and yes, it took a Herculean effort, but I managed to say, "What about overseas? Maybe she's foreign?"

Another pause.

Great. I half expected Adele to set up another roadblock in my case with some other tidbit of info that she'd gleaned about the woman. Actually, I really didn't know if Olivia had anything to do with my case.

Only going on my nursing premonition abilities and gut instincts.

"Adele?"

"Adele is very thorough, *chéri*. She always checks foreign and domestic before reporting to any of the investigators."

Oh, no. I had Adele back to her old habit of talking about herself in third person. When we first met, I found it kind of eerie, but now I was used to it. At first I thought it distanced us, but now I accepted it as friendly ... yet odd. "I am so sorry, Adele. I didn't mean to insult you. You know I think the world of you. Hey, have you eaten yet?"

"No. Lilla and I were going to go out as soon as Fabio rolled himself in, but the sheet hasn't shown up yet."

I loved the way she called Fabio the "sheet" instead of the "shit."

"Sit tight. I'm coming over with food." I clicked my phone shut and turned, smacking right into Jagger. Before I could apologize or yell for his invading my space, he looked at me.

"Interesting. Very interesting," he said.

I hurried into the kitchen with no idea what the

hell he was talking about, but figured it was the thing about Olivia since Jagger surely had eavesdropped on my entire conversation.

Good. Maybe he could be of help.

I'd learned early on in this profession not to be too proud to use him.

For work, that was.

And it sure was easier taking his suggestions for help when I thought *I* was using *him*.

After I'd made sure my entire family was set, including a few more lessons on using a pink cast for Mother, I had thrown together some pork sandwiches for Adele and Lilla.

Jagger had sat on the counter stool watching the entire time.

Good for him, and even better for me since it was a good lesson in ignoring him or anyone else so that I could concentrate. Okay, I was concentrating on pork, but I figured I could transfer the newly learned skill to my investigating.

I really couldn't wait to get back to work!

It was a comforting feeling to know that I loved my job that much, and no way was I going to let the notion that I partly wanted to leave 171 David Drive so very badly interfere with that thought.

On the way to Fabio's, Jagger and I exchanged very little words. I had been thinking more and more about what Adele had said about Olivia. Where the heck had she come from if Adele, snooper extraordinaire, couldn't find out?

"So, what are you thinking?" Jagger asked.

"Hm?" He'd taken me by surprise, and I wasn't

ready to discuss any of the case with him anyway. Truthfully, that was because I had nothing to discuss. Damn.

"I asked what you were thinking."

"In general?"

"Look, Sherlock, if you've got nothing, say you've got nothing."

I curled my lips as I turned away from him. "I'll have something very soon." There. That should shut him up.

But I noticed his reflection in the window. That stupid grin.

"I hope the pork is all right since it's probably cold by now," I said for the umpteenth time, and for the umpteenth time Adele said it was fine and Jagger shook his head. Oh well, I wasn't immune to making a fool of myself to get a conversation going. As I watched her eat, still with her white gloves on since her hands had been burned in the "joint," as she'd once told me, the front door opened.

Half expecting, and fully regretting, that it might be Fabio, I tried not to look. But then I noticed Jagger—staring.

Nothing about Fabio would cause a Jagger-look like that.

I turned to see that walking across the waiting room was a woman who looked like a Victoria's Secret model—dressed. Actually dressed in a black turtleneck, black jeans, and sunglasses propped on her head—very eerily Jagger-like in appearance.

Long brown hair bounced across her shoulders as she made her way closer until her spike—red spike, that is—heels clicked on the linoleum floor that bordered the stained carpet. Her eyes were enticingly large and deep brown, and I'm sure Jagger hadn't missed that she was proportioned just so and knew it.

Yet there was a friendly air about her, and I knew I liked her on the spot—which sure as hell stunned me.

Adele flew up from her seat, knocking over her cup of coffee but not caring as she grabbed the woman in a hug.

"Chéri, Jagger, this is my Lilla. Lilla Marcel. Lilla, she is my fourth child and also married four times!" Both mother and daughter broke out into laughter.

Jagger and I remained silent, but I forced a smile and held my hand out toward Lilla. "Nice to meet you. Your mother is a peach."

She eyed me with mascara-covered lashes, looking very chic, though a scent of cigarette smoke wafted from her. But I just knew she had a way of puffing that made her sexy.

Adele sat back down and started to tell Lilla to eat something. With her figure, I wondered if she ate more than once a year.

"What is this peach?" Lilla asked.

"Oh," I chuckled. "It means that your mother is a doll. Priceless. She finds things out that no one else could."

Lilla's eyes darkened.

Oops. Wonder what that was about but figured

I should keep my mouth shut since we'd just met. We made small talk, and I found out that Lilla, after signing her fourth set of divorce papers, moved in with Adele after leaving Canada to get away from ex-husbands two and four. Yikes. Talk about a double dose of trouble.

Both she and Adele seemed thankful that Lilla didn't have any offspring with any of the spouses. But she was near destitution, as hubby number four took her to the cleaners, and she had to move down here with her mother. Since it could only be temporarily until she got her emigration paperwork in order, she needed to work.

And somehow I got the impression that legal or not, Lilla was going to be working there.

First thing that popped into my mind was: *What can I get her to do to help with my case?*

Jagger almost tripped as he stood from his seat to shake hands with Lilla. Hm. Maybe Adele needed help filing. Nope. I wasn't the jealous type, and besides, what did I have to be jealous about?

Not that I thought I was some great beauty, but there was nothing between Jagger and me. Okay, a few rogue kisses, but possession apparently was *not* nine-tenths of the law when it came to men.

Lilla looked toward Jagger and mumbled, "Attaboy!"

He hadn't done a thing to warrant any congratulations and the way she'd said it sounded more like a "wow." I looked at Adele, who in fact mouthed the word "wow."

Apparently French Canadian wasn't that difficult to interpret.

"Okay, Adele, if you couldn't find anything out about Olivia, that must mean she wasn't around anywhere." I tapped a nail to my tooth. "Hm. You think she's not real?"

Jagger looked at me. "Ask Lydia."

"I know she's a real person, but is she really who she says she is? And why, if she isn't, is she pretending to be who she is?"

The entire room gave me a well-deserved collective look of confusion.

I raised my hands. "Okay. Okay. That didn't come out right, but you all know what I mean."

"If she is an imposter," Lilla said, "*ça suce*."

This time Jagger mouthed, *That sucks.*

I made a mental note to buy a French dictionary on my way back to Newport. Then again, I think the Canadians probably had a different version. And speaking of Newport, I stood up. "I really have to get going and back to my job. Goldie's surgery is tomorrow."

Adele gasped. "Oh, *chéri*, take good care of our Goldie. I know you will."

After hugging Adele and telling Lilla it was great to meet her, she walked us out to her "machine" (car) to have a smoke. When I looked inside the old gray Buick, I wondered just how long she'd been living in it, and why it took her that long to come to her mother.

Then again, this was Adele I was talking about. Not exactly Mother Goose mixed with Stella Sokol.

* * *

A woman should never sleep in her childhood bed when Jagger is in the next room.

I learned this hard lesson after getting my mother settled for the night and declaring that she was fit and well-adjusted to her pink cast, after spending the entire weekend working with her, so I could leave in the morning. But on my way to my old room, I happened to walk by my brother Peter's old room and there in one of the twin beds—was Jagger.

Dark hair slightly tousled. Yikes.

Softly snoring. Ah.

Pheromones dancing in the doorway. Wow.

Thus the sleepless night.

"Hey, sleepyhead." The voice seemed to come from a distance.

I turned over, ready to look at the clock to see if it was still the middle of the night. But the sun glowed on the numbers, and I could tell it was already Sunday morning.

The day I got to leave.

And Jagger was standing in my doorway watching *me* sleep!

My blonde hair looking very Rod Stewart. Oh damn.

Probably sawing wood like a three hundred pound man. Ah, shit.

And even while semiconscious, hormones at high alert for those stupid pheromones.

I rubbed my eyes, yanked the covers higher, although I was fully clothed in a jogging suit beneath, and said, "Oh, hey. Morning." *Please leave.* "I'll be up and ready in a few."

"We need to make it quicker, Sherlock."

"Oh." I yawned. "Okay. What's the rush?"

"The lieutenant from Newport called. They found out who killed Mr. Baines."

Fourteen

"Ian?" I said. "Ian?" I shouted, then yanked on the sleeve of Jagger's leather jacket. For springtime, it was still cool in the mornings.

"Maybe you need your hearing checked, Sherlock. Yes, Ian."

"Ian James killed Mr. Baines?" The horrifying thought still hadn't sunk in as Jagger took a right turn off the Newport Bridge ramp.

I'd asked pretty much the same question the entire two-hour trip but still said, "I can't believe it. Ian? Ian killed someone?"

"Mr. Baines."

We turned when the light changed, and Jagger weaved in and out of one-way streets through the narrow roads of Newport.

"You sound as if you are placating me with that tone."

At the next stop sign he turned and merely looked at me.

"Okay, so I'm having a hard time with this one.

He was such a nice guy. He really had fallen for Goldie." Damn! Could my dear friend have been in any danger? Naw. Obviously there was more to this fraud stuff than I knew about, and Ian never would have hurt Goldie.

But Ian was dead and the question remained: Who killed *him*?

And why? What did Ian know about the fraud?

Well, I could rest easier since obviously it was Ian who had knocked me down. At least that was what I was going to tell myself over and over so I could do my job.

As we pulled into the driveway of the lodge, I looked at Jagger. "Why? Why would Ian kill Mr. Baines? Did he even know him? I find it hard to believe."

"Weren't you the one who saw him running from the scene of the crime, Sherlock?"

Oops. I sat silent for a second. Not that I was so shocked at what Jagger had said, but I was trying my damnedest to try to remember if I had told him about the possible Ian sighting. I couldn't remember. Then how the hell did Jagger know?

Before I could ask, he was out of the car, took his duffel bag from the backseat and was walking along the front path. I figured anyone who wouldn't tell me the truth about his name was not giving away crime-related secrets.

I got out, grabbed my stuff and followed, but when I got inside, Jagger was nowhere to be seen, and Arlene was at the front desk doing some kind of paperwork.

Oh well, I figured, might as well get back to work as soon as I could. When I got closer, I said, "Morning, Arlene."

She kept her head down and didn't answer.

At first I thought she didn't hear me, and then, with all the death and murder lately, suddenly I worried that something might have happened to her! I reached over the counter and gently tapped her arm.

Arlene flew up, smacked me in the face (accidentally, I told myself) and screamed.

All of a sudden my arms were flailing about and that cold wind encircled us—while the doors and windows were tightly shut. "It's me! Arlene, it's Pauline."

She stopped screaming, looked at me and in the eeriest of tones calmly said, "Oh, hi, Pauline," as if we'd just shared a morning cup of coffee and nice chat. Never saw anyone snap out of fright that quickly.

I knew Sam was around but had no intention of feeding into his actions. There was way too much to do on my case and two murders so far for me to deal with the paranormal. "Sorry I startled you. I guess you didn't hear me. Anyway, did you know Mr. Baines?"

She gave me an odd look—which I was getting very used to in this business. "Know him?"

I nodded. Seemed like a pretty cut and dried question to me, but maybe she was still recovering from ghostly sightings.

"I knew *of* him."

I shook my head and waited for her to expound

on that statement, but she merely sat back down and stuck her nose in her paperwork. This case was getting tougher and tougher to work.

"Um, Arlene? About knowing of Mr. Baines. Could you tell me more?"

She seemed perturbed but that was another thing I was getting used to ignoring. People got angry with me. People shouted at me. People ignored me, and yet I had a job to do and was not going to let hurt feelings stop me.

Arlene got up, went to the stove and took the hot water pot. Then she refilled her teacup, which was next to her papers. Without offering me a drop—guess she figured I could get my own in the guest's dining room—she sat back down and stirred the used tea bag around a few times.

"Mr. Baines?" I repeated, getting anxious to go unpack and change, but I didn't want to lose Arlene to her paperwork.

"Real estate. The Baines family has been in Newport real estate for ages. Lots of money with the skyrocketing prices. They actually owned a fair bit of land themselves which was used to build condos near the water." She took a few sips of tea.

"Any children?"

She laughed.

I wondered why that was so funny, but being childless myself, had no clue. I sure didn't find anything funny about dirty diapers, baby drool or fresh adolescents who were my nieces and nephews.

"Baines probably had more kids than a Mormon. Not that he knew about them though," she said.

Hm. "Really. A real playboy, you mean?" Interesting indeed.

"Yep." She started writing something and certainly gave me the feeling that I was bothering her.

I figured I was and didn't want to antagonize a local, so I said goodbye for now and went to unpack. My room looked smaller, but very welcoming after the 171 David Drive weekend from hell.

I shuddered.

At least I knew my mother was fully functioning with her pink cast, so I didn't suffer any pangs of guilt. I did suffer annoyance at how Jagger got away with so much with Stella Sokol. Damn it.

After I'd unpacked, rested for a few hours and showered, I stuck on my black and white jogging outfit and decided I needed to do something mindless and physical. Of course something other than jogging came to mind, but being the good Catholic gal that I was, I stuck on my running shoes and headed out toward Cliff Walk.

After a few silent prayers for Ian's soul, I jogged along the path in the other direction so as not to have to see the scene of the murder.

Jogging always was a great time for thinking. Today I'd decided not to wear my CD player so I could run bits and pieces of my case through my thoughts.

Sadly that's all I had—bits and pieces.

I wondered if Jagger knew any more about Ian

killing Mr. Baines or about Ian's death. Certainly couldn't have been accidental.

Or could it?

Maybe he was so distraught over killing Mr. B that Ian leaped to his death? Or maybe he was trying to punish himself? Thoughts bombarded my brain, and before I knew it I was at the exact spot of Ian's demise, not even sure when I had turned around.

Yellow police tape was draped across the thorny bushes, as if that would keep locals and tourists out. For heaven sake, the damn bright color attracted attention. Mine at least.

I stood back and surveyed the area. Nothing looked that out of place. As a matter of fact, the spot where Ian must have been pushed or thrown, since he wasn't that huge a guy, wasn't very disturbed at all. I stepped a bit closer to see the bush's branches were slightly bent but not really broken. Couldn't hurt to do a bit of investigating to help out the police.

Maybe he went over at another spot?

Not that it could have been much farther away, but maybe a few feet and the current or waves impaled him on the rocks below? Or at least had impaled his clothing.

I walked several feet toward the end of Cliff Walk. It still went on about a half mile, but I nosed around near the ocean side for several minutes. One never knew what one would find.

Seagulls squawked in the distance, landing on the rocks below or like little dive-bombers into the water to snatch out a snack. When I got too close to the edge of the cliff, my foot slipped on a damp section of mud and I nearly followed Ian to that big ocean in the sky.

With my heart pounding, I grabbed onto a nearby bush, cursed as a thorn punctured my palm and then, all the while holding on for dear life, imagined maybe this was the scenario that Ian had followed. I eased myself back to safety, took a deep breath and put on my investigator cap once again.

I tried to re-create the moment, lying there and thinking about how it might have occurred. I looked around at everything in sight then noticed something in the bush.

A tiny scrap of color.

Once I was safely back on the path, I leaned over and picked it from amid the thorns. Deep red. Almost had a velvet feel to it. Obviously a material not within my budget, and obviously had been hidden deep inside the bush so the cops had missed it.

Of course, it could have been there for ages, but with the ocean winds up there and the winters along with rain, I was guessing it was newly skewered on the thorny branch.

It didn't, however, look like the same color as Ian's shirt.

I took out a tissue, wrapped the swatch in it and tucked it into my pants pocket to give to the police. If they looked at me as if I were nuts, so what?

Certainly they already had my number since Jagger was in touch with them.

My jog back was uneventful and I made it to Highcliff Manor in record time and luckily fast enough to see Miles about to get into his car. "Hey! Miles?" I ran across the parking lot and grabbed him by the shoulders. "Seems like so long!"

We hugged, kissed cheeks and hugged again.

"How was your weekend?" he asked.

I rolled my eyes, and he hugged me again.

"Yours?" I replied.

Even through his Foster Grants I could see tears forming. "Take good care of him, Pauline."

I kissed him on the cheek again and gave him a wink. Miles got into the car and drove off. I turned toward the front door to see Goldie standing in the window—I'm sure sniffling.

Ain't love grand, was my first thought, and then I told myself that at the rate I was going, I wouldn't know. But I was happy for my two roommates nonetheless.

I headed inside to give Goldie a much needed hug and told him about the material. As a matter of fact, I said, you probably might recognize it.

Goldie leaned near when I unwrapped the tissue with the "evidence" inside.

"Hmm," he said and kept looking.

"Expensive?"

He nodded.

Whoa boy. So whoever killed Ian, in my humble opinion, was rich.

Then again, so was half of Newport.

* * *

After listening to Goldie's detailed explanation of his fab weekend with Miles, and grunting and groaning about my weekend with the Sokol family and Jagger, I reviewed the surgery with Goldie. He seemed to understand, reiterated that he did not want to change his mind and seemed to have a real grip on his post-op care.

"So, by this time tomorrow you'll be sleeping off the beauty sleep of your life, Gold."

We both howled.

Then it dawned on me. Monday. Neal. Geez. "Oh, shoot."

Goldie flopped on his bed and hugged a mauve silk pillow. "What? What is wrong? Something about my surgery?"

"Oh. No. Oh, no, hon. No," I said to reassure him.

"Okay, I buy that. Then why the look of confusion?"

"Neal and I had made plans to go out tomorrow night. At the time, I didn't know it would be your first night post-op. I'll cancel."

Goldie sprung up and grabbed my arm. "The hell you will. Some hottie like that asks you out, could be a help to your case, and is cutting me tomorrow, and you're gonna break his heart tonight? Uh-uh. No way."

"But Gold—"

He waved a hand at me. I could tell his French manicured nails were recently done. Beautiful and sexy in a vixen sort of way. "Look. You yourself just said I'll be asleep most of the night. There are nurses here enough to staff an entire hospital. I've met a few already. Kerie Cetin and Jackie Wisherd. If they can take care of the real nasty-rich patients here, they can watch me for a few hours." He leaned forward and looked in my eyes. "No cancelling."

I saluted him, said, "Yes, sir," and kissed his cheek. "I'll make sure you're medicated and comfortable before I leave."

"Drugs. Yum. Sounds perfect."

I smacked his shoulder and got up to leave. "Call my cell if you want or need anything. Promise?"

He saluted me back, and I knew having Miles come visit had been the perfect medicine for our Gold.

Tomorrow would be a piece of cake.

Fifteen

Goldie's death grip had my hand turning white. Make that made my hand as white as his pale face. "Suga, Suga, Suga," he moaned.

I leaned forward and kissed his forehead. "I'm going to tell Neal that all bets are off on your surgery for today. You changed your mind."

"Noooooooooo!" Despite the fact I thought it impossible, his grip tightened. "No, Suga. I'm just being melodramatic—"

"So what's new?" a male said from behind me.

I swung around to see Miles, holding a bouquet of red roses.

"I thought that voice sounded familiar, but had no idea that you'd plan to come today. Then again—" I looked at Goldie, who was now smiling. My numb hand had been released. "—I should have known."

"He knew," Miles said, walking into the room and setting the roses on the bed next to Goldie.

I swung back to Gold. "What?"

He shrugged. "I didn't want the guy who'd be cutting me to pieces to be thinking his date might cancel tonight."

"So you called Miles to come all this way."

"Like I could have stayed home," Miles said, kissing Goldie on the forehead. "Who better to replace you tonight than an O.R. nurse—"

"Who I know will take the world's best care of my patient. Group hug, guys."

We all leaned in to hug each other, and I felt as if a weight had been lifted off my head. Goldie swore he really didn't want to change his mind yet again. I bought his story, and Miles settled into the room since he'd spend the night.

While I was "touring" Newport with the doc.

One could only hope he knew his way around ... *everyplace*.

"I'm going to ask if they can give you a little something to calm you down, Gold. A pre-op cocktail of sorts. They usually don't like to give too much prior to surgery, so you wake up faster, but no one should be too worried and uncomfortable." I touched his hand. How I hated seeing my friend like this. We'd been waiting for what seemed like hours for them to take him to the O.R.

Goldie, snuggled under the duvet in the fetal position, merely looked at me and blinked as if he'd forgotten how to talk.

I felt horrible putting him through this, so I told Miles to stay there—as if he'd leave—and headed out to find the anesthesia people.

When I came up to the front desk, my eyes grew

teary. Ian should have been working, but instead
the evening receptionist had filled in, I guessed
until they found a permanent replacement.

"Excuse me." I looked at her name tag. "Kim-
berly."

"Kim." She stuffed a few papers into a folder.
"Damnedest filing system I've even seen. I can't
work like this."

I wanted to say that since Ian was dead, she
probably could do what she wanted, but before
I could, she said, "Thank the good Lord I'm not
going to be here much longer."

Hm. "Oh? Have they found a permanent replacement?"

"Yeah, Pauline. Me."

I looked toward the door behind the reception
desk to see Lydia standing there. In her black
slacks and white blouse she looked a few years
older, but not any happier.

"Hey. Great, Lydia. You're taking over ... that's
great."

"Yeah. Ian's job. Will wonders never cease?"
With that she walked past me and said, "Kim will
help you. I'm officially in orientation, and it's my
tea break. See ya."

Interesting.

If her aunt owned this place and was so wealthy,
why would poor Lydia have to work here as a
receptionist—when obviously gigolo husband
Devin didn't punch a clock for anyone.

"Kim, I need to talk to whoever is doing the anesthesia for Mr. Goldie Perlman's eleven o'clock
rhinoplasty."

She looked as if my just standing there annoyed her, and now that I had a question that needed answering she was even more pissed. Geez. Folks around here were very complicated.

Maybe that's what money did to people.

Me, I wouldn't know.

"Okay, Gold, I'm going to give you a little sedative that will ease your anxiety." I lifted the IV tubing, wiped the rubber stopper part with an alcohol pad and stuck the needle in.

"Shouldn't I count or something?"

Miles and I chuckled. "Sure. Count if you want, but this may not knock you out, merely relax you." I pushed the medication in slowly.

Within a few minutes Goldie snored like a sailor, Miles was watching *The View*, and I sat by the window praying to Saint Theresa that all would go well for Goldie.

Even from the second floor I could see Lydia walk past the window, and right on her heels was ... Olivia Wheaton-Chandler. Although I could see they were talking—make that arguing—I couldn't read lips. However, Lydia looked furious.

My heart thudded.

The last person I'd seen arguing with Olivia was Ian, who promptly ended up dead a few hours later.

Yikes!

I added a quick prayer for Lydia as the door opened. An orderly said, "We're ready for Mr. Perlman," and the day began.

Tears were shed (mine). Goldie snored. And I insisted that Miles be allowed to walk to the O.R. with us.

When we got to the double doors of the surgical suite, we nudged Goldie awake, kissed him on the lips and turned to hug each other. "He's going to do spectacular, Miles. Spectacular."

He sniffled and nodded as they wheeled Goldie in. Not that I was happy Ian had been killed, but I was glad he wouldn't be there to snoop on Goldie's surgery. Sounded way too perverted.

When I let go of Miles, a hand touched my shoulder. Half expecting Jagger to be standing there, I spun around ready for a friendly hug.

"I'll take good care of him, Pauline," Neal said.

My heart did a little dance, which was a hell of a lot more fun than the earlier thudding experience. "I know you will. Thanks," I muttered, and then introduced him to Miles.

"That's perfect. We'll have a wonderful time tonight. Goldie will be in good hands and we'll ... make the rounds of the town."

Well, damn, didn't that just make my day?

"He looks like a sleeping angel," Miles said as he tucked the duvet under Goldie, who snored away with his nose covered in bandages and packed like a traveler's suitcase—only with surgical cotton packing.

I nodded. "At least he's comfortable. I couldn't stand to see him in pain, and I know neither could you."

Miles wiped his finger across Goldie's fore-head. "No."

Gold had to go to surgery sans drag, and without his wig, makeup and fantastic smile, he looked so very different, yet so very familiar. I almost suffered a maternal moment. Almost.

Miles turned toward me. "Don't you need to go get ready for your big hot date? He'll be fine."

"I know he will and my date is not a date nor is it hot. It's just a friend showing me around town."

Miles looked me in the eye. "Pauline dear, straight guys *do not* want to be friends with chicks."

I knew he was right but out of principle smacked him on the arm. "Okay. I'm off. I'll have my cell on if you need me, but I know you are capable of caring for him."

"Go."

I nodded, leaned over and kissed Goldie on the forehead. "You did great, Gold. Just great."

He muttered something, and I smiled at Miles before heading out the door.

If I thought I changed my outfits a lot to not embarrass myself in front of Jagger, the pile of clothing (every stitch that I'd brought with me including my pink scrubs) lay on the floor at my feet. Naked feet that went with my body. What the hell was I going to wear?

And was I really trying to impress Dr. Neal?

Jeans. I should just wear jeans and clean un-derwear without worrying about matching col-

ors. The clean part came from—who else?—Stella
Sokol. You know the drill. Clean underwear in
case you got into an accident. I smiled to myself,
missed my family a bit and decided I needn't
make such a big deal about what to wear. After all
it was merely a tour of Newport—with a swanky,
sexy, hot doctor.

I flopped onto the bed.

"You about ready for dinner, Sherlock?"

For a second I thought I'd dozed off and was
dreaming. Then I looked to see that I had on nothing and, knowing Jagger, he probably could see
through the wood door.

I flew up from the bed, grabbed the closest
things I could—my jogging shorts and tee—stuck
them on and walked toward the door.

When I opened it, Jagger looked at me. Was
that a grin?

"What? Do I have spinach in my teeth or something?" I held the door and leaned against it, not
inviting him in. Hopefully he couldn't see the
pile of my belongings on the floor—because then
there'd be questions with embarrassing, I was
sure, answers.

He leaned closer. "Or something."

I pushed at his chest so he wouldn't come in.
"You're not making any sense."

He gave me the once-over. After my toes un-
curled, I allowed myself to be ticked. Guys.

"Men don't have to make sense, Sherlock."

There *was* a grin. Jagger was in some kind of
mood!

I actually laughed. "True. Look, about dinner—"

"There's a great local place I want to go to. Portuguese. You up for Portuguese?"

I almost said *Sure*, but instead my sanity returned and I said, "No."

"Okay. You pick." He tried to step inside, all the while looking at my outfit.

Maybe the colors didn't match, but there was no need for him to stare like that. Men in all black were not exactly fashionadas. Sexy as hell, yep. "What I meant was, I'm not picking anything and stop assuming I'm going out to eat with you every night. I have a life."

I'd never noticed any hint of being taken aback in Jagger, but right now there was a teeny, tiny hint in his eyes. Jagger was surprised that I was busy.

Good!

He moved closer.

I stepped back.

Wrong move. Before I knew it he was in my room, noticing the pile of clothing and about to say something.

I waved my hands in the air. "Don't even ask. I'm busy. Reorganizing." I tried to turn him to push him toward the door, but he didn't budge. Not that that surprised me.

"Busy?"

I let out a long sigh. "Okay, Jagger. As if you didn't know, I have a date. Yes. A date with Dr. Neal Forsyth, Goldie's surgeon."

"And you've gone through your entire wardrobe several times and came up with red shorts and a purple tee."

It wasn't a question, but I started to explain, but only managed to dig myself deeper. "I'm going to be late. I'll see you tomorrow."

He did turn, and over his shoulder said, "You might want to rethink the underwear issue."

When the door shut, I yanked off my clothes.

No wonder he was staring.

Oh … my … God.

I'd settled on black slacks, a white top (thanks to Lydia today) and as much silver jewelry as I'd brought with me. When I stepped back from the bathroom mirror, I pronounced myself done. Goldie's past makeup techniques had made a world of difference for my looks. Very natural. I loved it.

It was then I realized I hadn't had any makeup on when Jagger'd "surprised" me.

I sighed and thought, *So what is new?*

The announcer on the radio said it was nearly seven. I decided this small room was nowhere for Neal to come get me so I hurried to get my wallet, cell phone and a tissue, stuck them in my pockets and went outside my room to go downstairs.

Jagger's door was open. He sat with his legs up on a cushioned ottoman and looked directly at me over his sailing magazine.

Then he gave me a thumbs-up.

I flew down the stairs in delight until I got to the bottom. A thumbs-up to go out on a date with someone else? What nerve!

"I hope old Samuel haunts you tonight," I mumbled.

The front door swung open. I half expected Neal to be standing there but would have actually been surprised that he would shove the door so. Instead ... there was no one.

Yikes.

In my head I offered an apology to Sam, telling him to do what the heck he pleased even if it meant hanging all my clothes back up. Before I could shiver at the thought, Neal, in fact, did appear, looking very suave and handsome in navy slacks, an off-white silken shirt, and I'm sure very expensive sunglasses.

We looked like two flight attendants.

"Hey," I said. "How's Goldie?"

He put his hand on the small of my back to guide me down the porch stairs and said, "Perfect. He's a perfect patient. Doing all that he is supposed to do."

"No bleeding?" I couldn't help myself. Once a nurse, always a nurse. Damn it.

He chuckled. "None. Normal swelling. Normal temp. Normal vitals, Nurse Sokol. Your patient is recovering nicely and Miles is only inches away."

I smiled. "Thanks."

He leaned over, kissed my cheek and whispered, "No thanks needed."

When I went to step into Neal's black Porsche, I noticed the curtains in the upstairs room, Jagger's room, move.

Hm. Samuel or Jagger?

* * *

"So this is the church where the Kennedys got married," Neal said as we pulled in the parking lot of the unpretentious St. Mary's Roman Catholic Church on the corner not too far from the center of town.

Neal held the door as I walked in. "Oh, my," I whispered. "You can almost feel their presence and picture them walking down the aisle." I stepped inside the seats and knelt down.

Neal joined me.

When I bent my head to say a quick prayer for Goldie, I noticed Neal doing the same. Hm. Nice guy. Good looking. And spiritual?

Stella Sokol would be stuffing almonds in lacy fabric for bridal shower table favors if she knew this.

Truthfully, even *I* was impressed with the doc.

We did a little walking tour around Bowen's Wharf, which was filled with shops and eateries—and also where I'd shared a meal with Jagger last night.

Damn.

Wish those reminders didn't pop up at such inopportune times. Neal was the perfect gentleman. Actually he reminded me a lot of Nick the freelance investigator, whom I'd dated a bit. And Neal certainly knew his way around this swanky town. He gave me a bit of culture along the tour.

"Slavery was actually very popular in this seaport," he said, sipping a glass of very expensive wine once we'd stopped for a drink.

Good thing because the brick and cobblestone

walks were getting to my feet. What on earth made me wear heels?

"Wow. Slavery. Huh? Stuff like that really fascinates me." I sipped on my wine, which Neal had insisted I get instead of beer. Not that I minded, but I wondered if Neal was the possessive male type. At first glance I'd have said no. But there were little hints.

However, after a self-imposed dating drought, a wee bit of possessiveness felt nice. Someone cared. Someone had taken the time to take me out. Yes!

We finished up, walked toward the marina section and back to Neal's car.

"We'll take Ocean Drive out past Fort Adams State Park. I'll show you Hammersmith Farm too." He again guided me by placing a hand on the small of my back.

I sighed.

"Isn't that where Jackie Kennedy grew up?"

"And the Kennedys' reception was there." He opened the door, I got in, and after I'd buckled up, he shut the door. How cute.

The drive was beautiful, especially when we got halfway out and the ocean popped into view. Neal continued his tour with all the local folklore then stuck on a Sting CD and paid attention to the road.

For a few seconds I thought I'd doze off in sheer relaxation.

Then I realized why I was there. Not there in Neal's car on a "tour" but there in Newport on a case. I looked at him from the corner of my eye and forced myself to say, "I see a new receptionist has been found to replace Ian."

Neal's hands tightened on the leather steering wheel.

Damn. It had to be painful for all the employees at Highcliff to accept that one of them had been murdered.

With his eyes straight ahead he said, "Lydia won't last long."

He knew her. He knew her? "Why do you say that?" I thought the question would force his hand and he'd have to say how he knew her.

"Spoiled rich kids don't have work ethics, Pauline."

Yikes. Was he generalizing about them or did he really know Lydia *personally*?

Sixteen

Neal took every turn of the winding Ocean Drive with expert precision. One would assume, or at least hope, that a surgeon would have pretty damn good control over a car, and this doc certainly did.

Along both sides of the road now were gigantic mansions or Tudor homes or quaint-looking cottages the size of skyscrapers. The place really was for the rich and famous.

Before I knew it, the sign said Bellevue Avenue. We'd made a gigantic circle on this tour. Then again, the section for the rich and famous really wasn't that large although it bordered the ocean on one side. There wasn't much more to this town other than small, mostly one-way streets with houses from the 1700s and 1800s. I actually preferred them to the mansions. They were so colorful and so New England.

"Hungry?" Neal asked.

I was famished and figured he'd heard my stomach growl a few times over darling Sting, but thought better than to mention that. "I could eat."

"Perfect." He took a right off of Bellevue Avenue. The residential section sure didn't look like a place where a restaurant would be located, but I figured Neal knew best—until he turned into a drive with a gigantic pr i va t e sign guarding the entry and wrought-iron gates that were shut until he poked a button on the dashboard.

"I'm guessing you've been here before."

He chuckled. "A few times."

No other explanation, but when an imposing Tudor structure came into view, I guessed this was home sweet home for the doc.

And the family crest of f o r syt h hanging from the gates was a bit daunting and impressive.

Oh … my … God.

Was I out of my league or what?

"You should have been a tour guide instead of a doctor," I teased as Neal showed me around his "place."

Despite the size (at least thirty rooms, although I couldn't make it around the place to count), it felt warm and cozy, until a butler appeared and offered to get us drinks. For a gal from Hope Valley, having a butler, no matter how nice he was, did not say cozy.

My mouth wouldn't work so Neal ordered us each another glass of wine. Not being a connoisseur, I had no idea of even the color, but figured it wasn't going to be Sangria.

The butler—Pierre, who else?—excused himself while Neal ushered me into a tiny little room off the foyer.

Suddenly it was my favorite room in the house—although he hadn't shown me the upstairs … yet. Yikes.

Mahogany paneling covered the walls, which had built-in bookshelves filled with what I guessed were first editions. A small section near a stained-glass window had some current paperbacks so I figured at least Doc Neal wasn't some eccentric. There was a flat screen television in the center with mahogany doors, which I guessed covered it to show proper Newport good taste.

Neal guided me to the burgundy leather couch, and when I sat, I thought I'd fallen onto a cloud. I ran my hand along the arm and had never felt such buttery soft leather in my life.

Having a fraud case in a place like this was actually fun.

Neal refilled my glass despite my protests—well, fake protests. I didn't want him to think I was some lush, but expensive wine was delicious. Okay. Okay. I couldn't help but take advantage of the freebie.

He sat next to me on the couch and smiled. "Wait a minute." He leaned forward, brushed the hair off my forehead and said, "That look. Worry."

"Worry? No—"

He waved his hand at me and said, "Hang on."

I sipped at my drink while he took out his cell phone and made a call. Trying not to eavesdrop, I started to hum and looked out the window.

"Ms. Wisherd, how's Mr. Perlman doing?"

I swung around and held my breath.

Neal winked at me, causing a whoosh of air to blow out of my mouth. Then he smiled and all was right with the world. "Okay, Jackie, let me know if he needs anything that's not ordered."

When he hung up, I leaned forward, grabbed him by the shoulders and planted a kiss on his cheek. "Thank you," came out in a rather hoarse, sexy tone.

Guess Neal noticed, since he leaned closer, took my face in his hands and kissed me. Gently. Softly. And on the lips.

And here I thought the wine had given me an internal glow.

Yikes.

After several more kisses Neal eased back. "Nice," he whispered.

All I could manage was a nod of agreement. How pathetic was I? Actually, this guy was perfect for me to take my mind off my case for a few moments and recharge my "female" batteries. Neal the Igniter. I chuckled.

"What? What's so funny, Pauline?"

I sipped my wine. "Nothing. This is delicious."

"Speaking of delicious, let me check on dinner." He stood, planted a kiss on my cheek, and walked out the door.

Who knows how long I sat there, touching my cheek. I sure didn't until I noticed the black, obviously expensive briefcase on the floor near the couch.

Don't even think about it, Pauline.

I was on a job though.

Everything and everyone needed to be checked out.

Slowly I leaned over, to see it slightly open. A sign from above. I took my glass of wine, sipped, then started to put it down when I sipped it again—and then polished it off.

Accidentally, my foot reached out about three yards away and bumped into the briefcase.

"Oh, my."

I eased closer to that side of the couch and looked down. Several papers spilled out onto the wooden floor. When I leaned down to put them back into the briefcase, my eyes widened.

"Oh … my … God."

Seventeen

"Can I help you with something, Pauline?"

I swung around to see Neal standing by the doorway. My body had been flat against the couch as if I were reaching for—his briefcase. Shit.

"Oh. No. I'm fine." I stood up and bent down to pick everything up. "I accidentally knocked this over. So sorry. I'm guessing it's yours?" Who else's? Pierre's?

Neal didn't exactly look angry with me or even suspicious. And truthfully he needn't be.

The papers that I read were his notes about Dr. Cook—as if Neal were gathering evidence!

I knew there was a very good reason for this date other than lust ... wait, that was a normal red-blooded American girl feeling.

"Here. I'll get those. The clasp doesn't always catch. You didn't hurt yourself. Did you?" He took me by the shoulders before I could get past him toward the door.

"Uh-uh. I'm fine." *Especially in your arms, Doc.*

"Good." He quickly kissed my cheek, let go and bent to stuff the papers into the briefcase.

Phew. Phew. Phew.

"Wow. This looks like a buffet set for the entire town." I glanced around the table Pierre and some maid Neal had called Marie had hustled about, setting dishes, silver trays and glass decanters of food, wine and delicacies, before us. Several times I had to remind myself not to act as if I were starving and to eat "ladylike" as Stella Sokol would say.

Neal chuckled. "I like to please my dates."

Date? Hm. Nice ring to that one. The word sounded familiar and made me wonder if the cliché about riding a bike applied. God, I hoped so.

I took a bite of something that looked like a little pansy. I think it was, but it tasted great. I only hoped it wasn't just a decoration, but Neal didn't look at me oddly or yell that it was something poisonous, so I chewed on it then swallowed. "I'm so relieved about Goldie. You guys do great work at Highcliff. No wonder you have such a booming business."

He sipped his wine and looked at me over the glass. "We do all right."

"All right? Look at this place!" I waved my hands around the ornate, mostly mahogany, mostly gold-leaf-decorated room.

Neal laughed. "I inherited Forsyth Manor, Pauline."

A house with a name. I loved that! "Oh. Well, I'm sure you and Doc Cook do pretty well. I've seen the results, and now Goldie will benefit too."

"Glad he's doing so well." He leaned over and took one of the hundreds of forks from near his plate and started on his salad.

Not wanting to appear "country hick," I did the same and decided I'd had enough of the flora arrangement for one night. "But," I said, swallowing, "I have seen some women there who look as if they are ... repeat customers." I'd almost used Ian's "frequent flier" term.

Neal paused his fork midair. "Yes, there are some."

Oh boy, I needed him to expound on that, but suddenly the salad was more interesting to him than my conversation as I watched him poke around the arugala. Okay, the tiny grape tomatoes, fresh buffalo mozzarella and red peppers were delicious, but that wouldn't get me anywhere.

I set my fork down for a minute. "I can't imagine having so much work done. I mean, I think I'd get therapy before I allowed the 'Michael Jackson' syndrome to run my life." I chuckled.

Neal ate his forkful and smiled. "People are strange sometimes, Pauline. Especially when it comes to appearance."

"Oh, no doubt. But do you ever refuse to operate on someone?" *Going for the gold*, I thought. *No time to waste.*

Neal set his fork down too. "Odd dinner conversation."

Damn! Did he suspect me of snooping? Did he

think I was trying to get a freebie nose job? Or did he think I was plain nuts?

"Then again, with two medical folks, I guess it's really expected." He laughed.

Phew again.

"Yeah. I've heard conversations during surgery. You guys. I mean, sometimes they border on risqué!"

"We have to do something to keep our minds occupied." He laughed and took his fork again.

While he ate, I said, "So, do you? Refuse some patients I mean?"

"Sure. Some of them become obsessed. Ever hear of BDD?"

"You mean that is a real disorder? I saw a show on it once on TV."

Neal told me everything I already knew about BDD, some about what I didn't know and then some about the practice. "So, sometimes I think of quitting when Dr. Cook gives in to those damn patients who need therapy more than plastic surgery."

Neal's eyes darkened. His hand shook as he set down his fork. Yikes. Not a good sign in a surgeon. But at least he was honest about not wanting to work with a crook. Well, he didn't out and out call Dr. Cook that, but I knew that was what he meant.

Progress in Newport tonight!

Pierre came in with a tray of lobsters all stuffed with what I guessed was plenty more shellfish like clams, scallops and shrimp. The maid carrying a dish of something that smelled heavenly followed him. Yum. *I could live like this*, I told myself.

I glanced over to see Neal thanking the servants. It impressed me how he treated them so well and not in any condescending way. Neal was the catch of the day. I wondered why he wasn't already caught, filleted, and married.

"Have you ever been married, Neal?" Okay, pressed for time, I was getting more brazen.

He looked up from his lobster. "Once. Long time ago. You?"

Eeks. That didn't sound amicable. "Nope. Never. Well not yet." I stuffed my mouth with stuffing.

He laughed. "Good for you. Wait for Mr. Jagger."

Did he say *Jagger*?

"Excuse me?"

"I said Mr. Right. You know, your soul mate."

"Oh, yeah. Soul … mate." *Jagger? Ha!*

What the hell? I pushed that stupid thought from my head, took a slice of French bread, dipped it in the drawn butter and shoved it into my mouth despite a trillion calories dripping off the end. Jagger indeed. "Yeah, I'll do that."

"I don't think I can move, Neal. I ate way too much. It was all so wonderful," I said to the servants as they hustled about cleaning up. "Thank you, guys."

Neal chuckled. "Let's have an after dinner drink in the library."

That sounded oh so very Newport chic.

I forced myself up, and before I got my chair moved, Neal was at my back, holding onto me and guiding me to the doorway. Yeah, Pauline Sokol could learn to live like this.

Once in the library, Neal poured us two glasses of some syrupy kind of liquid. I didn't even want to know what it was. After all the wine, I was already feeling way too happy.

He handed it to me; I sipped, took another and thought it was better than a hot fudge sundae. When I went to drink again, he touched my hand. "Easy does it. That stuff is pretty powerful."

Then I could have my way with you, I thought.

Pauline Sokol is a lush, I thought as I sipped the last drop of the fabulous after dinner drink Neal had poured me. I wanted to ask for seconds, but when the more than likely solid gold clock on the mantel chimed then started to wobble, I figured I'd had enough alcohol for the night.

Neal sat next to me observing. No doubt he thought I was snookered too. I took in a very deep breath, blowing it out slowly and hoping the alcohol would dissipate with every respiration. I really wasn't fall-down drunk, but merely feeling very good—and my tongue loosened with every word.

"How did you know where I was staying?" flew out of my mouth on one of those exhalations.

At first Neal looked puzzled. His forehead wrinkled.

How adorable. "I remember you mentioning

that I was at the lodge. Funny that just popped into my head." I waved my hand and hoped it looked genuine. "No need to answer."

"Ian ... Ian had mentioned it when I'd asked how I could get in touch with you."

"You wanted to ask me out?"

Neal smiled. "In all honesty, Pauline, what I meant was that if I needed to get in touch with you about Mr. Perlman."

Gulp. "Is my face red or what?" I tried to sink down into the expensive leather—this one burgundy—couch. No such luck.

"In all honesty again, I did want to ask you out too." He leaned near and touched my face.

"Careful. You could get third-degree burns by touching my skin."

He laughed, pulled me closer and whispered, "I love your wit. You make life seem so wonderful as you spread your charm."

Yikes. I took his face into my hands and planted a kiss smack on his lips—and what he returned with was not just a thank-you.

My insides had been toasty warm from the liquor, but with Neal so near, inhaling his expensive, I'm sure, cologne and his arms pulling me closer until I felt his heart beat against mine, I was damn *hot*.

He trailed his kisses along my cheek, hitting spots that jolted pleasure as he made his way down my neck.

I sighed.

He moaned.

Before I knew it, we were on the Aubusson carpet, Neal's chest was against mine and the buttery leather soothed my back as he eased me down— all the while kissing every part of me. With one swift movement he had the room darkened to a sensual dim. Sometimes, when he moved, I could barely see him ... but always felt him near.

Thoughts of fraud, liquor and ... Jagger suddenly became a fog of gray in my mind. *Nothing like the present,* I thought as Neal's lips caressed mine. I arched back and sighed.

"Will Pierre come in?" I whispered as I ran my fingers through Neal's hair. I wasn't used to sex in a servant-run mansion.

In all honesty, I wasn't used to sex—period.

Neal chuckled, tickling my skin. "Don't worry. Pierre is the height of tact." Light kisses that he worked up my cheeks then down to the base of my neck felt fabulous.

We came face-to-face; he kissed my lips then moved near my ear. As he nibbled and kissed me into Nirvana, I felt his warm breath and heard his soft breathing, which made the idea of lovemaking all the more intense. Even his eyebrows, tickling my skin like tiny butterflies, had me nearly unable to move.

When he lifted his head and paused, I leaned forward with my lips at the ready, but stopped before contact—so he could think he was in charge. Men liked that.

"Nice," he whispered seconds later.

Soon we were both up, kissing and moving toward the bed with my hand in Neal's as he kissed and licked my fingers one by one. Dizzy was the only word to use at the moment, until he reached into the drawer of the bedside table and took out a gold-foiled wrapper.

Gold. What else? I smiled to myself.

While endorphins swam through our bodies, the scent, the sound, the taste and the feel of Doc Forsyth melded into a culmination of pleasure. Soon there'd be no turning back.

Dr. Forsyth.

Dr. Forsyth!

I was on a case.

Suddenly I didn't feel all too professional.

Thank goodness I still had my wits about me after accepting this "date." I eased back, reluctantly explained to Neal that it was too soon, which he accepted like a gentleman, and we stopped before possibly making a mistake.

But it sure felt good to knock on *that* door.

I smiled to myself and thought I'd nearly had the chance to remember how to ride a bike.

Neal held the car door for me as I stepped inside. He leaned near and kissed me. "I had a wonderful time, Pauline—"

"Wonderful, Neal," I said, and then we both laughed.

He shut the door, walked around the other side and sat next to me. "Fantastic. You're right. It was fantastic. How about tomorrow?"

About ready to accept, again the stark reality that I was on a case hit me. I blew out a breath, wishing I were here in town on vacation. "You know, I'll have to see. Let me tell you tomorrow.

Depends a lot on how Goldie is doing. If that's all right with you?"

He winked.

I nearly had an orgasm—I wish.

If there was a next time, I'd pass on the syrupy, expensive alcohol.

Thank goodness he drove rather quickly since I needed to get to my room and back to reality.

After he pulled into the parking lot of the lodge, he opened my door, I stepped out and threw my arms around his neck, planting a kiss on his lips. He held me for a few minutes, whispered "Good night," and was gone before I made it up the walkway.

Something drew my attention to the second floor, where I noticed the curtains of Jagger's room move.

He knows! was all I could think.

"Oooooooh!" Goldie moaned as I touched his arm, tickling his skin for comfort.

"In another hour it will be time for your pain med, Gold. Sorry I can't give it sooner." I tickled faster, hoping the soothing touch would take his mind off the discomfort.

Dear Gold didn't have the highest level of pain tolerance around.

"Tell me a story, Suga," he whined like one of my nephews.

I sat on the edge of his bed. "I'm fresh out unless you want a rerun. I think we're on story number gazillion now, Gold. Sure you don't want to sleep?"

He took my hand in his. "Can't. Too painful. Tell me about last night. You and the doc."

My face grew hot. Very hot.

Goldie peeked out from one eye above his bandaged nose. "Oh ... my ... God. *Those* details should take my mind off things."

I slapped him very gently on the arm.

"I'm not the kiss and tell type. Use your imagination ... and then add about two degrees of X-rated separation, then—" I sighed. "—subtract one."

Goldie finally laughed. "Aye!"

"Hey, Gold. Listen to this." I told him about Neal's papers "falling" out of his briefcase.

"Brilliant, Suga. I'm very proud of you."

"What do you think?"

Goldie ran his hand across his chin. "Maybe Doc Neal would be a real asset to your case. I'd say you have to go out with him again. You need to, Suga. You're way too young to die a born-again virgin."

I curled my lips at him. "You're not talking fraud investigation here. Are you?"

He chuckled and took my hand in his. "Thanks for being you, Suga. I feel a bit better already."

I figured a little attention—no, make that a lot of attention—paid toward my Gold would take his mind off his pain.

Once I had Goldie comfortably medicated and snoring away, I gently placed the mauve duvet over him, made sure the nurse's call bell was within reach, and went to get a cup of tea. I knew

Goldie would be asleep for hours, and he knew where I'd be.

I headed to the door, took one more look at him and pronounced him recovering splendidly, turned and went down the hallway to the staff's kitchen.

Mugs hung from racks on the back of the counter, and as long as you rinsed them out and stuck them in the dishwasher, you were free to use them. Sadly I took a mug down, thinking that was Ian's rule.

"Make sure you wash that out and stick it into the dishwasher."

For a second I thought Ian was talking to me. I swung around to see Lydia standing in the doorway.

"How's your patient?" she asked.

"Oh, hey, Lydia. He's fine. Goldie is a real trouper. And, I will definitely wash out my mug."

She took one herself and started to fix a cup of Earl Grey tea. "He's an interesting person. Seems like a real doll. I got to spend some time with him Sunday before his surgery once you'd left."

"Oh. Yeah, he's one of a kind." I wondered how much time Lydia spent around there. A young girl should be out with friends. Sailing. Eating. Talking. Laughing. But poor Lydia, today in a black silken blouse and black trousers, looked way too serious and solemn for a young girl.

She held the milk container out toward me. "Here."

I chuckled. "You remembered that I take mine with milk. Neat."

She didn't crack a smile. "If nothing else, Pauline, I'm observant."

Yikes! That sounded like some kind of warning. Did Lydia know about me? Who I really was? Naw. No way that she could.

As I sipped my too hot tea, Lydia set hers down on the counter. Only thing was, she didn't just set it down in any casual fashion. I was talking *thud* with a splash here.

Anger? Was that anger that had her tea puddling onto the countertop?

Trying to change the subject so she wouldn't start questioning me, I asked, "So, how do you like your new job? I'm sure it helps your aunt's peace of mind to know that she has a relative working here."

Silently Lydia turned toward me. I'd never noticed how dark black her eyes were, or maybe it was the lethal look in them when she said, "*Who else* can one trust?"

Eighteen

Yikes! Who else could one trust? Did Lydia know some deep, dark secret of Highcliff Manor? Sure seemed that way. Only thing was, as I watched her pick up her mug and take a drink of her tea, I certainly didn't feel as if she'd willingly share any secrets with me.

Time to review Investigating 101.

And maybe time to meet dear Auntie—outside of this place.

I forced a laugh to lighten the mood and hopefully get Lydia talking more. "I hear you. Family is very important."

She remained silent for a few seconds as if she were studying me. Slowly she drank her tea then said, "One would think."

Oh, my. "Lydia, do you go to school?"

One would think dear Lydia imagined me a nutcase by her look. "I graduated from high school."

"Not interested in college?" With her financial backing, I would have thought Lydia could get away from her aunt and Devin, with college being a godsend.

Tears welled in her eyes, making me feel horrible. "I'm sorry I brought that up. So, any plans for tonight?" I asked.

Lydia's eyes cleared, then darkened. "Don't try to change the subject. Ian must have told you about me."

Yikes! "No. No, Lydia. He never said a word. Are you talking about college?"

Robotically, Lydia stood, set her mug, gently, on the counter and turned toward me. "I was accepted to Yale. In New Haven, Connecticut."

I nodded. "I know where Yale is." Who didn't? But she was young and probably felt the need to explain.

"My grades weren't that good, but I was accepted because of who I am. My father had gone there."

All sounded great to me. A little nepotism didn't hurt anyone.

"But ... here I am." She turned to walk toward the door.

Here I am? That was it? "Er, Lydia, I don't get it. Why didn't you go to college?"

When she turned to look at me, tears spilled out of her eyes, she sniffled and wiped her sleeve across her face—then spun around and walked out.

Oh ... my ... God.

Lydia couldn't get away from Newport. But why? And why not go to Yale like her dad?

I finished my tea, all the while watching the

door as if I half expected Lydia to come bouncing back to explain.

What the hell had made that child so unhappy?

"What's that noise, Pauline?" Miles asked into my cell phone as I turned toward the window in Goldie's room.

"That's our boy snoring his way through La La Land."

After a pause, Miles asked, "How is he?" in the softest, most concerned tone.

Someday I wished some guy would ask about me like that.

"He's doing great. I'm about to take my lunch break so the staff nurses will keep an eye on him."

"I know you need to leave to eat, and I'm so glad I got to meet a few of them. Kerie Cetin on today?"

"I think the second shift. Jackie Wisherd will cover me in a few—"

The door opened and Jackie stuck her head in. I waved for her to come in. "She's here now, Miles. I'll call you later. Love ya."

"Love ya too and thanks."

I smiled and flipped my phone closed then walked toward the door. "Hey. He's doing fine. No more drainage. No more swelling. And I med-icated him about twenty minutes ago. Should sleep the entire hour."

"Great. I'll be in and out, Pauline. And take your time. There's no need to rush back in an hour. Sometimes the lines at The Market can be long. Oh, I assume that's where you go for your lunch?" She smiled.

Hm. Why did my worst-case scenario mind suddenly wonder if Jackie had been spying on me. Had she coincidently seen me at The Market, or innocently assumed I'd eat there since it was so good?

"Yeah. I'm getting their clam chowder. May I get you something?"

She shook her head. "I always bring lunch. Can't afford that place on a regular basis."

Interesting.

I smiled, blew a kiss to Sleeping Beauty Perlman and walked out after making sure Jackie knew my cell phone number even though it was on every chart and document around.

When I stepped into the elevator, I told myself I wasn't that hungry at the moment, and if Jackie wasn't going to time me, I might have to make one teeny, tiny stop first.

I stood near the elevator on the main floor and watched until Lydia had walked away from the desk and out the door. She stuck a little plastic clock on the counter that said she'd be back in fifteen minutes. After looking around to make sure the coast was clear, I nonchalantly walked toward the reception area, praying no one would come around.

Surely everyone was dining on caviar and champagne for their usual lunch. That was, except Lydia and me.

All clear, I thought, and moved in for the kill.

Hoping my stomach wouldn't suddenly growl from hunger pangs, I walked around the desk as if I belonged there. The more innocent one looked, the more innocent they'd appear.

At least that was my motto as I snooped around—and constantly prayed.

The computer files apparently had been cleaned out, as evidenced by the new file names. No more cutesy names from poor Ian. Damn. Even the "frequent flier" title was gone, so it was going to take some time for me to find it. I looked at the clock. My stomach did in fact growl, and I told myself that I'd have to pass on computer nosing around. I clicked the mouse until the screen was back to its original desktop—so Lydia would not be the wiser.

Footsteps took my attention. I looked up to see one of the patients walking into the living room, her face a veritable ball of bandages. It was a wonder she could find her way around. Figured she wasn't interested in me as she sat down and leaned back in the brocade chair. Probably taking a snooze sitting up was easier on her breathing. I'd seen her around before, and she never paid me any attention. Good thing.

I got up and went into the back room. Things were neatly arranged on the two desks and the bookshelves surrounding the room. Ian must have set it up like that, since Lydia didn't strike me as the neatest teen on the block.

I walked behind one desk to find a black metal

file cabinet with only two drawers. When I yanked on the top one, nothing happened. Locked. Damn. Yet good. Regular patient files weren't locked up around there so whatever was inside this gem might be of help.

I flopped down into the chair and decided I needed to find the key. In order for that miracle, I needed to think like Jagger. The guy had such a knack for things like this! Slowly I looked around the desk area. Not much except a picture of Cliff Walk, a sailboat in a bottle (go figure) and a pen holder next to a little box that held letters. I assumed outgoing mail.

There was a tiny drawer in the bottom of the box. Bingo? Maybe?

Gingerly I opened it. Two Cross pens that looked expensive, a black comb (probably left from Ian since Lydia didn't look like a teen fashionista who cared about her hair) and a key. But my heart didn't leap in my chest since it was the old-fashioned kind—long, slender, brass, actually an antique skeleton one that opened old-fashioned doors.

However, I picked up the key and twisted it in my hand, kinda hoping to get some positive vibes from it or even a premonition.

After several minutes I started to set it back in the box when I noticed that part of the built-in shelving had a pull-out section. Much like a rolltop desk cover, only flatter and in the center of the shelves.

As if it had called to me, I got up, took the key and held it toward the lock part. An exact match.

When I stuck the key in, my heart did in fact leap in my chest as the lock clicked, and I eased the cover down like a makeshift desk.

Two papers flew to the floor. The rest of the inside had what looked like personal letters stacked and tied in blue ribbon and a few photographs. Old ones. I lifted one up. A handsome man holding a toddler—who looked very much like she'd grow into the teen Lydia—stared out at me. Had to be her late father. Wow. Olivia was definitely the lady in the next picture, holding the baby. Lydia? This time her hair looked too light. Then again, Lydia could have dyed it or her hair had darkened with age.

"Ah choo!"

I swung around to see the bandaged patient standing at the desk. "May I help you, ma'am? Oh, and God bless you."

"Where's Lydia?"

I nonchalantly picked up the papers, put them back, then eased the desk closed, locked it, and set the key back in the box—but not before "borrowing" the stack of letters. I *would* return them tomorrow.

"At lunch." I looked at the clock as I stuffed the letters into the pocket of my scrubs. "I'm sure she'll be—" As I made my way around the reception desk, Lydia walked in the front door.

Saved by the sneeze.

"Oh, here she is, ma'am. See you later," I said to both of them and hurried out, ignoring the odd look on Lydia's face.

I had to ignore it or—with my damn honest conscience—I might spill my guts about what I'd been doing, or at the very least spill the letters.

Wow. I couldn't wait to look at them!

Even though the letters were burning a hole in my pocket, I couldn't risk taking them out in a public place like The Market nor could I take too much longer since I needed to get back to my Goldie.

"Next?" Sheila said in her nifty brogue.

"Hey, Sheila. Guess I'm next. Clam chowder, to go. Please."

As she fixed my chowder, I touched the stack of papers, pulling my pocket back just enough to read the address.

Mrs. Olivia Wheaton. No Chandler yet.

Great. There might be something very useful for me in these correspondences. I only hoped they weren't some steamy love notes from Devin. Then again, Devin looked as if he didn't know how to write.

After grabbing a stack of napkins, plastic spoon and package of oyster crackers, I paid for my lunch and hurried back the several blocks to Highcliff Manor.

Neal's car wasn't in the parking lot, which made me relax a bit. Not sure if I was up to seeing him after last night when he'd seen me—*all* of me. I smiled to myself and went inside.

Lydia was at the computer, so I quickly said hi and went to the elevator. It felt as if she was staring at me. At my pocket. As if she knew I had "borrowed" the letters. Yikes! Quickly I got onto the elevator that seemed to open its doors just in time as I heard Lydia call my name.

I stepped inside the elevator, pretending that I didn't hear. Hey, I knew myself well enough to know that lying about taking personal property was not up my alley. I would have spilled my guts to her even if she had no suspicions at all.

When I opened the door to Goldie's room, I was relieved to hear him snoring away. Thank goodness. Jackie was bustling about the room and stopped to look up when she heard me.

Hm?

Had she been snooping around Goldie's personal belongings? Did she suspect us or was she more of a thief, since I recalled her making that comment about not being able to afford eating out for lunch.

Damn it. My mind was reeling out of control. Had to be guilt eating away at me. I walked in and smiled at her. "Hey. How is he?"

"Sleeping like a baby since you left. I was just straightening out the place." She lifted a pillow from the chaise lounge, fluffed it and set it back.

I looked around. "The place looks perfect." As it had when I left.

Seemed Jackie needed watching.

I let out a breath and wondered if I was overly suspicious of everyone around there. They all couldn't be involved!

Or could they?

Goldie moaned.

Jackie and I swung around in his direction. I hurried to his side and leaned over. "Hey."

"Suga?"

"None other. How you doing, Gold?" Before he could answer, I looked up to see Jackie gone—without a word. Hm again. Weird if nothing else.

"Do you need anything?" I asked, sitting down on the chair next to him.

"Water. Maybe water."

"Sure, hon." I poured some fresh ice water into a cup and held it out toward him. "Take it slow."

He did, then leaned back and sighed. "Hell of a dream after taking those narcs, Suga."

I laughed. "Oh yeah? Spill. Was I in it?"

"Ouch. Don't make me laugh. Yes, you were in it—" He looked around the empty room. "And you and you and even Toto."

"Oh, stop. Hey, Gold, listen to this." I proceeded to tell him about my snooping, the letters, and whatever I'd learned about Lydia. Not wanting him to worry, I left out my suspicions about Jackie. I'd keep my eye on her myself.

"Wow. Read me the letters." He lifted himself up on his elbows then flopped back down.

"You're still too high on your meds, silly, and besides, I wouldn't want someone walking in or listening outside the door. For several reasons, Gold, I don't trust too many folks around here."

"I hear you, but what about the good doc?" He chuckled then said "Ouch" again.

"Well, I trust him," I said.

Goldie looked at me, whistled and said, "Good for you."

"Stop trying to get my mind off delicious Jagger."

"Touché." He rolled over and moaned.

"Get some more rest, Gold. I'll be in the chair by the window if you need me."

"Perfect. Peek at a letter or two and let me know what you find out. If anyone comes in, they'll never suspect you took the letters from the office.

I walked to the chair, sat down, put my feet up on the ottoman and thought Goldie had a good point.

Except for the heavily bandaged woman—who even I didn't recognize.

Nineteen

After making sure Goldie was set for the night, I hurried out and jogged back to the lodge. Thank goodness no one was around as I ran up the stairs—oh so eager to read the letters. Even if old Samuel flew past me, I'd ignore him.

A cold breeze touched my cheek as I opened my door. "Okay. I get it. You read minds. I'm busy now though. Beat it."

My skin warmed. I laughed out loud and flopped onto my bed but not before pulling all the letters from my pocket. Turned out that there were only seven of them, but someone had lovingly packaged them up in a ribbon.

For a few seconds I contemplated not opening them.

It was so prying to read someone else's personal letters. They had to be personal and probably sensual by the ribbon, the handwriting and the fact that they were snail mail and not e-mail.

Still, two men were dead and fraud was being committed here in Newport.

And someone had followed me and Ian had knocked me out.

I slowly untied the ribbon, not wanting to cause any damage. After all, I had committed a crime even if they were only letters, so no need to do any damage.

My hands shook as if they knew we shouldn't be doing this. But I managed to get the first one open. It was over twenty years old and the hand-writing rather messy. Had to be from the guy. The lover.

My darling…

Soon my vision blurred and a tear dropped onto my pillow. The guy had really been in love with the woman, but it sounded as if their parents wouldn't allow them to be together. Wow. Sure sounded like some movie of the week or a Brontë novel. It went on to say that they could meet secretly on Cliff Walk near the Chinese pagoda.

"I've seen it," I whispered.

How romantic! I got the sense that these two were very young, probably still teenagers since he talked about movies and television shows. After three more letters I sat up, blew my nose for the thousandth time and decided they hadn't gotten me anywhere other than a romantic read. Not even any names or return address on the letters.

Obviously two forbidden teen lovers. I called them Romeo and Juliet in my head and hoped they actually didn't do away with themselves.

Before I could wrap the letters back up exactly as they were, there was a knock at the door.

"You eating tonight?" Jagger asked.

My Romeo, I thought, and then told myself the letters had made me crazy. Crazier than usual. "Come in."

"You should lock your door," he said as he opened it and stepped in. "What's wrong?"

There was genuine concern in his voice. Nice. "I'm fine. Work related. What are you up to eating?" I asked.

"Whatever. What type of work related thing makes your eyes bloodshot?"

I rubbed my eyes. "I'll explain over dinner. I'm actually hungry. Let's just go to The Market. I don't want to fuss."

Jagger took me by the shoulders, leaned forward and kissed my forehead. Then he moved to my cheeks.

How sweet, I thought, until his lips met mine—and sweet would not be the word I'd use to explain how I felt—because for a fleeting moment I felt as if I'd *cheated* on Jagger and should confess.

Within seconds, and still in Jagger's arms, I told myself that was ridiculous. We had no commitment to each other. No words of feelings had ever been spoken. Hell, who even *knew* what our feelings were? I sure didn't, although if he kept me in this embrace much longer I'd be professing my supposed love and asking him to get hitched.

I eased back.

He seemed reluctant as he let go then he turned toward the door. "The Market it is," he said as if nothing had happened.

I thought of Neal, Jagger, Neal, Jagger, and decided *nothing* indeed had happened.

* * *

I took a sip of my clam chowder while I looked at Jagger across the table at The Market. If Neal popped into my head one more time I'd dive into my chowder and drown myself. Even though I'd had the same menu over and over here, I still hadn't gotten tired of it yet.

"So, what do you think about the letters?" I asked him after telling him in great detail all about them, including my opinion. Were his eyes always that glassy?

He took a bit of his beef tenderloin, chewed, swallowed, sipped at his bottled water then said, "Interesting."

I set my spoon down rather abruptly. "Interesting? That's it? What the hell does that mean?"

"Look, Sherlock, I think it's great that you found them and thought they might help your case, but do they?"

Shit. "No," I said in a whiny tone. "No, they don't. But they *could* have."

He shook his head. "Yes, Pauline, they could have. Now how do you plan to put them back?"

Yikes. I hadn't exactly worked that one out in my head. Maybe I should have thought it through a bit better. But what I did get was Jagger's "lesson" not to take the evidence—or possible evidence—next time, but to leave everything as is and snoop ... investigate on the spot.

Jagger lesson number one million learned.

We finished our meal and headed back to the lodge. I half expected Samuel to be waiting for us in the lobby, or at the very least to see Arlene puttering around behind the desk. However, the place was empty. Eerily empty.

"Good night," I said and turned toward the steps.

Jagger stepped forward.

Oh, boy. Another kiss!

There was something so sensual about Newport.

I positioned myself against the banister and waited.

"I stopped in to see Goldie today," he said. "Olivia is having a fund-raiser at her home tonight. She's funding a scholarship in Ian's name. Your buddy Doc Neal made a point of telling Goldie and me about it. Might be a good place to check out. I'll meet you back down here in fifteen."

My jaw did its thing.

"What? You waited until now to tell me that? I'm exhausted. I'm going to sleep." I turned to go.

"This gig is upper crust. Wear something nice," he said, and sprinted up the stairs.

"Samuel, if you don't kill him. I will."

The front door swung open, the breeze blew my hair into my face, and I turned toward the stairs. "Okay, I'll do it then."

"I feel like a fish out of freaking water, Jagger," I said as we walked into the foyer of Olivia Wheaton-Chandler's home. Home? It really had to be about forty rooms, decorated in gold and silk, and even the dust bunnies looked elegant. Since

I hadn't planned to attend any social functions, I only had a plain little black dress in my wardrobe that Goldie had made me pack. Something about dating the wealthy and how simplicity would make me look less obvious.

Obvious about what?

Knowing Gold, he probably meant obvious about snagging myself a billionaire. I shook my head this time and smiled inside, knowing dear Goldie had meant well and that after I'd called Highcliff and had spoken to Kerie Cetin, Goldie's post-op recovery course was running smoothly.

Of course, hearing him snoring in the background helped to allay any fears or worries from me.

Jagger took my arm and led me into a gigantic ballroom where the crowd had gathered.

"You act as if you've been here before," I whispered, and then thought, *He probably has.* I was talking Jagger here.

No response except for me to stay put as he walked away to get us something to drink. I looked around the room and after noting the grandeur of the ballroom from the wood floors to the mural of clouds and angels on the ceiling, I realized I knew no one there. Probably even Lydia was holed up in her room.

Charity events did not seem up a teen's alley.

While waiters walked around, offering silver trays of fabulous hors d'oeuvres to the crowd, Mrs. Wheaton-Chandler took center stage. Of course there was no real stage, but she stood near a set up area next to a white baby grand piano, potted palms and gigantic white flowered arrangements.

"Thank you all so much for coming," she started, as I scanned the room for Jagger.

Knowing him, he might have hightailed it out of the place and left me to my investigating all alone. Half of the time I think Jagger actually liked teaching me the ropes and the other half I think he felt obligated and probably annoyed at coming to save me when I hung myself on one of those ropes.

"Here."

I swung around to see Jagger standing there with a glass of champagne held out toward me.

"Where the hell did you go?" I took the champagne, sipped it, and wrinkled my face. "Ick. Do they have any sugar I can stick in this stuff?"

He shook his head.

"What? So I don't like expensive champagne."

"They don't have Coors in bottles at these things. And I was working before, Sherlock," he said, looked me in the eye and then walked away.

Walked away!

While Olivia went on about what a wonderful cause this was in the name of her past employee, Ian James, I moved about the guests. As she sang Ian's praise, I scanned the crowd. No one even looked familiar until I got close enough to two women. From behind they could have passed for twins.

Daphne Baines and Babette LaPierre.

For a second I debated sneaking away before they noticed me. Then I decided, what the hell? Maybe I'd learn something from them. "Ladies," I said, causing them to turn around.

Both gave me a "who the hell are you" kind of look until Babette said, "Oh, the nurse."

Daphne added, "What are you doing here? I can't imagine you make a good enough salary to win any auction tonight."

After squeezing my champagne goblet so tight I thought it would shatter in my grasp, I smiled and said, "I'm not into antiques anyway."

"Then you wouldn't want to bid on old Doc Harrington, the heart specialist," Babette said.

Both women laughed hysterically.

I was ready to say that I'd noted a few new laugh lines on each of them, but my Catholic-school-induced conscience wouldn't let me. Shit. What the hell was Babette talking about anyway?

Before I could ask, I heard a man say, "First bachelor of the night. A fantastic catch ladies and certainly going to be our biggest moneymaker."

I followed both Babette's and Daphne's drooling stares to the podium to come eye-to-eye with ... *Dr. Neal Forsyth.*

Twenty

Neal? Neal? Neal was up for *auction*?
Apparently so, as the gentleman who'd introduced Neal started taking bids—starting at ten grand!

Wow. *Last night I'd nearly gotten a real bargain*, I thought, and would have loved to shove that in the perfect man-made faces of the two women ... who were no longer next to me.

"Fifteen thousand!" Babette yelled out.

Suddenly she and Daphne were way up front bidding against each other along with plenty of other women in the room. Make that *every* woman in the room. However, one of the voices from the back sounded rather deep, and kept outbidding everyone.

I sipped my champagne, decided it actually tasted delicious and laughed and enjoyed the festivities, as everyone else in the room seemed to be doing.

"Going once, twice, three times," the auctioneer said, finishing with, "Two hundred fifty-five thousand to the anonymous bidder in the rear."

Everyone in the room turned around. No one was there except two waiters with half empty trays.

The auctioneer laughed. "Of course we won't take that bid out of those gentlemen's salaries. No, the bidding is complete and anonymous, however the bidder informed us that I am to announce who the winner is right now."

For rowdy, snooty rich folks, the room hushed instantly.

"The bidder has already paid up, and the winner of the date with Dr. Forsyth is ... Ms. Pauline Sokol."

Along with everyone else, I looked around the room to see who the hell she was.

Hands covered my eyes so I gave a swift slug behind me with my elbow.

"Ouch! Hey, Pauline. It's me. Your *prize.*"

My eyes were uncovered as I swung around to come face-to-face with Neal.

"*I* won you? I *won* you, Neal?"

He laughed and kissed my cheek. "Don't be so shocked, Pauline. I had Marie do the bidding. I thought it a great surprise for you. It's for a good cause, you know. The scholarship goes to a high school student who is underprivileged."

Hm. Guess I could have sex with Neal for such a worthy cause. I would have figured the entire thing out, but I never got to see Marie. Oh, those upstairs or downstairs maids were so discreet!

Suddenly I had a strong urge to go to confession. Damn that morality-induced upbringing. I looked at Neal, allowed myself a little hot flash and said, "Guess I could suck it up."

We laughed as he hugged me—and over his shoulder I saw Jagger ... approaching.

Damn. Now I didn't have any time to question Neal to see if he knew who paid for our date.

Trying not to be too obvious, I eased myself free of a rather surprised Neal, and why wouldn't he be? After last night's antics, I shouldn't have been embarrassed to be held by him in public, but there was Jagger, approaching!

"Oh, Neal, have you met Jagger?" I asked before he got close enough to even hear.

Neal turned around, and I'm sure suddenly had second thoughts about dating me, even for 255 grand. "Um. No. Jagger?"

Jagger came up to me and eyed Neal. "Hey."

I introduced the two as "he's also staying at the lodge," that'd be Jagger, and "Goldie's doctor," that'd be Neal. Sounded very noncommittal I thought and mentally patted myself on the back.

The two kinda growled at each other, then Neal was called up to the "stage" area to announce the grand total made for the auction and Jagger stood silently next to me—and I could *feel* every second of him staring at me.

The crowd yelled and clapped after Neal announced a staggering number that had been paid for the bachelors. I couldn't help myself as I leaned toward Jagger, who still looked at me, and said, "They could have doubled it if you were auctioned off." Then I laughed.

He glared at me.

Oops. "Lighten up, Jagger. It's for a good cause."

I know he wanted to say something about my "winning" Neal, but probably didn't want me to think he cared. "Who paid for your 'date'?"

Damn. I'd nearly forgotten about that. "Hm. You know I have no idea. Do you?"

Jagger looked down at me, and I'm sure wanted to roll his eyes. "You need to find out. Could be related to your case."

"My case? What the hell does this have to do with my case?"

Jagger stood silent.

I punched his chest. Not that he probably even felt it, but I said, "Do you know something you're not sharing with me? Something about Mr. Baines's murder?"

"That case is closed."

Then Ian really did kill him. But why? "Aren't the cops even looking for motive?"

"What for? They can't prosecute a corpse."

I punched him again. "Ian was a person—"

"Who killed Mr. Baines."

I went to punch him again, but this time his reflexes came into play and he grabbed my arm.

"But then who killed Ian?"

Jagger looked out past me as if he were thinking. "The cops have ruled his death a suicide."

"Suicide?" My heart sank. How awful, yet, knowing Ian, it did sound believable. "Oh," was all I could manage.

"Get to work, Sherlock. Why the hell do you think I brought you here? To win ..."

He let go of my arm, turned and walked away. Yikes.

What the hell did that mean? Instead of facing the daunting task of figuring out Jagger, I decided to look around the room for someone to talk to who might have something to do with my case.

"Congratulations, Ms. Sokol."

I swung around to come face-to-scowling-face with none other than Olivia Wheaton-Chandler!

"Oh. Thanks. Thank you, Mrs. Chandler. Mrs. Wheaton-Chandler."

She raised one eyebrow ever so slightly. "Olivia. Please."

"Oh, yeah. Olivia please. I mean Olivia. Thanks." For a few seconds I couldn't even remember what she was thanking me for, but faced with critical situations all my nursing career, my mind snapped back. "Winning Dr. Forsyth—that is, a date with Dr. Forsyth—well, that was quite a surprise." I stepped back to get a better look at her this close.

Olivia was beautiful and for someone her age looked rather young. I figured she had to be past fifty to be Lydia's aunt from the stuff Lydia had shared with me, but there were only tiny crow's-feet near Olivia's eyes and the slightest droop to one eyelid.

Her hair had to be fashioned daily by a beautician, and the coloring, deep golden blonde tones, looked perfectly highlighted. Strong, high cheekbones gave her not only an air of being wealthy, she looked as if she were born to be.

A handsome woman one might say.

"Yes, dear. I'm sure it was a surprise," she said,

and then sipped on her goblet of champagne.

What was a surprise? I thought after I'd been studying her up close and personal. Oh, yeah. The Neal date. "Hey, do you know how it came about? I mean who coughed up all that dough for me?"

She leaned near. Earlier I hadn't noticed how dark her eyes were. Very much like Lydia's. Olivia's, however, darkened further as she said, "I have no idea who *coughed* up the dough ... or *why*."

In seconds the crowd parted and Olivia Wheaton-Chandler walked graciously away as I stood there with my jaw resting on my chest—and everyone staring at me.

"One thing is for sure, Jagger, old lady Wheaton-Chandler is not a nice person," I repeated in a whiny tone as Jagger walked in front of me into the lodge.

Okay, I'd said the same thing over and over all the way back, but he didn't have to run away like that. "Hey, I'm not done!"

Over his shoulder he said, "Yes, you are, Pauline. Get some sleep."

Damn it. I wasn't done, I thought as I walked up to my room and opened the door. The window was closed but the room felt about thirty degrees. "Hey, Sam, I could use some help."

The curtains ruffled.

For some reason I didn't feel frightened and said, "You're invisible. Maybe you could help with my case. Who the hell paid for that bid and why?"

The newspaper that the maid left on the bedside table each day, and I never had time to read, fluttered to the floor. I chuckled as if it were a sign from old Samuel as I bent to pick it up. It read:

Bachelor auction this evening. Dr. Neal Forsyth, the number one draw.

I looked up and laughed. "Why Sam, you dog you, are you telling me Neal had the hots for me and bid the money himself so I would date him again? Ha! Nice to be that rich that you could afford it!"

The room warmed ... no, make that heated to an unusually warm temperature.

After tossing and turning most of the night and blaming it on the champagne and not the woo woo actions of Samuel, I finally got up and dressed for work. I didn't want to be late for taking care of Goldie, although I was certain he was in good hands.

When I went down to the dining room for breakfast, I noticed several settings had been used, but no one else was about. When the maid came to ask me if I wanted "savory or sweet," I asked if Jagger had come down yet.

"Hours ago, ma'am. He had his suitcase with him too."

"He left?" That rat! He wouldn't leave without a word, or would he?

Yes, Pauline, I told myself, *Jagger would do whatever the hell he pleased.*

"Savory. No, sweet," I muttered as I contemplated the fact that if Jagger felt he could leave

Newport, I was perfectly safe, but still needed something sweet.

Yeah, I also entertained the idea that he left—jealous of Neal—and didn't want to be around to see me go on another date.

"Is something funny, ma'am?" the maid asked.

I looked at her and realized I actually had been laughing—hysterically.

"Hey, Gold," I whispered as I touched his hand. "It's me, Pauline."

He opened one eye and smiled. "Morning, Suga."

"How you doing, buddy?" I sat on the edge of the bed and studied the bruising on his face and knew that was all par for the course. "Any pain?" Suddenly I wanted to bite my tongue. Old nursing trick: With patients like my dear Goldie, who had a low tolerance for pain, one should never bring up the subject of any discomfort and put it into their heads! How many times had I asked a patient if they had a headache and suddenly they did.

He moaned. "Some. Maybe I should take something?"

"Well, you were sleeping pretty soundly, Gold. I only woke you because your breakfast is here and I don't want it to get cold. How about you eat and then we'll see if you need something." I stood up and Goldie grabbed my hand.

"Thank you, Suga."

I winked at him and fixed the tray so he could

sit up in his bed and eat while I promptly told him all about last night, including the auction and the Samuel newspaper incident.

"Don't make me laugh with these damn bandages on my face, Suga. A ghost!"

"Hey, I'm really buying into it, Gold. He's so real. And the strange thing is, he seems to know Jagger so well!"

We both laughed, and I sat in the stuffed chair near the window, fairly certain that dear Goldie, in his Burberry nightgown, false eyelashes and a silken bed jacket, was not in dire pain.

Since Goldie had assured me that he was fine while he ate breakfast in bed and watched Martha Stewart on television, I headed downstairs to return my stolen goods. Dear Goldie had given me some tips on how to sneak them back into the desk, and to make sure I'd wiped off any fingerprints—just in case.

Lydia was sitting at the computer, obviously lost in work. When I came around the side of the reception desk, I smiled. Solitaire. The kid was playing a game of Solitaire.

Actually, it then struck me as sad.

She should have been out with friends or in college and having the best time of her life, not holed up in this dead-end job because she was a relative.

What the hell did Olivia, and probably Devin, I'd bet my last dime, and Dr. Cook all have to hide that they needed to involve Lydia?

*   *   *

"Hey, Lydia. How about a tea? I made you some Earl Grey." I set her mug of tea next to her computer. Getting the tea was part one of my getting the letters back. If nothing else, Lydia would be preoccupied, or at least have to leave for a few seconds since I purposely didn't fix her tea correctly.

"Thanks." She looked at her tea. "No milk, Pauline."

"Oh. Sorry. I forgot how you take it," I lied. "I'm fussy about my tea too, so why don't you go refix it. I'll watch the desk for you."

She hesitated a second, looked at her cup and said, "Don't touch the computer."

Bingo.

I smiled to myself at my success and only frowned when I thought that I wished Jagger were there to give me an "atta girl." Oh, well. I was on my own and apparently doing fine. No. Spectacular!

I hurried into the back room, looked around several times to make sure no one snuck up on me, and got the key to the desk. Before the clock's handle could move, I had the desktop opened, the letters safely tucked back inside, and eased the cover closed.

Then I swung around to see that heavily bandaged woman standing at the desk—watching *me*.

Twenty-One

When I got back to Goldie's room, I shoved the door closed so hard, he shouted. "It's just me, Gold. Damn. That was close." I told him about getting caught by "Lady Bandage" and how Lydia had come around the corner just in time for me to hightail it out of the office area—without an explanation or lie needed.

"Got the letters back safely then?" he asked, pulling the covers up tighter over his shoulders.

I helped tuck them behind his arms. "Yep. Phew. I'm not sure my heart can take that kind of investigating!"

We laughed until Goldie said his nose hurt. "I can't wait to see it, Gold! You are going to look so fab. Not that you didn't already!" *Vanity wins out*, I thought as Gold started to talk about his new nose and how he too couldn't wait to get the packing out and the bandages off.

Then I thought of Neal and my heart did a little jig of excitement—and not because I had a new nose.

Suddenly I was glad old Jagger had left New-port.

"Goldie, I need to find out more about Mrs. Olivia Wheaton-Chandler. Any suggestions?"

He looked at me over the bruises on his face. My insides knotted. He'd done this for me. Sure he'd benefit, but I was still feeling badly about his discomfort.

He shifted in the bed. "Let's see. Lydia is her niece. There's your connection. You need to bud-dy up to her to get to the old lady."

"I'd thought about that already, but Lydia is a strange child. I'm not sure I could penetrate her teen armor." I chuckled.

Goldie reached out and touched my hand. "With all your nieces and nephews? You can do it, Suga. You can."

Feeling as if I really could, I made sure the call bell was within reach, the phone nearby and the remote in Goldie's hand, and went back to "visit" darling Lydia.

This time when I got off the elevator, I noticed "Lady Bandages" walking out the back door to the solarium. Good. At least I wouldn't have to worry about her eavesdropping, whoever she was. Ac-tually, by the looks of her bandages, she probably had other things on her mind besides watching me. I'm guessing a fast, pain-free recovery.

Lydia was still sipping her tea and looking at the computer. Perfect. Maybe the soothing warm liquid would make her feel more comfortable with me since I'd gotten it for her. Make her feel as if I cared. I really did, in a friendly sort of way.

How I hoped she wasn't involved in any nefarious activity.

"Getting hungry, Lydia?" I asked, walking up to the desk.

Her head swung around, the tea splashing out onto the computer, and she cursed like a sailor. Oops.

"Sorry. Here let me get something to wipe that with," I said.

"I got it," she said as she took a tissue from the box. "Yeah. I'm about to go eat. One of the stupid nurses is supposed to cover for me but no one's shown up yet. Jerks."

I shook my head inside. Poor Lydia really was an unhappy teen—which would seem very common, but her pain went deeper than acne, boys or weight.

Lydia seemed like some tortured soul.

And what would cause such hurting?

After Jackie Wisherd had shown up to cover the reception area for Lydia, I followed the kid out the doorway, fast on her heels. "Can I walk with you to The Market?" I asked.

She didn't even turn around.

Hm. "Lydia?"

Nothing. She was already out the long driveway.

I hurried closer. "Lydia!"

Stopping, she looked over her shoulder. "What?"

I noticed she had earphones on and the music was so earsplitting that I could suddenly understand the words to a rap song—then wished I couldn't. "Oh, didn't mean to be so loud, but I'd called you a few times and asked if we could walk together to The Market."

Okay, she looked at me as if I were nuts, but something about me must have made her a little comfortable or at least trust me a bit. "I'm not going there, but ... umm ... you can come with me to eat."

"Fine." I figured I could find something I'd like on any menu. "Where to?"

"My aunt's house."

My aunt's house! What a bonus for me, yet how sad for the kid to not even call where she lived home.

Since Lydia kept her music playing as we walked, conversation was kept to a minimum. But when we turned into the Chandler place, she yanked the earphones off as if she'd get hollered at for wearing them.

I followed her around the gigantic mansion to the back where a tiny door faced a driveway. Along one side ran tall hedges with animal topiaries nestled in between. I could tell there were long paths of floral gardens leading away from the house too. It looked very much like a well-kept private park.

Lydia rang the bell. A servant woman opened the door, nodded and stepped back inside while I stood there with my mouth gaping.

Lydia had to use the servant's entry?

"Take a seat," she said to me as I looked at the huge kitchen with thousands of copper pots hanging from the ceiling, three gas stoves that were the size of my living room, and rows and rows of utensils, dishes and supplies. This place could feed an army.

Several cooks bustled about, one making some kind of cookies that smelled heavenly while another chopped vegetables. Both smiled at Lydia, asked how her day was going, but kept working.

"Pauline?" Lydia said. "Sit down."

"Thanks," I mumbled and sat while she went to the refrigerator.

The cooks weren't even going to fix the kid's lunch.

But as I watched, I noticed a good rapport between them all, and Lydia actually looked more at home fixing us two ham sandwiches. This was probably her "Pollyanna" refuge from her family. And more than likely she felt "at home" enough to help herself.

"Mayo or mustard?" she asked me.

"Mayo please, and can't I help?" I started to get up just as the door opened—and Mr. Perfect came in.

Not Mr. Perfect in a good sense either.

Devin.

He looked at Lydia and ignored her, told the cooks that Olivia wanted her lunch right now and then turned toward me. "What the hell are you doing here?"

Whoa. Don't mince any words, buddy.

Before I could lie, Lydia was in his face, saying, "She's with me. Got a problem with that?"

At first I thought he'd smack her, so I started to

get up to help, but he backed down, cursed and turned to go out.

Lydia had something on Mr. Perfect.

She had to or why else would some macho guy like him back down from a skinny, petite teenage girl?

I studied Lydia as we ate our ham sandwiches. She was quite a good little chef, even adding fresh mozzarella and red peppers to the sandwiches. When I looked at the cooks bustling about, probably so Ms. Olivia's food would get done in seconds, I thought they must have taught Lydia. Without a word one actually handed her the mayonnaise, which she mumbled a thanks for.

And I also thought about Devin backing down.

She handed me my sandwich, for which I nodded in appreciation and then took a small bite. "These are fantastic, Lydia." I took another taste to reinforce how good they were.

Somewhere in the recesses of her darkened eyes, a glimmer shone. No one paid much attention to the kid—which could be my saving grace—although I didn't want to hurt her in any way with false hopes.

She nodded as if in thanks.

"How the heck did you learn to make them? I can just about open a can of tuna, throw in some mayo, stick it on rye bread and call it a sandwich." I started to laugh, and soon she joined in.

Then Lydia confirmed my suspicions. She spent much of her time in the kitchen or in the laundry room or in her bedroom. Not her fancy bedroom on the second floor, but a rather stark one on the third floor where all the staff lived. It was her special getaway, she'd said, and always spent time with the servants. They really were her family. *How sad*, I thought. So sad that such a young life could not be happier.

"Devin seemed as if he were in a hurry," I lied, having no inkling as to what Devin seemed other than a jerk.

She hesitated. "Aunt Olivia likes to get her own way."

Interesting.

"Ha. Don't we all?" I chuckled.

This time Lydia stared into space. "I wouldn't know."

Damn. "Come on, Lyd. You must get your own way lots. I mean, you're a teenager!"

She set her sandwich down with a thud. Geez. I hoped I hadn't taken her appetite away. The kid was rather thin and needed to eat.

"Sorry if I said something wrong. You all right?"

"Fine. I'm fine. It's just that …"

Once again she stared into space.

Once again I felt her pain and felt sorry for her.

Lydia continued, "It's that I don't get much of what I want. And I'm not talking material things, Pauline."

I touched her hand. "I figured that."

She smiled. "Ever since Devin married my aunt, things haven't been the same around here."

"Were they better before ... before the marriage?"

She pulled her hand free and looked me in the eye. "I never really knew my parents."

Then how could things have been any better?

I helped Lydia clean up and took my damn time to try to get more info out of her, although I didn't want to see more hurt in her eyes. She did, however, say how Devin had spent so much of Olivia's money—no great surprise there. On more than one occasion, Lydia had heard them arguing that money was tight.

However, a damn good reason for Olivia to try to recoup.

But how?

Was she somehow involved in the medical fraud?

Now that I had that tidbit to work with, I told Lydia that I really needed to get back to Goldie. We said goodbye and I turned to go out the door. I figured the buffalo mozzarella had a gazillion calories in it so I would jog back to work.

When I came around the corner of the mansion, a form lunged out of the bushes!

After stumbling backward, and before I knew it, I was on the ground. I tried to kick and scream, but suddenly the threatening voice had me mute—and he wasn't even touching me.

"Shut the hell up, Nurse," Devin said. "I'm not going to hurt you. Just a word of advice. Stay the hell away from Lydia."

I shielded my eyes from the sunlight and said, "Those words of wisdom from you or someone else?" I pushed him away, got up, ignored the pain in my back and wiped gravel from my scrubs.

"What the hell difference does it make?" He stepped back as if he didn't have the nerve to attack me again. Every so often he looked up at the mansion.

I tried to nonchalantly turn to see if Olivia were standing watch in some window like old Samuel was wont to do, but I didn't want to seem obvious. Anything that I did could cause more problems—thus pain—for Lydia.

When I stepped to his side, I said, "It doesn't matter. Leave me the hell alone, and if you ever threaten me again, I'll go to the cops." Unless dear Olivia owns them.

He grumbled something and started to walk away.

"Keep out of the sun, Devin. Your crow's-feet are deepening." With that I started my jog out of the driveway and thought I heard him screech.

"Hey, good to see you sitting up," I said as I hurried into Goldie's room.

From the chair by the window he forced a half smile and said, "Feels good to get out of that bed. I'm not doing too well, am I, Suga?"

I shook my head. "You are the perfect post-op patient, Gold. Stop beating yourself up. You are doing fantastic. These things take time." I sat on the arm of his chair and told him about my lunch escapade.

"Wow. Sounds like lots of covering up going on. Too bad the kid is caught in the middle of something. No idea what?"

I shook my head. "Other than the insurance fraud, which they all could be involved with. I have to find out more and get more about Olivia—"

"Perhaps I can be of help?" Neal said, walking in the door.

Oops! I sprung up. "Oh, hey. We didn't hear you come in." The guy was like a stealth doctor.

He chuckled. "I like to surprise my women, Pauline."

Your women? Goldie and I exchanged glances that said, "Interesting." But I chuckled, very ladylike, and turned toward Goldie. "He's doing great, Doc. Really great." I winked at Goldie. And stupidly could imagine myself living at Forsyth Manor. I mean, a house with a name!

"I am," Gold managed.

Neal examined him and with my assistance changed the outside bandage, promising that in a few days Goldie would get to see his accomplishments, although there would still be swelling and bruising involved.

Gold's eyes lit up like a kid's on Christmas Eve.

I felt ten years younger, knowing Goldie's pain was not in vain.

Neal turned to me. "May I speak with you, Pauline?"

Goldie made a little sound. Kinda sounded like a cat, a scaredy cat.

Neal, the doll, touched Goldie's arm. "Nothing about you. You fit into the textbook recovery scenario for your procedure. No. Nothing about you, sir. It's personal."

Goldie let out a sigh, and I walked Neal to the door.

"I'm free tomorrow night for our date," he whispered.

Geez. So soon?

After today's visit with Lydia I wanted to cancel. Just not in any mood for ... "Tomorrow would be perfect," I heard myself say and mentally shook my head.

Suddenly I missed ... Jagger.

Twenty-Two

Back in my room, I flopped onto my bed and looked at the door, expecting a knock and a "Are you ready to eat?" But nothing.

Even Samuel seemed to be gone. I couldn't feel his presence or any cold draft. Damn. Kinda missed the guy. This was lonely! For a few seconds I shut my eyes and reviewed my case, or what little info that I had. One thing for certain was that I had to make another trip to the office and snoop around the files.

I needed to find the "frequent flier" patients' records. The files might just tell me whom the fraud was being committed for. Seemed logical to me that those patients would have been spending the most money at Highcliff, and they were almost a guarantee to spend more.

My stomach growled, but I didn't want to go out to eat all by myself. I sat up and took out my cell phone, dialing Fabio's office. When I looked at my watch, I curled my lips. "Damn. I'll bet

Adele has gone home already." Just as I started to
flip the cell closed, I heard a voice.

"Hello?"

"Adele?" Didn't really sound like her though.
Maybe I had the wrong number.

"*Chéri*? This is Lilla. You are Pauline?"

I leaned back on the bed not feeling so alone
anymore. "Yeah, it's me. Lilla?"

"*Oui*. My mother, she has gone home already.
May I give her a message from you?"

"Well, truthfully I was just calling to see if Jagger was around. Do you know him?"

I could hear the hitch in her voice—a very Jagger-like reaction to the guy.

"*Oui*," rolled off her lips, and suddenly, despite
the fact that I liked Lilla, I felt a wee bit jealous.
She was, in all honesty, a real looker.

"Umm. Then he's not there?"

"No, Pauline. He has not returned from Newport as far as I know."

"Well, I think he did. No sign of him. Huh?"

"None."

I thanked her and selfishly was glad Jagger
hadn't shown up there, but couldn't help but
wonder, where the hell was he?

Hey, I was a red-blooded, healthy woman!

After eating two slices of a pizza I foolishly had
delivered to my room, I offered the rest to the evening staff. Then I dressed in my black turtleneck
with black jeans, took my camera that was dis-
guised as a beeper and clipped it onto my belt,

grabbed my thin black gloves and stuffed a flash-light into my pocket. I also carefully removed the pink locket that Jagger had given me as a gift from my makeup case. At first I'd thought the locket was jewelry, but it turned out to be pepper spray for protection. What a guy.

Thank goodness Stella Sokol had always made us kids take a travel-sized flashlight wherever we went, "in case the power goes out."

I shook my head, thought about Jagger, ignored that thought and walked downstairs and out the door—feeling a rush of cold breeze behind me.

"I'll be fine, Sam. Go haunt someone else," I said, then laughed as I turned out the walkway, heading to Highcliff Manor.

This was a rather safe neighborhood and filled with walkers or other joggers, so I didn't worry about going out alone—since Ian was no longer around. *I will, however, stay off Cliff Walk at this time of the night*, I thought as I turned down the street with Highcliff in view.

Neal's car turned out of the parking lot, heading toward Bellevue Avenue. Suddenly my hormones went into overdrive. Damn, I just missed him. *You are bad, Pauline*, I told myself. *You have a date tomorrow. Tonight is investigating time.* With that, I walked along the driveway and up to the main door. No one was around, so I figured that was a good sign from up above.

For a second I considered going to see how Goldie was doing, but decided not to risk it. One of the staff might see me and know I was in the building. No. Gold was progressing fantastically and, in fact, would be more beautiful in a few more weeks.

So I walked into the foyer, looked around and headed toward the reception desk area.

The evening clerk was sitting at the computer—probably playing Solitaire like Lydia. I didn't recognize the woman, but she was much older than me and, frankly, looked bored. That could be helpful. Maybe she'd need a cup of coffee soon. I tucked myself into an alcove near the door, behind a gigantic Fica tree, and waited.

The receptionist's eyes started to close!

Great. Could I sneak past a sleeping woman and get into the files? That wasn't my strong point, but if need be, I'd give it a try. Waiting for several more minutes, I watched her head bob back and forth. Damn. I needed to get her out of the reception area since I wasn't feeling lucky enough to work around her.

I took out my cell phone and dialed, knowing I was far enough away that she couldn't hear me speaking. When the phone in front of her rang, she jumped, nearly plummeting out of her chair. I would have felt horrible if she'd fallen.

"Yeah," she said, sounding very confused.

"I'm calling for Mrs. Olivia Wheaton-Chandler."

I never saw anyone come to attention so fast as the poor receptionist. "She ... she's not here at the moment."

"I know that, you fool," I said, feeling badly about being so rude but figuring anyone working for Olivia would act that way. "She wanted me to check and see how things are going there. Any problems? You are paying attention, aren't you?"

Suddenly the woman was up from her seat, blinking her eyes and carrying on that everything was fine. I then hung up and waited.

Perfect. She shoved the phone back in its cradle, stretched and set the back in fifteen minutes sign up on the desk. Great. Caffeine it is, I thought as she walked around the front of the desk. But before she headed toward the staff's kitchen, she went to the front doors, jiggled the handles and … locked them! She used a key that she then tucked back into her pocket. That had to be against the fire code, but she probably didn't care and did it to keep out Olivia's spy.

I was locked in Highcliff Manor!

Oh, well, I'd been in tougher situations, often with Jagger, so I decided to get to the files and worry about my escape later.

When I got into the back office, I took out my flashlight, deciding it was safer than turning on the light. Then I stuck on my gloves, thinking Jagger would be proud that I'd remembered. Probably no patients would be about at this time, and certainly no visitors could get in, and the doc had left, so until "Rip Van Winkle" herself returned, I was safe.

I felt certain that was what Jagger would have done.

That lonely feeling started to creep into my thoughts, so I hurried to the locked file cabinet and refused to give in to that sentiment. Again I needed to find a key. I already knew the file cabinet key was not in the same box as the desk one. It would have stood out the other day when I was there. Nope. Had to be somewhere else.

I walked closer and accidentally bumped my knee on the edge. After a silent mumble of pain, I shone my flashlight onto the desk to see if there might be another box.

Papers were strewn across the desktop.

Old Rip Van must have been filing and gotten the urge for Solitaire. Perfect. I moved the light toward the file cabinet.

It was open.

Looking upward I thought, *Thanks, but this is way too easy for me, but thanks again. I'm not complaining.*

Hey, I was still fairly inexperienced at this job and took all the help I could get.

I sat down at the desk and shone the light onto the files. Some had Ian's old names on them, but they were crossed out and had more normal sounding patient names written above. No one had taken the time to replace them neatly. I bet poor Ian would be turning over in his grave, if he hadn't been cremated.

Slowly I read through the files as I held the flashlight in my mouth. Some of the names I recognized as women or men whom Goldie had spoken about meeting since being there.

Frequent fliers had been replaced with BDDs.

I lifted a file and rolled my chair back away from the desk. Before I opened the folder, I looked up to make sure no one was around. Hopefully Rip would take her time. Something told me she wasn't up for employee of the month anytime soon.

When I leaned forward to open the file, an unexpected breeze blew a paper off the desk. My heart stopped. Geez. Old Samuel must have followed me. I laughed to myself and stuck the paper back but not before reading it.

Over due was stamped on it. Then a handwritten note: "Payment refused to be paid by husband" across the top of the bill ... for one Daphne Baines—wife of the murdered Mr. Baines. Wow!

I set the paper back on the desk, hopefully where it'd been before but thinking Rip wouldn't know any different, and opened the frequent flier file.

"Wow," I muttered, followed by "Hmm," then a few more "wows" until I took out my beeper camera and started to click away. Thank goodness I'd invested in it for my first case.

Seemed as if the frequent fliers *were* the ones bilking the insurance company. Handwritten notes, and I wasn't sure whose hand had written them, said the spouses of each patient had refused to make any more payments. Mr. LaPierre had even said that his wife was a "sick woman" and needed therapy not more surgery. His credit card number had been crossed out.

But what interested me the most was that the surgeries were still preformed with a diagnosis of "deviated septum," so dear, perfect Babette could get yet another nose job.

After reading through all of them, I found similar "made up" medical diagnoses so that the insurance companies did, in fact, reimburse Highcliff Manor for their work.

What I couldn't tell was who preformed all the surgery—and who was behind this whole scam. These files had been tampered with and lots of potential evidence covered up.

A *whirring* sound struck the air.

The elevator descending!

I shoved the files back, not too worried about the order because Rip Van Winkle surely wouldn't notice, and ran out the door back to the safety of my alcove.

Two nurses came off the elevator and old Rip walked around the corner at that very minute . . . and my heart started to beat once again.

Solitary surveillance was no fun.

I'd been on cases where I had to hide and watch the goings-on of suspects before, but most of the time I had Jagger to keep me company. Enough said.

Right now, though, my back hurt. I was also sweating in my jeans, but I couldn't even take my gloves off for fear of leaving any fingerprints, so I just stood there watching the damn receptionist, again back at the computer, playing games!

It seemed hours passed before she finally got up. Thank goodness! She walked around the desk area and took a left down the hallway. She was probably headed toward the ladies' room, but I couldn't care less as I finally stepped from my alcove and looked at the front door, only steps away.

What to do? What to do?

Not wanting to draw any suspicions, I ran toward the elevator, but opened the door to the stairs instead. I hurried up to the second floor, looked around before I stepped out from the stairwell and turned toward Goldie's room.

"Visiting hours are over, Ms. Sokol," someone said—and in a not too pleasant tone.

Twenty-Three

Mentally I reviewed the symptoms of a heart attack—because getting caught right now, I believed I was having one. Chest pain, neck pain, shortness of breath, no heartbeat! Yeah, I could pass out right about now.

Quickly I slipped off my gloves then turned around to see Neal standing there. How the hell had he gotten back in? Duh. There had to be a staff entrance. That's right. Doctors and nurses came in through a door that was on the south side of the building where their parking lot was located. Geez. I never parked there since I always walked here.

"Oh, hey." I stepped forward. Thank goodness he was smiling ... or make that ogling me. Maybe the all black outfit looked weird. Sure it did.

"Hey. Is there a problem, Pauline?"

Problem? How did he know? Oh, wait. "Problem with Goldie?"

Neal shook his head. I realized he looked oh so casual for him. Brown suede jacket. Blue jeans, snuggly fitting in all the right places, and brown boots. Yum. He looked yummy.

"Did he call you or something?" Neal stepped forward and placed his hand on the small of my back.

"Oh, yeah. Something. I better go see him. I didn't want to wake anyone so I was sneaking around. Like I'm some kind of spy!" I laughed and thank goodness he joined me. "Oops. We should be quiet." I leaned forward and forced myself to kiss him on the lips. Really. It *was* forced.

He eased me back and looked around. I guessed he didn't want any of the staff to see us ... you know. Then he guided me toward Goldie's room, and I suddenly realized that my patient was snoring away. What the hell was I going to use for an excuse?

It was then that I realized it paid to be a good person in one's life. Kerie Cetin walked around the corner and saw us. She hurried closer and said, "Oh, Dr. Forsyth. This is so strange. I was just about to page you. Mrs. Seymour is having some excessive swelling. Can you come take a look at her?"

"Excuse me," Neal said to me.

I nodded and smiled. "No problem. I hope she's fine."

Kerie hurried away with him.

And I looked upward and winked. "Thanks."

I turned and walked back to the elevator, realizing I wouldn't have to crawl out of Goldie's second story room window. I'd use the staff entrance—and no one would be the wiser.

With Jagger MIA, I gave myself a mental "atta girl," knowing he'd do the same. However, it really didn't feel the same. In other words I didn't feel it down to my toes.

The digital clock said two and I groaned, realizing it was actually 2:00 A.M. Jogging back after my Neal scare had me revved up and falling asleep didn't come easily. I'd have to nap in Goldie's room tomorrow at the rate I was going.

Thank goodness the night had turned out profitably ... and having nearly slept with the guy who caught you sneaking around had to be a plus.

I smiled, turned over, hugged my pillow and decided I'd force myself to sleep, and before I knew it the sun was glaring in my window, the damn clock had only moved four hours, and I had to get up for the day.

"Are you shitting me, Suga?" Goldie asked, then made some kind of surprised noise. It was difficult to identify sounds with old Gold.

"No. Neal caught me right outside your door. You do snore like a lumberjack, Gold."

We both laughed and went over the evidence that I'd found last night. Goldie was so proud of me, I felt like a little kid getting a gold star on my homework.

"So, Jagger disappeared, huh?" Goldie asked.

"Don't start on him, Gold. I have no idea where he went. All I know is, I don't *need* him."

Goldie gave me a nod, but it was followed by

a "but you *want* him" kind of look. Thank goodness he didn't verbalize, cause there was no way I could lie to my best friend.

I waved my hands in the air. "Enough about that. What the hell am I going to do about my date with Neal tonight?"

Goldie walked to the window, sat in the chair and looked at me. "Do, Suga? I'd think you would know what to *do*."

"If you were closer, I'd smack you, but I'm too tired to get up." I rolled over onto my side as I pulled the duvet up on Goldie's bed. "I mean, I should be wrapping this investigation up, Gold. I really don't have time for a date."

"A $255,000 date?"

I peeked at him from under the duvet. "I hope I don't have to spring for the damn dinner!"

What does one wear to a 255 grand date? I asked myself that question a gazillion times and even looked around my empty room and asked Samuel. "You're no help, Sam," I said then laughed.

A gentle breeze touched my face.

I laughed again. "Okay. You're a guy anyway. I'm sure we'd never agree on what looked good for me to wear. Only Goldie and Miles have that market cornered."

I lifted my black dress and decided that was the only decent thing I had. Then again, I'd worn it the other night and Neal never did say how dressy we were going to get. There was nothing worse than showing up for a date under- or over-dressed.

I flopped onto my bed, pulled my cell from my scrubs top and poked in the numbers.

"Hey," I started to say then realized it was Neal's voice mail. So I left the "what to wear tonight" message, flipped the cell closed and pulled the blanket over me. There wasn't much I could do until I heard from him.

For a few seconds I stared at my cell phone, and then picked it up. "Damn it. I shouldn't do this, but—" I pressed the contacts button, scrolled down and pressed Talk.

"The Nextel subscriber you are trying to reach is not available," the disembodied voice said in my ear.

I slammed the phone shut—as if Jagger could see that I'd tried to reach him.

Strictly for business purposes.

Really.

Ring. Ring.

My eyes flew open to see the red light blinking on my cell phone. I had a voice-mail message. Jagger? I pressed the button, listened to the female voice go through her rigmarole and then heard, "Casual. Jeans are fine. Bring a sweater or jacket."

Neal.

Okay, he wasn't Jagger, but my stomach fluttered at the sound of his voice and my mind flashed back to imagining a near-miss of pretty damn decent sex (remember, I had no recent comparisons). I sat up in bed—feeling as if Samuel were right next to me, jeering.

"Damn it. I wouldn't be surprised if you're a long lost descendent of none other than my Jagger." I laughed and realized how easily the word "my" had come out. Then I jumped out of bed and headed for a shower—a cold one.

"You look fantastic, Pauline," Neal said as he put his arm around me and kissed my cheek.

I purred. Purred? Geez how unlike me, but it felt kinda good. "Thanks. You don't look so bad yourself, although for 255,000 bucks, I'd expect maybe a tuxedo."

We both laughed, and I realized the little crow's-feet at the ends of Neal's eyes deepened significantly when he laughed—and the damn things were way too sexy. He probably spent a bit too much time out in the sun, and guys were notorious for not using sunscreen. But then again, it did look good on him.

"So, Doc, where are we headed in our casuals?" Neal's hand moved to the small of my back and he led me out the door. I could get used to this. Really.

"It's a surprise."

Yikes. He'd leaned closer to my ear, as if I couldn't hear normal talking, and when his breath tickled my cheek, I sighed and mumbled, "A surprise sounds ... surprising."

A surprise sounds surprising?

What the hell? I really needed to take a deep breath and to get out more. I let Neal guide me to his car. After I got in, I took several long, slow breaths to get my wits about me. This was way too much excitement for a gal from Hope Valley.

Newport. Money. House with a name. Handsome doc. Wow.

I'm there.

As we drove along Bellevue, Neal cranked up the CD on his stereo. Not much into music except the few country songs I liked by Trisha Yearwood and Tim McGraw's "Live Like You Were Dying," I was not any kind of expert.

By the time we made it down to America's Cup Avenue, I couldn't stand the suspense. "Come on, Neal. Give me a clue."

He laughed.

My heart danced and hormones surged.

"We're almost there. Patience is a virtue, Pauline."

"Ha! You just enjoy being in charge!" We laughed some more and soon Neal turned into a parking lot at the marina. "We're going on a boat?"

Yikes. Water. Not a good swimmer. Maybe seasickness.

"No." He shut the car off, leaned near, touched my hair, gently pushing it behind my ear, and said, "We're going on *my* boat."

"Oh … my … God … that   sounds … fantastic," I whispered, as if I could swim to save my life if the boat capsized.

Something that large is not going to capsize, Pauline, I told myself, looking at the gigantic white yacht bobbing gracefully before me, all the while twisting my pink locket in my hands. I'd forgotten to take it off when changing, but it came in handy for nervous energy.

Neal bustled about with lines and carrying stuff from the car. A picnic basket of sorts that I wondered might be filled with food was the first thing he'd brought out.

The boat bobbed.

My stomach lurched.

Damn. "I wish I had some Dramamine in my purse," I mumbled.

"Prone to seasickness?" Neal asked.

I swung around, ready to jump in the water and drown myself. "Umm."

"We could head back to a drugstore and get some, but then I'll be late making my post-op rounds tonight."

I thought of Goldie. "No. I don't want you to do that." I opened my purse and started to look inside.

"Well, what do you have in there? Anything of use?" he asked.

I dug around until I found my pill case, opened it and took out a little pink and white capsule.

"Well, there you go. Benadryl. Should help. Take that," he said and eased my hand toward me. "Good thing you had it."

"I carry Benadryl in case I ever have some weird allergic reaction."

"Even though it's not for motion sickness, Pauline, it might help alleviate any nausea because it has the histamine blocker ability." His eyes kind of sparkled when he said it. I smiled to myself. Doc Neal looked so proud of himself. Then again, maybe he just wanted me to enjoy the boat ride.

Made sense coming from a doctor, so I promptly popped it into my mouth.

He looked at me and smiled.

I smiled back then thought, *Shit. I only hope the Benadryl doesn't make me sleepy!*

The pictures on the wall shifted—as did my stomach.

I looked up from my comfy spot in the cabin near Neal and watched him sail or drive or whatever the yacht until we were out in the Atlantic far enough that I couldn't see any land.

How romantic ... if I didn't barf.

If I didn't watch the pictures sway, hear the swells of water outside the front window or acknowledge that this teeny, tiny boat could actually flip over like the *Poseidon*, I would be enjoying myself.

Then I yawned.

"Is it the company?" Neal asked, turning around to look at me.

"Hey, keep your eye on the road, water, whatever. And, no, it isn't the company." I yawned two more times. "I think yawning is a sign of lack of oxygen."

He did something with some parts on what I called the dashboard of this vessel and walked over to me, bent down and took my hands in his. "Then we need to do something about that. Maybe mouth-to-mouth?"

As his delicious lips covered mine, I muttered, "Shouldn't someone be at the helm ... what the hell is a helm ... or ..."

Neal took my head in his hands, kissed me several times and kissed me again. "No need. We're fine."

"Umm. Fine. We're ..." Suddenly he lifted me up and all my motion worries vanished.

The bright sun had settled below the horizon, casting a reddish-pink glow across the sky and water. The waves seemed to calm in order to give us a few special minutes to...

How fabulous!

I figured Neal knew what he was talking about by letting the boat float around all by itself. What's the worst that could happen anyway?

We'd drift out to sea and have to spend more time together?

"I seem to be getting my money's worth—" I kissed him behind the ear and amid his moans finished with, "—out of this date."

A deep chuckle tickled my cheek. Neal's arms were around me, over me, and like some testosterone-soaked octopus, on every wonderful part of me. Getting a little rough, but guys will be guys.

This time we moaned in pleasure together.

"Ever made love out at sea?" he asked against my cheek.

I paused. There was that one cruise I'd taken, but with all the murders, making love had not been on my itinerary. "Nope."

Neal lifted me up and carried me toward the stairs, which led down to a cabin—the likes of which were fancier than my condo at home, and I'd never tell Miles that since he owned and decorated it.

The sandstone walls were circular, as were the mahogany dressers built into said walls, which surrounded a—you guessed it—circular bed. Gold, brown and navy striped covers neatly sat on the mattress with pillow shams, with drapes and two stuffed chairs to match.

Very nautical bachelor.

"Beautiful," I said as he set me down on the duvet. "You the interior decorator?"

He chuckled. "Surgeons—make that most men in general—are not very good at that stuff."

Then who was? Damn it! I had no business asking that question.

While I chastised myself, Neal busied himself with removing my jacket, unbuttoning my blouse and slipping it off. He then very gently set it on the bedside chair. How cute.

Not the most spontaneous person around, I asked again, "Are you sure no one needs to be upstairs driving this thing?"

"I'm sure, Pauline. I've been sailing since I was about nine." Oops. I thought I'd just insulted him. He gently undid my pink locket and carefully set it on the pile of my clothing.

"But you're not sailing." He nuzzled my neck at the spot just below my jawline. Oh ... wow. Good thing he'd taken off the locket or it might have accidentally sprayed him. That would be a real sexual deal breaker for sure.

"She's well-equipped with instruments, lights, an anchor and all kinds of fancy stuff so that we can ... do what the hell we want down here. Besides, it's a quiet night, but with the bright full moon any other boats that pass by will clearly see us. Stop worrying."

I hadn't even thought of another boat ramming into us. "Thanks for that," I said.

Neal lifted me up slightly to yank the duvet and covers down. The sheets had to have been woven with a thousand thread count. I felt as if I could slide right off the side with the tilt and roll of the boat.

And my mind had been too preoccupied with Neal to remember that earlier I'd felt like seasick crap.

I did yawn again.

"No, it's not the company," I said as I undid the zipper on Neal's jacket.

Soon he was only in his jeans—and I realized I had a real "thing" for shirtless, well-built jean-clad guys.

I, however, had my jeans gingerly removed in one sensual moment by Neal. Hey, he was a doctor for crying out loud!

My vision blurred a bit as another damn yawn snuck out. Although I didn't want to admit it, the damn Benadryl had knocked me for a loop. Shit. I decided staying "active" would help keep me awake.

Neal bent over to lift his jacket and shirt up from the floor. I had to smile to myself at the guy's perfection qualities. Jagger would have walked all over both of our clothing without a thought.

But the doc pulled his red shirt from the jacket, folded it, stuck it on the bedside stand and started to fold the shirt.

"Force of habit. I'll be right with ..."

Neal was talking. I knew it because I could hear his voice. But I wasn't comprehending a thing as I watched him fold his shirt so carefully.

Red.

Expensive looking.

Hmm. Intriguing.

Shirt with the one side pocket ... missing a tiny piece.

Twenty-Four

I knew it wasn't the Benadryl that had my mouth drier than the sandy beaches of Newport. No. It was Neal. Neal folding his shirt. The red, expensive shirt. The fabric that looked exactly like the swatch I'd found on the bushes of Cliff Walk where Ian had died.

Suicide?

I didn't think so.

Perfect Neal was wearing this particular red shirt as if mocking me. Giving me some kind of signal. Yikes.

Neal set the shirt on top of his jacket and turned back.

My jaw dropped.

Apparently he was better at reading body language than I was at hiding my reaction. His look became rather ominous, eyes darkening, face scowling.

He knew, just *knew*, that I had caught on about the shirt.

"Goddamn it, Pauline."

I wrinkled my forehead and tried to chuckle. "What?" I asked, moving to the side with the hopes that maybe I was wrong. Maybe he wasn't as crafty as I'd given him credit for. Or should I say devious? "I'm fine." I tried to sit, but he pulled me back. "I have to use the powder room." And get my pepper spray.

He looked at me and shook his head.

This time that body language said, "Doesn't matter. You ain't going anywhere. We have things to do."

In my gut I knew Dr. Neal Forsyth wasn't talking sex here.

And in my medical opinion, Neal brought me out there for one *specific* reason, and in the interim he snapped. Snapped like a twig. I could see it in his eyes. The guy was nuts.

I had to think fast.

"Let me go, Neal." I leaned over and tried to kiss him on the cheek (as a diversion despite my nearly gagging), but he pushed me away.

Oh, boy.

This was not looking good.

Suddenly Neal was standing above me, and with his shirt off looked more like my older brother than the young doctor that he was. I pushed myself over to the other side of the bed and stared at him.

That ominous, dark look deepened in his eyes ... and I realized ... Neal Forsyth was *not* as young as I thought he was.

The guy must have had plastic surgery.

Oh, yeah. Neal probably had BDD too—or was hiding something.

Or had plastic surgery to change his appearance. Oh … my … God.

How could I have not noticed before? Okay, I cut myself some slack since it was so dark in Forsyth Manor the other night, Neal didn't take off his shirt, which should have been some kind of clue, and I'd had … maybe a bit too much expensive alcohol.

I moved one way.

He followed.

I had to do something fast. "Oh, are we role playing here?" The words slipped out of my mouth in hopes that Neal would believe that I thought he was kidding. Then I could get away from him—and go where?

"Yeah, Pauline. We're role playing." He came to my side of the bed and looked down.

I tried to ease back and grab my jeans.

If something menacing was going to happen— and my gut was screaming that it was—I certainly didn't want to be found in my floral pink undies.

I knew I needn't worry since shark bait didn't need to follow any fashion trends. Who the hell would ever see? I gave up trying to grab my pants and concentrated on what to do.

Save my life came to mind.

I yawned and felt my body getting lighter. My arms actually felt heavy, and I knew if I had to get up and run, my legs would fight me. The Benadryl could be my undoing here.

Benadryl that Neal had "encouraged" me to take.

All right, I'd been in this situation before. Facing the murderer and probably fraud criminal too. But despite my getting through it unscathed before, my mind was so woozy that I couldn't remember what I'd done.

So I said a silent prayer.

Neal grabbed my arm. "Get up."

"I'm cold. At least let me stick my jeans back on." I tried to pull away, but he held me tightly. I told myself I should poke his eyes with my nails, but the damn antihistamine really had done a number on me and I could barely focus.

Why was I so vain that I didn't want to barf in front of a hunky doctor?

"What are you doing, Neal? I thought we were … I mean … I really wanted to—" I leaned forward and whispered in his ear (all the while fighting back the nausea my words caused), "—make love to you. Real hot, naughty nurse sex, I'm talking."

Long shot. Sure. But a guy was a guy was a guy.

For a few seconds he started to cave. I could feel him stiffening next to me so I continued prostituting myself in order to … live … and stiffen him.

I kissed him behind the ear and his grip loosened.

Sometimes survival was all out sickening.

"Neal, what happened? I mean, I thought you were younger than you appear." I ran my fingers through his hair and nearly groaned in disgust. But a girl had to do what a girl had to do to get out of this treacherous situation. "Um, not that you still aren't a hunk," I lied, trying to appeal to his vanity.

He started kissing me back.

Bingo.

I swallowed hard so bile wouldn't rise up in my throat. When faced in a life or death situation, I realized it was an out-of-body experience and pretended this really wasn't me.

It wasn't *me* he was kissing.

It wasn't *my* neck he was breathing heavily on.

It wasn't *me* Neal would have sex with—then flip overboard.

It *was* me thinking over my dead body.

But I did keep my mind on the problem at hand, all the while fighting like hell to stay coherent. I knew I could never take him, especially on the Benadryl jag, so I had to keep my wits about me and use my brain.

"What is really going on, sweetie? You were kinda scaring me for a few minutes." I tried to chuckle, but it came out a strangled sound.

He eased back as he tried to undo the buttons on my top.

To buy time, I took his fingers from the clothing and kissed each one very slowly and deliberately. Ick.

"It has to end, Pauline. It has to end," he whispered near my ear.

He wasn't talking finger kissing, that much I was certain—and hoped to hell that *I* wasn't the "it" he'd just mentioned. "What, Neal? What has to end?"

Slowly his hands relaxed and he eased me

down on the bed. But thank goodness he balanced himself on his arms. Then he looked so very odd. Almost as if in another world. Neal really wasn't with me right then as he said, "The deception. The killing. My own *brother*."

My heart stopped.

When it started again, my hands were shaking so badly I worried Neal would notice. *Don't show fear to the enemy* became my motto—although it was much easier to repeat in my head than to actually do. "Deception?" The killing could wait since I figured out that he must have pushed Ian off the cliff. But was Ian his *brother*? How to get away from this wacko?

"I told Mother this could never work. She's never left me alone in my life. Never." Tears streamed down his cheeks, falling onto my chest.

How I wanted to push him away before I vomited, but my strength hadn't returned despite the adrenaline that pulsed through my body. Besides, Neal had gotten me confused. Mother? In past cases I'd learned to get the murderers, who usually loved to brag, to confess more and more once they got on a roll.

Neal was almost there.

And Neal was no longer rational.

The question was, what the hell would I do with the information since getting off this yacht alive looked … like a slim chance.

For a second I shut my eyes and prayed again, asking Saint Theresa for a miracle.

Neal looked up, his tear-filled eyes eerily

glassy. He wasn't seeing me any longer. But he was still talking.

"She should have stayed in Europe where she could have made a life for us. Damn her for dragging me here. I could have been a doctor in Austria and never gotten into this mess."

This mess? I needed to know more about this mess. "I'm not following, Neal. Mess?"

He didn't acknowledge me talking, but as if in a trance continued, "Killing Ian because the fool fell in love with Mr. Perlman."

I gasped. *My Goldie!*

On one hand it was handy that Neal had snapped and started confessing, but on the other … I sure didn't like his admissions.

Neal shifted his weight from one arm to the other. I glanced down to see he was in no "readiness" for sex (thank you, Saint Theresa), so I didn't try to push him off but lay there listening.

"Because they are gay?" I asked, fishing for clues.

Neal scowled at me. "Because Ian's loyalty shifted. He was going to risk our moneymaking surgical scheme for love. Love. Ha!"

I tried to weed through what he'd said, clearly admitting to the fraud, yet what else?

"Mother could have been set for life if she could only control herself."

"Control," I muttered in a subliminal sort of way so as not to pull Neal from his rambling.

He relaxed a bit, crushing into my chest, but I took a long deep breath and remained silent. "I did all that surgery on her, and when she came to America and married Chandler I was nearly twenty ..."

Chandler? Olivia Wheaton-Chandler was Neal's *mother*!

Wait a minute! Nearly twenty? That would make Neal closer to fifty than thirty. Eek! I shivered at the thought. Thank goodness we didn't do more the other day, but too bad it was so dark, I would have noticed that he was older then.

"What happened to Chandler?"

Neal looked at me oddly, as if I should have known. "Heart attack is what the autopsy said." He grinned an evil look, and I knew he and Olivia had probably given Mr. Chandler some medication to cause the attack—so she could get all his money. How convenient to have a doctor for a son. One who could invent a person. No wonder Adele couldn't find anything about Olivia's earlier life.

There was no Olivia.

Probably Olivia—not even her real name, I imagined—married for money—and murdered for the same.

"Your mother looks much younger." I didn't expound since I wanted to just shift his direction. The locket was still too far out of reach. Damn it.

In a rather testy tone he said, "You know I am a board certified, exemplary plastic surgeon. Mother has a penchant for younger men. Mother needs to be kept happy."

I'll just bet. So Olivia was made to look younger

and younger but in a very clever way so as not to attract attention to her—and so she attracted young guys like Devin. Men and money. What a combo.

"Did she love Devin?" I asked, holding my breath as if Neal would snap out of this episode and strangle me in a second.

"Ha, that bastard. Olivia doesn't love anyone. She uses him as much as he uses her. But the bastard spent way beyond their means and ... that's why I had to step in to take care of Mother."

Made me wonder why he didn't just "off" Devin. Maybe Mommy put the kibosh on that idea so she could keep her boy toy. Eeeeeeyew.

So, Neal was committing fraud so that his mother could live her life of luxury. But what about Forsyth Manor?

"Where did you get your house from?" At first I even stunned myself with that question, but faced with death, I figured I had nothing to lose. Then I had a thought: Maybe my cell would work out here, and I could at least leave a voice mail for Jagger.

Jagger.

Tears seeped out of the corners of my eyes. I refused to allow myself to think of any of my loved ones—as that would be my undoing. Nope. I had to keep my wits about me, fight the damn Benadryl and find out everything from Neal.

Neal looked off into the distance. "I really did love her. Emily. She gave birth to our daughter seventeen years ago, but died from hemorrhage, leaving me all of her inheritance. Emily was the only heir left to the Forsyth money—but it wasn't nearly enough for Mother."

So to disguise himself, Neal took his wife's maiden name and their baby. Oh … my … God. I looked him in the eye. "You are the father? Of … Lydia."

He didn't even acknowledge the fact but merely said, "She was too much a reminder of her mother. I couldn't love her." He looked off into space and muttered, "The goddamn baby was too much of a reminder of what I could have had. What I'd lost. Well, at least I got all of the Forsyth money and house."

That's it, Neal. The old glass was half full in theory.

So Lydia's grandmother, not aunt, raised her. Or at least let her live in the same mansion, but grow up unloved.

But why not let her go to Yale?

I asked Neal that question, and after him mumbling a few seconds learned that Olivia kept all of them—Neal, Devin, Ian, and Lydia—on a very short rope. If Lydia moved away, she could draw attention to the family, such as it were, and maybe even uncover their moneymaking scheme.

That's what Lydia had meant by only trusting family.

She knew about the fraud, but had no choice in the matter.

Poor kid. No wonder she talked of suicide.

"Does your daughter know who you are?" I asked through clenched teeth.

"No."

"Good," I mumbled. She was better off not knowing.

"So you pushed your brother off Cliff Walk so he wouldn't go to the authorities?"

"He already had. How ironic. He knocks off Baines, who refused to pay for Daphne's multiple surgeries, and then found out about the diagnosis scheme we used, yet Ian too was going to bail. Poor Mother." Neal looked me in the eyes. "And you, Ms. Sokol, investigator, are the reason we are out here. You too are not going to be allowed to ruin Mother's scheme."

"How ... why me, Neal? Why pay all that fund-raiser money to get me out here?"

He laughed. The eerie sound had me stiffen.

"Ah. The Chandlers are known for their generosity, Pauline. We needed to make sure to keep up our stellar image."

Stellar my ass.

"Mother kept a close eye on things recently. She'd sent Ian to check out your room at the lodge." He laughed. "He thought he'd scare you off with the lipstick message."

Ian? Knowing he tried to scare me made it somehow hurt more. I thought back to the pictures in the office. Ian must have been the blond child with Olivia. And I guess nurse Jackie was innocent, and it was Ian who had knocked me out.

"Mother found out about you in her spying. Very smart lady my mother. Oh, don't flatter yourself that I spend all that money on you. There is no scholarship, the ruse was merely to make you feel as if you had to go out with me at least one more time. You might say we 'killed two birds with one stone' by having all of Newport admire our generosity, and getting you out here. Sealed your fate, you did, you fool."

Fool? Hey! Wait. Spying? I let my mind wander backward. "Lady Bandage," I murmured and had to stop myself from clocking him after that "fool" comment. "So Dr. Cook worked with you on all this?"

"Ha. He's what kept the suspicion *from* us."

I had to agree with him there. Damn, even I'd fallen for believing Dr. Cook was the crook when Neal had obviously set it up that way. The guy was smart. I'd give him that. Sick but smart and the true meaning of the words "mama's boy."

My eyes shut a second as I tried to think. This guy was off the deep end, and if I didn't do something soon, I'd be off the deep end of the boat. With all my force I kicked my knee into his groin, opened my eyes and pushed at his chest, sliding from under him just enough to grab the pink locket with its pepper spray.

Neal screamed out in pain and, taken off guard, fell to the floor where his head smacked against the bedside table. Blood spurted out onto the beige carpet, but I told myself that head wounds bled a lot and that I had to save myself.

No nursing the killers, Jagger had once said.

I needed my miracle.

Neal lay silently still.

I grabbed the pull rope of the drapes and yanked with strength I had no idea that I had.

Ring. Ring.

In the pocket of my jeans my cell phone went off. Neal started to moan.

I grabbed my cell phone out, pushed the speaker button on and talked nonstop to whoever was on the line, telling him or her exactly what had happened and where I was—not even knowing the real location. I chattered on and on, never letting the other person say a word—then the line went blank.

But for a miracle, you don't have to fill in all the blanks. You merely have to *believe.*

I pushed Neal over, ignored the gaping wound on the back of his head and tried to tie his hands together. In my nervousness my hands shook and I fumbled several times. Soon I had Neal's hands near each other.

One hand reached out and *grabbed* me!

I screamed.

Neal swung around and with blood trickling down his forehead cursed at me in a low, guttural tone that sent chills racing up my spine and fear into my heart.

"You bitch!" he shouted and started to get up.

I pushed him back with all the Benadryl-laced strength that I could muster. Then I relied on my self-defense moves that Jagger had taught me— and stuck my fingers into Neal's nostrils.

Barely able to complete the gross action, I did as I'd learned, and before I knew it, Neal was once again doubled over in pain. I then grabbed the rope, tied as tightly as I could, not forgetting his feet, and ran out of the room.

At the top of the stairs a set of arms seized me. I screamed.

And I knew I was then going overboard to my death.

All went black.

"What the hell possessed you to come out on a boat? You couldn't swim to save your life, Sherlock!"

I opened one eye, realized I was on Jagger's lap still on Neal's boat and must have died. If this was Heaven, I'd wasted way too many years of diligently going to church each Sunday.

Not that being on Jagger's lap wasn't Heaven, but he was chastising me and the setting was all wrong.

I rubbed at my forehead. "Don't yell so loudly."

Suddenly his voice softened, "I'm just so pissed that you could have ... you could have—"

I looked up at Jagger to see his eyes teary and him not able to finish.

Worrying about me had Jagger speechless.

Oh ... my ... God.

This rush of pleasure made living through the experience with Neal all worth it.

As the Coast Guard called out from some bullhorn—since Jagger had called them right after my rambling cell phone call with him—he leaned over and kissed my lips, then tucked the pink locket into my hand.

"I can't even take off a few days to go sailing on a quick trip to Martha's Vineyard without you getting into trouble."

"Hey, I didn't get hurt."

"Yeah, you did good, Sherlock."

My heart soared.

Jagger blew out a deep breath. "I'd told Samuel to look after you."

I chuckled. "I guess that's why you called when you did. Who is he, Jagger?"

He looked off into the distance. "He lives in the lodge that I'd inherited many years ago. Samuel was my great-grandfather. Samuel Freeman Tonelli. He started the insurance company years ago...."

I knew Jagger was talking but I'd fixated on the word "Tonelli."

Jagger Tonelli.

My boss.

My *boss*?

Shark bait was sounding better and better by the second.

My boss!

Epilogue

"On your mark, get set ..." I turned to look at the crowd in my parents' living room. All the family, my favorite uncle, Walt, Miles, Lilla and Adele, freaking Fabio, and ... Jagger. Not to mention the star of the day, Goldie. I touched his shoulder as he stood with his back to the crowd. "Go!"

Goldie, the one with the new nose, turned around.

The room let out a collective "Wow!"

I threw my arms around him. "You look fantastic!" Sometimes one had to lie to their friends in order not to hurt their feelings.

Goldie's damn nose looked pretty much the same to me.

Yikes!

If I stood a bit closer, which I did, I noted the slight bump he used to have was gone. Okay, I'd give him that. But there was no drastic change—which gave me a comforting feeling.

The old Goldie really was perfect, and despite

all his faults—and there were plenty—criminal Neal must have known and decided not to disfigure Goldie in any way.

I'd thank Neal for that, but not the fact that he tried to kill me and all the other stuff that'd happened, however. No way was I going to visit him in jail.

"Hey." I felt a set of arms wrap around me and knew instantly whom they belonged to.

"Jagger," I murmured.

"Why the shiver? Cold?"

"In my mother's house?"

Jagger chuckled against me. Ah.

"You're right, Sherlock. This place is always so warm and cozy."

I couldn't tell him that I'd momentarily relived the boat incident and my near-imminent death with Neal so I said, "Goldie looks great. Doesn't he?"

Jagger turned me to face him and stood silent.

"Don't ever tell him," I whispered. "Please."

He nodded then leaned forward. When his lips touched mine, I, of course, melted. Suddenly, while still feeling his touch, tasting his deliciousness, and momentarily losing my mind, I found my arms around his head, found my hands running through his hair. And found myself leaning in.

Oh … my … God.

A tingling started in my fingers and spread, ever so slowly, so sensually, down my arms that I actually let go. Damn, but this guy had some effect on me.

He stepped back.

Shit. Why did my extremities have to be so tak-
en with the enigmatic guy too? Seems when Jagger came near, every part of my body felt him.

"I spoke to the Newport cops today," he said.
"Lydia has been placed in foster care since she's
only seventeen."

I winced.

"Foster care in Newport, Sherlock. How bad
could it be?"

I smiled. "And school?"

"She's registered for Yale in the fall."

I smiled again. "I'm so glad."

"Oh, in all the celebration of Goldie's nose revealing, I almost forgot. Here." He took an envelope from his pocket and handed it to me. "I'll get
us a drink." With that he walked away.

I opened the envelope to see the biggest payment that I'd ever received in this job. While my
jaw dropped, I pulled out a Jagger handwritten
note that said, "Case number six. Practice your
driving skills, Sherlock. We'll talk in the morning—at our spot."

Our spot.

Those two words had me so shaken, in a good
way, that I could barely think about the next case.
Practice your driving skills?

Oh ... my ... God again.

Coming from delicious Jagger, who the hell
knew what *that* meant?

Experience other
comical and clever adventures
of nurse turned p.i.
Pauline Sokol

The
World of Lori Avocato

A Dose of Murder

Pauline Sokol's adventures first began in this hilarious debut novel, so open wide and say AHHHHHHHHRRRGGGGHHHHhhhhhh-hhhhh!

After years of chasing around sniffly munchkins with a tongue depressor, nurse Pauline Sokol has had it. She's sick of being an "angel of mercy"—she'd like to raise some hell for once! But finding a new career won't be easy for someone who's had no experience beyond thermometers and bed-pans.

Luckily, the smarmy head of a medical insurance fraud agency hires her, mostly because of her killer pair of legs. Soon, Pauline is going undercover as a nurse at a local clinic, and the healers around her start dropping dead! Luckily, the hunky and mysterious Jagger is there to step in and teach her the ropes before her own continued wellness is in jeopardy!

The Stiff and the Dead

Pauline has a drug problem . . .

Pauline's second case finds her going undercover at a senior citizens' center, where prescriptions are being filled for a patient who just happens to be dead. A little snooping reveals that the recently deceased oldster was up to his jowls in an illegal Viagra ring!

Not that Pauline begrudges these elderly gents their newfound virility, but it becomes a bit unnerving to be in the middle of a group of sex-mad lotharios, especially when people keep turning up dead! Hopefully, her handsome co-worker Nick and the enigmatic Jagger will make sure that the next prescription for murder doesn't have Pauline's name on it!

One Dead Under the Cuckoo's Nest

Former nurse-turned-insurance fraud p.i. Pauline Sokol's current undercover investigation into a sleazy scam has hit a small snag: She's been forcibly committed to a mental institution! Pauline's certainly sane, but try telling that to the nuns who run the place. Even her cohort Jagger is unwilling to spring her until she digs deeper into the scam that the mental institution is running. When the strange death of a gender-confused "sister" further complicates matters, Pauline realizes she may need the help of her own very kooky family to find a way out of Wacko Town . . . alive!

Deep Sea Dead

Book a cruise to paradise! Enjoy an incredible escape from everyday life with extraordinary views, first-class dining, deluxe accommodations, and no more than one corpse per stateroom.

When fraud investigator Pauline Sokol discovers that her next case requires snooping on a giant cruise ship miles away from dry land and safety, she tries to squelch her feelings of unease. For a nice Polish girl who has never been out of New England, cruising in the Bermuda triangle isn't Pauline's idea of a good time. And to add to her distress, she finds a dead body in her quarters. Now Pauline must juggle her duties as a cruise ship nurse with her new role of ship snoop. And when a fellow nurse goes missing, only hunky fellow investigator Jagger can help Pauline sort out the mystery before more bodies start piling up . . . including her own!